CW00376095

# THE DEALER & THE DEVIL

by

**Rex Merchant**

**Published by Rex Merchant**

***@***

**Norman Cottage.**

Copyright © Rex Merchant 2012
ISBN 9781902474267

All rights reserved. No part of this book may be reproduced or stored in an information retrieval system other than short extracts for review purposes or cross reference., without the express permission of the Publisher given in writing.

Published by Rex Merchant
Norman Cottage
89 West Road
Oakham
Rutland LE15 6LT   UK


rexmerchant@btinternet.com
www.rexmerchant.co.uk

British Library Cataloguing - in - Publication Data.
A catalogue record of this book is available from the British Library.

Typeset, printed and bound by Rex Merchant @ Norman Cottage.

Cover design by Rex Merchant. Based on a Tarot pack designed by him.

All characters in this publication are fictitious and any resemblance to real persons, living or dead, is purely coincidental.

# THE DEALER & THE DEVIL

*by*

**Rex Merchant**

*Hope you enjoy.*

*Rex Merchant*

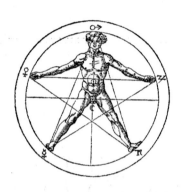

# Chapter One

'Alright! Alright! Don't knock the door down! I'm coming!' Christopher Doughty had just decided to go out for lunch when the hammering started on the shop door. He threw his coat onto the workbench and hurried into the front shop to answer the persistent banging. Only minutes before, he had put up the Closed sign and pulled down the blind as he prepared to leave his antique shop to get something to eat.

Chris unlocked the door, hoping it was a punter who would buy something but he was to be disappointed. He immediately recognised his visitor by the man's dishevelled appearance, by the tatty army coat and the worn blue trainers he wore on his feet. It was Steve Mattock, one of the dealer's neighbours who lived at the far end of the village. From his vacant expression and his unsteady stance it was obvious the man was drunk, as usual.

'Can I...can I...come in?' Steve, who was over six feet tall, loomed over Chris and slurred the request.

Chris stood his ground, blocking the entrance. 'I'm just off for lunch, Steve. Come back another day.'

The drunk didn't move; he seemed to be turning the reply over in his fuddled mind. Eventually he said. 'Mr...Mr... Doughty, I...I...I 'ave something to...to... sell you.'

Chris shook his head in disbelief but decided it would be better to let the man into the shop instead of confronting him on the doorstep.

In the past, Steve Mattock had been a useful contact. When Chris was in business in Stamford, Steve had been a runner, picking up the occasional bargains at auction, at car boot sales and at house clearances, and selling them on for a small profit to the local antique dealers. They did quite a lot of business together but that was a few years ago. Steve's drinking had got worse since his wife left him and now he was seldom sober. Most people avoided him, but a few of his old friends took pity on him and still acknowledged him. Chris had given him that pair of old blue trainers when he had no shoes to wear.

When Chris stepped aside, Steve staggered to the nearest chair, flopped down on it and gazed vacantly around the shop, uncertain of where he was.

'Well?' Chris tried to bring Steve's attention back to business. 'What have you got for me?'

Steve closed his eyes and groaned.

1

Getting no sensible answer, Chris leaned over his visitor, put his mouth close to the man's ear and asked again in a louder voice. 'Come on Steve, what exactly have you got to sell?'

With an effort, Steve pulled himself together, fished out a small sack from under his tattered coat and let it fall to the floor. The contents fell out of the bag with a metallic clang.

Chris looked down at the meagre offering and frowned. There was a brass paper knife and a brass bowl on a stem lying on the shop floor. Both of them looked tarnished and needed a good clean. They were not very interesting. He took a quick glance at them, decided they were cheap Victorian ornaments and turned to his visitor, trying to hurry him out of the shop so he could go to lunch.

'Is that it? How much do you want for them?'

'I want...' Steve stopped to gather his wits. 'I want... fifty...fifty pounds for them.'

Chris couldn't control himself and laughed out loud. 'You must be bloody joking!'

'Well, well...what...what...what... will you give me for 'em, Mr. Doughty?'

The dealer looked at the sorry state of his visitor and took pity on him once more, after all, they had known each other for some years and had been quite good friends. 'How about twenty? That's more than they're worth, but for old time's sake I'll give you twenty pounds.' He knew full well the money would be wasted on booze but he felt sorry for the man.

Steve closed his eyes and leaned back in the chair, ignoring the question.

Chris was not sure if the runner was falling asleep or considering his offer, so he waited a few seconds then leaned over again and shouted, 'Twenty pounds. Will that do you, Steve?'

Steve came to his senses with a start. 'Ya...ya...ya. That'll do me. Twenty pounds.'

Chris paid his visitor with a twenty pound note then picked up the two brass items and pushed them back into the sack. He was about to throw them onto a side table when he suddenly felt unaccountably apprehensive. Chris wasn't prone to flights of fancy but he felt an overwhelming sense of foreboding. He hadn't experienced anything like that since his army days, when he'd been in the heat of battle in Afghanistan. He shuddered involuntarily, shook off the feeling and carefully placed the sack on the table. Turning to his visitor he said. 'Now you'd better be going home.

2

I'm locking up shop. It's my lunch time. Use that money to get some food down you. You could do with a meal judging by the state of you.' He pulled Steve to his feet and propelled him to the door. At close quarters it was even more obvious that he had been drinking heavily that morning. Steve leaned against the door frame, turned towards Chris and belched loudly, breathing alcohol fumes in his face. 'I...I...I wan ya to know ya my best friend...Mr.Doughty.'

'Go home and sleep it off.' Chris advised him, but Steve turned to step back into the shop his arms held out to hug the dealer.

'I wanna...I...wanna...thank you, Chris.'

'No you don't, Steve. Get out and sleep it off. Go home. Go down by the reservoir. Go anywhere, but you can't stay here!' Chris turned the man around, put a firm hand on his back and deftly propelled him out of the shop, quickly locking the door behind him.

With the door locked and the shop empty, Chris stood and eyed the hessian bag on the table. It looked innocuous enough laying there. He could see no reason for the strange feelings he had experienced a few minutes before. Dismissing it from his mind, he went up to his flat to wash his hands and make himself more presentable.

Chris checked his reflection in the bathroom mirror. His sandy hair looked white; it was covered with fine dust from sanding a pine clock case. He fluffed his hair with his fingers, sending a cloud of dust into the air, then combed it with a damp comb. His face, which was normally freckled and fresh looking, was dirty. There was a clean circle over his mouth and nose where his dust mask had been, but the rest of it was grey. He filled the washbasin with warm water and washed. Finally he patted his clothes with his hands and stood coughing in the cloud of dust that rose from them.

Satisfied he'd removed the worst of the dust, he went downstairs and retrieved his coat from the back room. He brushed the jacket down, taking his time as he was in no hurry to leave. Honeysuckle Cottage, the house Steve rented in Barrowick village, was a few doors past the pub where Chris would have his lunch. The dealer had no intention of catching up with Steve, walking along with him and listening to his rambling conversation. He'd heard too much of the drink talking when he was a lad.

Steve reminded Chris of his late father, who was a widower and an alcoholic. He always talked a load of rubbish when he was drunk. He would come home from the pub at closing time and ramble on just like Steve had. 'Are you alright? What's the matter?

3

Are you alright then? Don't pull a face at me, lad. I'm happy. What's your problem, lad?' Then his mood would suddenly turn nasty and he'd belt the kids if they didn't get quickly out of his way. That's why Chris had left home. He gave up his apprenticeship to a local joiner and went into the army as soon as he turned eighteen. He volunteered for the parachute regiment to escape his life at home. Steve Mattock wasn't to know, but he reminded Chris too much of his old dad and his unstable childhood. Maybe that was the cause of the strange foreboding Chris had experienced earlier.

Chris served four years in the paratroop regiment then resigned when his father died from liver failure. He had no close relatives left in the country; his brother had emigrated to Australia as soon as he'd turned eighteen. Chris would have followed him but he'd met Vickie when he was serving his last year in the army and they married soon afterwards. His new wife wouldn't leave the Stamford area where she had been brought up.

Vickie! His thoughts turned to his ex wife. They had married in haste and definitely repented soon afterwards. After he left the army they had gone into business together in Stamford, restoring and selling antiques. With his joinery experience, he did the restoration while she ran the shop, but it hadn't worked out and they had divorced.

As Chris locked his premises, the church clock struck one. The sound carried far over the quiet village as he made his way to the Barrowick Arms for some lunch. His morning had been boring. There was no business and no one had called at the shop to view the stock, let alone to offer to buy something. After three months in the old butcher's shop in the tiny Rutland village of Barrowick he was beginning to think he'd made a big mistake ever leasing the place.

As Chris walked the length of Main Street, hands thrust deep into his jacket pockets, he mulled over his personal problems. How had he come to that dead end? The divorce settlement meant the Stamford shop went to Vickie. She had kept their thriving antique business, with the goodwill and regular clientele, which they'd built up together, while he had to look for new premise. He had to start all over again. The split from Vickie cost him dear and it wasn't just the business side of things that upset him. Vickie had married him when he was still serving in the army. When he left the service and they set up the antique business together, he found she had played around with other blokes. She had married too young, was not really ready to settle down and had fallen out of love with him.

'And she got most of the best stock.' He muttered under his breath. For him the timing of their split had been particularly difficult. When he'd been forced to look for alternative premises, the country was in the grip of a recession and money was tight. The only shop he could find, which he could afford, was the empty butcher's shop in Barrowick.

'If only my solicitor had done a better job... If only Vickie hadn't been so bloody minded... If only the bank manager had been a bit more understanding... If only...' He kicked a loose stone off the pavement, putting all his frustrations into that single explosive action. The pebble sped across the road and ricocheted off the dry stone wall, which separated the village from the woodland and grassland surrounding the Rutland Water reservoir.

Barrowick was a small village set on the South shore of Rutland Water and completely off the beaten track. It took Chris only five minutes to walk the length of Main Street, from his antique shop at the top of the hill to the church and pub near the far end. He stopped outside the Barrowick Arms and checked the billboard advertising their lunch menu, but he really needn't have bothered because the choice of food was always the same. Nothing much changed in Barrowick.

Before going into the pub, Chris hesitated and felt in his jacket pockets to check he had enough money to pay for a meal. As he searched, he glanced idly across the street at the old vicarage. Now there was a surprise! It seemed that some things did change in Barrowick! The tattered sign, which declared the house, the large plot of land and the outbuildings were for sale, had a brand new 'Sold' sign nailed across it. That bright new banner contrasted starkly with the 'For Sale' sign it covered. He shook his head in disbelief. When had that happened? The vicarage had been empty for ages. Judging by the general unkempt air of the place, he guessed it must have been up for sale for some years. Chris groaned to himself as he imagined all the work needed to make that house into a home again. He'd had a lot of work in the old butcher's shop, opening it as an antique business and renovating the upstairs flat. Like the vicarage, it had been neglected for years. He didn't envy the new owners.

It was really no surprise that the sandstone vicarage had remained empty. It was a huge rambling house. Chris guessed it had at least six bedrooms. With several outbuildings and a stone barn at the back of it, it was far too big for a modern family home. It might have attracted a business buyer if the village had not been such a quiet backwater. He knew to his cost that Barrowick was not on the main road. It was bypassed by all the through traffic. He wondered if the vicarage had been bought by a speculator to convert into flats. Turning on his heels, he crunched across the gravel car park to the pub and walked into the empty bar.

'Good afternoon, Mr Doughty.' Mrs Goodacre, the elderly landlady, looked him up and down, not bothering to hide her disapproval of his appearance.

Chris was acutely aware of his dusty work clothes but he had no intention of changing them just to have lunch at his local. He smiled sweetly at the landlady, ignored her black looks, and cheerily returned the greeting .

'Hello, Chris.' Sara, the landlady's daughter gave him a much warmer welcome. 'Your usual?' She handed him a menu and started to pull a pint of beer.

The landlady sniffed and took one last withering look at her solitary customer. 'I'll get to Oakham and do the shopping.' She marched out of the front door.

Sara relaxed as soon as her mother had left the premises. 'Had a good morning, Chris?'

'No...Have you?' He put on a sad face to underline his disappointment .

'No.' She burst out laughing at his doleful expression.

'It's no laughing matter, Sara. I don't know how long I can keep the shop open if there's no money coming in.'

She smiled apologetically. 'Sorry, Chris. Here, have this one on the house.' She placed a pint of best bitter on the bar in front of him.

He took a long draught of the beer and automatically reached to pick up a menu.

Sara didn't wait for his decision, she already knew his tastes. 'Ham salad, as usual?'

He placed the menu back on the bar.

Sara left the bar for a few minutes. Chris could hear her clattering about in the kitchen before she returned with a plate overflowing with food.

'Now sir, let's find you a vacant table and somewhere to sit?' She stood in the centre of the room and made a show of looking around the empty bar at all the vacant tables, pretending the place was full of customers.

'I'll sit here at the bar. At least I can chat to you as I eat. I haven't spoken to a living soul all morning! Tell a lie...I've just spoken to Steve Mattock but he was drunk as usual and didn't make any sense, so he doesn't count.'

'Ah! Steve. He's a sad case. Mother ordered him out of here again only last night.'

Chris munched his ham salad and chatted about the weather and the lack of business. Sara listened politely to him as she polished the newly washed glasses and stacked them on the shelves under the counter. At last he pushed his empty plate away and wiped his lips with the back of his hand. 'What about the vicarage then?... I see it's sold....That was a surprise.'.

'Ah yes! The estate agent nailed up that 'sold' sign first thing this morning. Mother and I heard the hammering and came out to see what the noise was all about. We were as surprised as you are. It seems someone has already moved some of their stuff in though. I didn't see it myself but I'm told there was a furniture van here only last evening.'

He pushed his empty glass across the bar. 'I'll have another pint, please... How long has the place been empty? I understand it was up for sale long before I moved here.'

'Nearly two years. When the old vicar died it wasn't wanted as they didn't have a permanent replacement for him. We get a church service now about once a month when a retired vicar comes over from Oakham to take the services.'

The dealer shook his head dismissively; he wasn't one for church going. He'd attended church parade in the army as a matter of duty; it was expected of him then, but he hadn't bothered since he'd returned to civvy street.

Sara understood the gesture. 'Me neither. But mother goes regularly. In fact, she cleans and looks after the church.'

'Do you know who's bought the old place?' Chris was genuinely curious about the vicarage. Just maybe, there could be some business for him with the new owners.

'No idea. But I understand they did have a lot of wooden cases delivered. I'll tell you this, they'll have a big job on their hands, clearing the outbuildings and getting them fit to use.'

'Is the house bad inside, then?'

'No, not it. The agent has been looking after the inside of the house and keeping it habitable. The inside is fine but I guess it will be a bit dusty. It's the outbuildings that are the worst. The large barn is chock a block with old bits of furniture and timber. All that rubbish will have to be cleared out before it can be used.'

7

The dealer's ears pricked up at this news. He'd passed by the house hundreds of times but he had never given it a second thought.

The mention of bits of old furniture raised his interest in the place. Pushing his empty plate further across the bar, he said. 'That was lovely, as usual. You do a smashing ham salad, Sara.'

'Another pint?'

Chris hesitated. He really had no reason to hurry back to the shop as he'd been stripping and sanding a painted pine grandfather clock all morning, and would be returning to that same boring job after lunch. As the clock was for stock and there wasn't a customer actually waiting for it, he almost weakened and accepted the offer of another drink but the mention of old furniture at the vicarage had set his mind racing.

'No thanks. I must be getting back.' He smiled at the barmaid and blew her a kiss as he left. Sara was an attractive girl and about his age. She was a credit to the place and she had drawn his attention to the possibility of antique furniture languishing in the barn behind the vicarage. That was a chance too good to ignore.

## Chapter Two

After lunch, back at the shop, Chris made a coffee and took it upstairs to his flat Up above the shop he had a large sitting room with a pair of glazed doors for windows. These opened onto a balcony on the flat roof above the showroom, affording him a good view over the whole of the village. He unlocked these French windows and stepped out into the afternoon.

From the balcony there was an excellent view over the surrounding countryside. Immediately opposite the shop was a lane leading down to Rutland Water. The reservoir could be seen above the treetops, gleaming in the early afternoon sunlight. Geese, Duck, Grebes and other waterfowl floated serenely on the clear water. A rowing boat with two fishermen lazily casting their lines over the lake, drifted into view then slowly vanished again behind the thick foliage of the trees lining the foreshore. Chris lifted his gaze above the treetops to look across the lake to the far side where traffic was busily speeding along the main Oakham to Stamford road. All those people, so near but yet so far! He shook his head in despair and muttered 'All those punters over there. How the hell do I attract them over here?

As he sipped his coffee, Chris turned to look along the main street at the old stone vicarage and its surrounds. From his high viewpoint he could really appreciate what a large site it was. The house occupied a plot next to the churchyard and close to the road. The whole area was surrounded by dry-stone walls built from the honey coloured, local sandstone. The churchyard was separated from the vicarage by a low stone wall with a gate linking the two. Behind the main house was a large barn and some smaller outbuildings, filling the yard, which led down towards Rutland Water. Between the back wall of the vicarage garden and the lake was an area of mature woodland, which skirted the foreshore and had a public footpath running through it, allowing access to the lakeside. He stroked his chin thoughtfully. It struck him how easy it would be for him to walk that footpath and take a closer look at the back of the vicarage and the outbuildings, especially at that barn. Sara's chance comments on the contents of the barn had really aroused his interest.

Chris's thoughts were brought back to reality by a shout from a boat on the water. One of the fishermen had hooked a large trout. Chris realised he would be in full view of anyone on the water if he chose to walk

9

the footpath that afternoon and enter the vicarage grounds. Maybe late evening would prove a better time to explore the area, when all the fishermen had returned their boats to the boatyard.

With his mind made up to take a look at the vicarage outbuildings after dusk, he returned downstairs to his workshop behind the showroom. Tuning in his portable to Rutland Radio, he carried on working on the pine clock case. Having removed all the old paint and varnish from the light coloured wood, he washed it down with white spirit to remove any last traces of the old finish and the chemical paint stripper. There were a few broken pine beadings to replace and a bit of woodworm infestation to treat and fill, but those were minor repairs. When the solvent had dried from the pine carcass he applied a honey coloured stain. While this stain dried he had another coffee then ran a duster over the furniture in the shop, for the dust settled daily from the walls and ceilings of the old building and coated the darker woods in a layer thick enough to allow him write his name on them. There were some mahogany pieces and an old carved oak misericord, which looked particularly good after a wax polish. He placed that oak piece in the centre of the front window display.

By tea time, Chris had sealed the pine case with button polish and rubbed in a good coat of beeswax with a fine wire-wool pad. He was just wondering what to do next to pass the time until dusk fell, when the shop door opened, announcing another visitor. He wiped the wood stain and wax from his fingers on an old towel and walked through to the showroom.

A well built, elderly gentleman, with white hair, stood in the shop peering at the items in the window. He had his back turned towards the sales area and the dealer. At Chris's approach he turned around. It was immediately obvious he was a vicar, from the white clerical collar and black shirt he was wearing.

Chris greeted the man. 'What can I do for you, vicar?'

The clergyman shook the dealer's outstretched hand vigorously and introduced himself. 'I'm John Smyth. Vicar of All Saints church, across the road.'

Chris frowned. Sara had said the church was practically redundant and they had services only once a month with a visiting clergyman from Oakham. Could this fellow be the part-time vicar?

Seeing his doubtful expression and guessing the reason for it, the man smiled broadly and held his hands out each side of his portly stomach in a gesture of apology.          'Well, I'm actually retired but I hold a monthly service at All Saint's Barrowick, to keep my hand in, you might say, and to keep the church in use.'

Chris returned his smile. The vicar seemed to be a likeable character. He was a rotund figure; almost Dickensian looking, with a weathered red face and sparse white hair.

'I was looking at that misericord panel you have in the window. It is made of oak with a carving of the face of the Green Man, if I'm not mistaken.' John Smyth spoke in an educated voice, enunciating every word as clearly as if he was delivering a sermon from the pulpit.

'Ah! That's a nice piece.' Chris hastened to lift the oak panel out of the display.

The vicar explained. 'I have a small collection of old, carved, church oak and I'm always looking out for bits to add to my collection.'

The dealer placed the panel on the table with the carving uppermost, pushing to one side Steve's sack, which fell open revealing the items he'd recently bought.

'It looks like continental work.' The Reverend. Smyth had put on his reading glasses, which were hanging on a blue chord around his neck. He checked the carving closely.

Chris volunteered some information. 'Well, vicar. I understand it came from an English church here in the midlands. I bought it at auction a few weeks ago.'

'Oh do call me John, that's my name after all. Now, as far as this misericord is concerned, it may well have been in an English church but many foreign craftsmen travelled from church to church in the old days, following the work. It's definitely continental in my opinion. How much is it?'

Before Chris could answer, the vicar noticed the brass paper knife and bowl, which sat on the table beside the panel. He instantly dropped the misericord back onto the table and recoiled in horror, holding his hands to his mouth.

'What's the matter? You OK?'

The old man turned and looked at Chris afresh, a stern look on his face. 'What have you there?' He pointed to the two items that Steve had brought into the shop only hours before.

'Oh those! I've just bought them from a local contact. A Victorian brass letter opener and a bowl.'

John Smyth gingerly picked up the knife and turned it over in his hands then he replaced it on the table and picked up the brass bowl. 'These are definitely not Victorian or brass. They are medieval and made of bronze. They are witchcraft implements.'

Chris was stunned and dumbstruck. He'd not bothered to look properly at the items when he'd bought them so he reached out and picked up the knife. It had a black wooden handle and a curved bronze blade. On closer examination he could see there was a pentagram inlaid in bronze on the pommel of the handle and there were curious symbols engraved all along the blade. He looked questioningly at the clergyman. 'Witchcraft things? Are you sure?'

'Certain. That is an Athame, a witch's sword or dagger.' The vicar picked up the bronze bowl and tilted it to show Chris the inside. 'That stained inner lining is bone. It's the inside of a human skull, if I'm not mistaken.'

'A human skull? Why?'

'Witches and warlocks often use a human skull as a travesty of the chalice that we in the church use to hold the wine in the communion service.'

Chris took the chalice from John, intending to inspect it more closely, but was instantly overcome by feelings of intense dread. He hurriedly replaced the bowl on the table and sat down heavily on a nearby chair.

The vicar noticed the change in his companion. 'You've gone quite pale young man. Are you alright?'

Chris apologised. 'Sorry. I suddenly felt very strange. That's the second time I've had these weird feelings when I've handled those items. I don't know what came over me.'

The vicar frowned then reassured Chris. 'Those bronze artifacts will have an aura of evil about them. You must be sensitive to such matters. Heaven knows what evil that knife and chalice have been involved in, or for that matter, may still be involved in. Witchcraft adepts still use them when they celebrate the Black Mass.'

'I notice you said 'still use' in the present tense. Surely this is medieval and isn't in use today?'

The vicar shook his head but didn't immediately answer.

The dealer's curiosity was aroused. He asked again, rephrasing his question. 'Are you suggesting these witchcraft items are still used today?'

'Yes. I know they are. It may seem very unlikely to you but I have had regular contact with demonology. I have had first hand experience of such things. I was the Deliverance Priest for a midland's diocese until I retired last year. I held regular exorcisms on behalf of the Church of England.'

Chris was unable to believe what he was hearing. 'In this modern day? Demons and exorcisms? Whatever next? It sounds like some X rated Hollywood film. Surely not?'

'Surely yes. The church holds several hundred such services every year. The problems of demonic possession are on the increase because people will dabble with Ouija boards, Tarot cards and other occult paraphernalia. I still get a lot of referrals from the Samaritans. Unfortunately gullible people get mixed up in the occult and then they pay the price. That's when I, and other Deliverance Priests, have to pick up the pieces.'

'Oh! So you are still involved in the work then?'

'Only while my successor gets more experience.'

Chris stared at the knife and bowl. 'I suppose they must be valuable but I am put off stocking them now you've told me what they really are.'

'Be careful, young man. I would advise you to destroy them, but they are your stock, which you have no doubt spent a lot of money on. But do be careful.' With that warning the Reverend Smyth let himself out of the shop with no further mention of buying the misericord. Chris stood in the doorway, disappointed at the lack of a sale, and watched the portly vicar retreat to the church.

The dealer was at a loss what to think or what to do with the bronze Athame and chalice. It was unlikely there would be a demand for them in Barrowick. How the devil Steve had come by them was a complete mystery. The items made him feel very uneasy but he couldn't really afford to destroy them or throw them out. After some thought, he quickly wrapped them in the sacking and locked them in the safe in the back shop until he had time to consider his options properly. He knew there must be collectors out there who would pay handsomely for genuine medieval items like those, but he wasn't sure he wanted the things in his shop. 'God knows where Steve picked those up,' He muttered aloud as he turned the safe key on them. As he sipped another coffee and wondered what to do with the medieval witchcraft items, the sound of the shop door opening interrupted his thoughts, announcing yet another visitor. Business was looking up.

'Oh! Hello Sara.' He was pleasantly surprised to see it was the barmaid from the local pub.

'Hi. I thought it was time I paid you another visit. I wondered what you'd had in new since I last looked.'

Chris cast his eyes around the shop trying to recall what was in stock when she last called and what might appeal to her. 'I'm working on a pine grandfather clock in the back. That will be ready for sale in a day or two. That writing box is new and that Victorian sewing box has only just come in.' He went over to an inlaid walnut box and lifted the lid to show her the green velvet interior.

'That's nice. I have always fancied an antique box to keep my jewelry in... not that I've got a lot of jewelry, mind you...' She grinned apologetically and walked away from the box.

Chris could only shrug his shoulders and return her smile for he had the impression she had not come to his shop just to look at his stock. There had to be another reason. Her next request confirmed his suspicions.

'I wondered if you were interested in folk music?' She handed him a poster.

He read the advertisement but said nothing.

Sara hurried on. 'I'm singing with a local folk group at the pub next Friday night. Will you come?'

Chris looked up at this invitation. 'I didn't realise you were a singer, Sara. Do you do a lot of it?'

'No. I'm relatively new at it but the band thinks I'm good...Do say you'll come... It'll be a good night I'm sure, and I need some friends there to support me.'

Friends eh? It was nice she regarded him as a friend. He looked at her with renewed interest. She was a good-looking girl, probably in her thirties like him. She seemed eager to please. Seeing her full length in a dress instead of jeans, and not hidden behind the bar, he realised she had a good figure and a very shapely pair of legs. Perhaps it would be worth his while passing some of Friday evening at the Barrowick Arms. He had rather shunned female company since his divorce. Anyway, he'd nothing better to do with his time once the shop was closed. 'I'd love to come, Sara. Save me a seat near the band.'

'I doubt if it will be that busy!' She looked pleased that he had agreed to support her. 'Do you think you could put this poster in your window for me?'

When the girl had gone, Chris pinned the poster in the shop window and considered the idea of a folk night at his local. It might just bring a few new faces into the village, and that couldn't be a bad thing for trade. It was just a pity they weren't performing during his opening hours but he could leave the window lights on later than usual. He had to give Sara full marks for trying to drum up trade, but wondered how she had ever persuaded her straight-laced mother to agree to the idea. Now he needed to think up some business ideas of his own to bring in the punters, but thoughts of marketing and selling were driven from his mind by speculation on the contents of his safe and by the possibility of those unwanted antiques in the vicarage barn.

## Chapter Three

Chris carried on restoring the pine clock case until the daylight began to fail. He became very engrossed in the work. When he finally checked his watch he was surprised to see it had gone nine o'clock. It was time to have something to eat then think about a walk by the reservoir to the back of the old vicarage.

He wasn't much of a cook. He made a cheese sandwich and another mug of coffee, took them into the sitting room and sat by the French windows. Outside, the evening was fine. The light was failing, but not fast enough for his plans. Swifts and Swallows could be seen skimming over the surface of the lake, catching the abundant flies that bred there. Some small Pipistrelle bats fluttered around the rooftops chasing the insects that rose in clouds from the reservoir. Chris took his time finishing the coffee and reading the Antique Gazette, checking the small ads for anything he might have missed. He particularly noticed there was a full page of photographs of stolen items that had been taken from a house in Stamford, which was just over the county border from Barrowick. He needed to keep an eye out for those and make sure he didn't buy them in the trade.

As he turned the pages, he studied the sales reports and noticed that clocks were making good prices at auction. That meant the pine clock he was restoring, should make a good profit for him, especially if he could sell it to a private punter. The problem was, few private buyers came his way as the shop was so far off the beaten track. He knew he could move the clock in the trade or sell it through the local auction room but for the best return on his work he needed to sell it privately. The clock works and dial stood against the wall near his bed in the next room. He'd propped them there to avoid the dust in the workshop while he worked on the case. The dial was nothing exceptional, just a white painted example with gilded sea shells painted in the corners, typical of its period. He dated it to about 1840, which was late for a desirable grandfather clock, being into the Victorian period. Chris went into the bedroom and checked the clock dial. As well as the sea shells on the corners it had a maker's name painted on it - William Aris of Uppingham. He thought it would be worth advertising in the Rutland Times and trying to sell it in the local area as there was the connection to Uppingham, which was a village only a few miles south of Barrowick. With his mind made up about the clock, he went to the bedroom window and checked the state of the daylight. By that time the birds had all gone to roost leaving the bats to hunt in the dark.

Chris watched the tiny bats until it was time for him to take a walk along the reservoir path. They flitted around the old butchery like small pieces of charred paper in an updraught, catching the flies that hovered above the roof where the heat of the day was still radiating from the pantiles.

He strolled across the road from the shop in the failing evening light, and took the lane towards the lake. There were still a few fishing boats on the water but happily most of them had gone back to the boatyard or were already heading in that direction.

Chris hesitated at the water's edge and watched a lone fishing boat on the far side of the lake. While he waited for the last of the fishermen to go, he stood and watched a pair of Mute swans feeding in the shallow water.

The dealer met no cyclists or walkers on the footpath at that late hour. He was pleased to find it completely deserted as he walked through the wooded area behind the churchyard then made his way along the section of footpath that ran past the back of the vicarage.

His walk soon brought him to the back of the vicarage, where there was a small wooden gate set in the dry stone wall. Taking one last look around to check he was not observed, he vaulted the gate and walked into the vicarage grounds. Sara was right about the numerous outbuildings. There was one substantial stone structure, which looked like the barn, and there was a large wooden stable block. In addition there were two smaller buildings, which could have been workshops or garages. Chris realised the vicars of Barrowick must have been well off in the past. It must have been a well paid post. In the old days they would have had a pony and trap, a groom and a gardener; certainly, one or two other servants would be needed to run a house of that size. It must indeed have been a well-endowed church providing a good living. No wonder the younger sons of the gentry, who didn't inherit their family estates, turned to the church or the army for a comfortable future. He hesitated and checked the vicarage for signs of life. Satisfied there were no people or lights showing in the house, he made his way quietly up the yard

The first building he came to had its door swinging open. He switched on his torch and looked inside but could see nothing of interest. By the wall was a pile of old straw and a few empty sacks, just the place for rats to thrive. Chris shuddered at the thoughts of that. He didn't like rats, they had a habit of moving fast and running over his feet. He stood very still and listened for any signs of vermin but heard nothing.

17

The stable block had been converted into a garage with the addition of large double wooden doors and the removal of all the partitions and stalls. That made sense as the last vicar would have needed a car, living out in Barrowick, away from most of his parishioners, and by his time the days of ponies and traps would have long passed. That left the other outbuildings and the large barn, which were much nearer the house and the main road, to be searched. He switched off his torch to avoid being detected.

He moved cautiously across the yard to the large stone barn, checking that he could not be seen from the road, then walked around the building looking for the entrance. This time he found the stout wooden double doors were intact and securely locked. He tried to pull them open but the lock held firm, so he stood back and considered his options. The building had no windows to speak of, just triangular slits set high up in the stone walls to allow the air to circulate inside and keep the hay fresh. He realised those narrow openings probably gave access to the bats he'd seen that evening. The slits were of no use to him, being too high to afford a view inside and too small to be used as a means of entry, so he turned his attention again to the double doors and tried to force them apart with a length of discarded timber he found lying in the yard. Although they were firmly locked, the old doors had warped and didn't fit properly together so they gave him a restricted view into the building. Sure enough, the barn was full of dark, regular shapes, which he suspected could be furniture. Sara could well be right!

Chris stood peering into the gloomy barn trying to see what the contents could be. Gradually, as his eyes became accustomed to the poor light, he could make out the things nearest to the doors. There was a table and chairs stacked onto a bow fronted chest of drawers. If that chest was made of Cuban mahogany he knew it could be worth quite a bit. He moved his head and put his other eye to the slit, trying to see more. What was that lying under the table? It looked like a small coffin or a long box, lying with its narrow end towards the door. He crouched down on his haunches and used his torch. His heart leapt! The end of the box was hollow and it had four feet attached to it, and they were not bracket feet. They were bun feet! It dawned on him then what he'd discovered: it had to be the trunk of a small longcase clock. But it was not just any run of the mill grandfather clock, it was a very dainty and very early case. He knew from his reference books that bun feet were only used at the very beginning of longcase clock making, in the 17<sup>th</sup> century.

Chris switched off the torch, stepped back from the door and tried to force it open once again but his wooden lever broke. The barn door and the iron lock were much too stout to give in to that sort of pressure. What he needed was a metal crowbar. He silently cursed for not thinking to bring one with him.

By this time the daylight had gone and it was getting quite dark. A car drew up outside the Barrowick Arms. Its headlights illuminating the vicarage yard as it backed onto the pub's gravel forecourt. Chris pressed himself against the barn wall to avoid being seen. The driver of the car walked over to the sale notice on the vicarage wall and read the Sold sign.

'Looks as if someone has bought the old place at last.' He shouted to his companions.

The dealer crouched down out of sight and cursed the interruption under his breath.

'Come on. I'm dying for a drink.' A girl's voice called from the car park. 'And me.' A second young man added. The driver turned and joined the group. The three of them went into the Barrowick Arms. At least Sara looked like being busy that evening.

As soon as the coast was clear, Chris walked quietly back to the gate of the vicarage and onto the reservoir pathway. He took the path along the water's edge and through the dark woodland towards home. As he walked, the moon came out from behind a cloud and lit up the whole scene with a silvery light, casting eerie shadows across his path. From far off he heard a Tawny Owl calling its mate and an answering call, much nearer to him. Through the trees, Rutland Water shone like a polished pewter plate. The occasional ripple of water murmured as it broke on the shoreline. From somewhere in the deepest shadows, some water birds made quiet, reassuring, noises as they settled in their night roosts. He slowed his brisk walk to a gentle amble and enjoyed the night. After all, he was in no hurry. If that was a valuable clock case he'd spied, it had been in the barn for years and a few more hours wouldn't matter.

Back at the shop, Chris checked his reference books and was even more certain that what he'd seen was an early grandfather clock case. Maybe it was just an empty case but maybe the works and face were still in it, hidden under the table in the deep shadow. That thought excited him even more, for not only was the clock likely to be very valuable, but he had a thing about old clocks and loved to restore them: the cases, the movements and the dials. When he was a young apprentice he had spent some time working at a farmhouse where the owner had a grandfather

19

clock in the hall. Chris had shown an interest in it. The proud owner, who was a knowledgeable clock collector, had taken off the hood of the clock and showed him the movement, explaining the time and strike mechanisms and telling him the history of it. Chris was hooked on longcase clocks from that day onwards. When he left the army and set up his own antique business he'd specialised in restoring grandfather clocks, learning to clean and repair the movements as well as restoring their wooden cases. He would love to work on an early example and bring it back to life. With those thoughts filling his head, he made himself a strong black coffee and considered his options.

The vicarage was sold and the new owners had already moved some items into the main house. That meant Chris had only a few days to get into the barn and check out the furniture. As it was obviously very neglected, he had few qualms about taking anything valuable he found there. The antique business thrived on shady deals. Most successful dealers bought as cheaply as possible and sold for as high a price as they could get. Most of them would pick up a bargain from any unsuspecting person and sell it to an equally gullible punter at a greatly inflated price. Sleepers at auctions, when the auctioneer hadn't recognised their true value, were the life blood of the business. It wasn't strictly honest but that is how the trade worked. Some of the more unscrupulous dealers would have diddled their own grandmothers for a fiver!

Chris regarded himself as above that sort of shady business but reasoned that this opportunity was different. No one knew the furniture was there. The owners, presumably the old vicar's heirs, had chosen to ignore the stuff and leave it to rot or get eaten by woodworm in the barn and reduced to a pile of useless sawdust. He convinced himself they deserved to lose it and the clock deserved to be restored. The new owners wouldn't have a clue it was there, so its loss was nothing to them. It wasn't so much stealing as recycling lost antiques, giving them the useful life they deserved. That sort of reasoning salved his conscience; that and the fact he was very short of stock and the money to pay for it.

When the wall clock for sale in the shop struck eleven o'clock, he stirred. The pub closed at 10.30 so they should be well and truly shut; especially as Mrs Goodacre never allowed drinking after time was called. The village was always deserted at night. His neighbours usually took their dogs for a walk in the early evening then settled down to watch TV before going to bed at about 11 o'clock. He was confident he would not be seen or disturbed at the back of the vicarage.

Tucking a crowbar and his torch under his jacket, Chris retraced his steps along the reservoir path, through the rustling woodland. At night his hearing and sense of smell was more acute. There were intriguing sounds all around him. He guessed they were probably badgers or foxes on the prowl. In one area he smelled the acrid odour of a fox but saw nothing of it. Finally he climbed over the gate and into the vicarage yard. The moon was riding high by that time and lit up the area with a ghostly white light. He checked the house was still in complete darkness then made his way to the locked barn and inserted the end of the crowbar between the wooden doors. He was about to turn on his torch to see what he was doing, when he heard a faint noise from the direction of the vicarage. He pressed himself up against the barn wall into an area of deeper shadow and held his breath while he listened.

'Careful...' A female voice giggled drunkenly. 'I'll take 'em off... if you'll only wait. You are an impatient boy.' There were more giggles and scuffling sounds from the direction of the vicarage.

Chris cursed silently to himself. Just his bad luck! There was a courting couple necking in the privacy of the vicarage porch. He settled back into the shadows and waited for them to finish their lovemaking and leave. Meanwhile, in the porch things hotted up. He heard the girl speak again. 'You are always in too much of a hurry, Garry. Slow down.'

A man's voice mumbled something inaudible and there was the rustle of clothing and deep breathing. Chris resigned himself to waiting while the courting couple enjoyed themselves, listening while her giggles turned into moans and groans. The sound of their breathing became more laboured, ending in a stifled scream from the girl and a gasp from the young man.

Thank God for that, he thought angrily, now go home. Zip up your trousers, put your knickers back on and leave me in peace!

Suddenly, to one side of the courting couple, a yellow flame pierced the darkness. Someone else was standing there and they were using a cigarette lighter. Chris was taken completely by surprise: that flame had alerted him to a third person standing in the shadow of the porch, the freshly glowing end of a cigarette pinpointed their exact position in the darkness.

'Come on Garry. You've had your fun. It's my turn now.' The second man spoke in a deeper voice.

Chris clenched his fists in frustration and waited impatiently as the two men changed places. In the porch, the girl groans were renewed as the

21

lovemaking started all over again.

The dealer waited in the shadows, growing more and more impatient. This could take all night. After a further ten minutes of whispering and rustling, he decided he would have to forget breaking into the barn that night, and he must creep back to the shop the way he had come. He waited for the moon to vanish behind some dark clouds then crept backwards, feeling his way along the barn wall towards the gate but keeping a watchful eye on the shadowy figures in the porch. Unfortunately, he'd forgotten about the piece of wood he'd discarded when he'd first attempted to break into the barn. Chris stumbled on it just as the loving couple paused for breath. The timber broke with a resounding crack.

'What's that?' The girl asked breathlessly, panic sounding in her voice.

There was a long silence as everyone listened. Chris stood stock still, pressing his body against the wall and praying the moon stayed behind the clouds long enough for him to make his escape unseen.

Finally a deep voice assured her. 'It's nothing.'

Someone struck a match and waved it in front of himself. Chris could see concern clearly etched on a young man's face as it was illuminated in the brief light. Realising the light from the match was too weak to reach where he was standing, Chris continued creeping away from the trio.

'A fox or a cat.' One of the men volunteered. 'Yes, it's a fox or a cat. They always hunt down by the reservoir. They're after the sleeping birds.'

The girl giggled, reassured by his explanation.

Chris climbed over the back gate and walked quickly back along the pathway towards his antique shop. He cursed under his breath at his bad luck. Thanks to that trio of lovers he would have to try again another night.

**Chapter Four.**

Next morning, the insistent ring of his bedside telephone woke Chris from a deep and disturbed sleep. He rolled over and checked the time. It was already 8am. He'd slept in after his late night escapade at the vicarage barn. He stretched and yawned as his mind got into gear. The telephone was still ringing so he reached out and answered it.

'Chris Doughty antiques.' He yawned as he said it but tried to sound perky and wide awake.

'I thought I'd get you out of bed.'

He recognised the caller immediately; it was Vickie, his ex wife. 'Ugh! What the devil do you want?' He glanced at the clock beside the bed. 'And at this time of the morning'

'Just to let you know I've finished sorting the last of the stock we had in store. Your bits are out in the yard behind the shop, if you can be bothered to fetch them.'

'Oh! What's that supposed to mean?' He could feel the anger rising in him.

'Just that it's dustbin day tomorrow so you'd better get here today if you want them. Otherwise the dustmen will think they're rubbish and take them away.' She didn't wait for a reply and put the phone down.

He stared at his phone, tightlipped and angry. 'That woman. She is bloody vindictive!'

Vickie's call had altered his plans for the day. It meant he would have to take his van over to Stamford and pick up the antiques she had thrown out. Chris glance out of the window at the morning, anxious to check if it was raining or if it looked like rain. With relief, he saw the sun was already up and shining, reflecting on the ripples of the lake. A few early fishermen were already on the water casting their flies for trout. Work on the pine clock would have to wait until he came back. He knew he couldn't afford to lose the stock Vickie had mentioned, even if it was second-rate stuff. He couldn't afford to be choosey.

A quarter of an hour later, shaved, washed and dressed, he sat in his kitchen eating toast and sipping hot black coffee    That phone call had been an abrupt wake-up call for him. He took the opportunity to gather his thoughts as he ate the last crust. He'd had a disturbed night. He remembered waking once or twice from lurid nightmares and frowned as the details flooded back to him.   He remembered dreaming he was making

23

love to Sara, the barmaid at his local. They were in the porch at the back of the old vicarage. This was obviously a reminder of his escapade the previous evening. Then the girl changed into Vickie, who laughed at him like some demented Harpy. He tried to run away but couldn't seem to get anywhere; it was like running into a high wind with his feet stuck in bird lime. Finally, the police arrived and arrested him for stealing hundreds of priceless antiques from the vicarage barn. When he protested his innocence, they showed him his van, which was parked behind the barn and full of fine inlaid chests, ebonised grandfather clocks, mahogany, Chippendale chairs and a bronze Athame and chalice. Chris scratched his head and grinned; that would teach him not to eat cheese and pickle sandwiches for supper.

The bad dream was very vivid and no matter how much he tried he couldn't dismiss it entirely from his mind. Maybe his subconscious was trying to tell him something important. He smiled to himself for there was no doubt he really fancied Sara. There was also no doubt, at that precise minute he really hated Vickie. Harpy was an apt description for her. Where had that sweet girl gone, the one that he'd married? The bit of his dream where he was arrested by the police, he shrugged off as simple anxiety. That sort of worry had never stopped him taking chances before; not that he usually agreed with thieving, but times were desperate. The new owners of the vicarage probably didn't even know there were old bits of furniture in their barn. The average punter would probably be pleased to get rid of the rubbish. He wasn't put off by that part of his dream. That night, he'd try his luck again. He was unlucky to have run into an impromptu menage a trois the previous night. Hopefully he'd have better luck next time.

As he had to go into Stamford that morning, he checked in the Antique Gazette and saw there was a sale on in the town. It wasn't one of the regular antique sales, it was a general sale, held the week after an antique sale, which meant there may be a few leftovers of interest that would find their way into that day's offering. Often sale rooms would put the remainders up for sale at the very next opportunity, especially if they were not the best examples of antiques.

Stamford was busy by the time he parked his white van at the rear of his old shop premises. True to her word, his ex wife had piled the remaining furniture in an untidy heap in the yard, right next to the dustbins. He loaded the items into the back of the van, covering each one with an old blanket. It was a bit late to prevent any damage as Vickie hadn't bothered how she'd stacked them, but this precaution was a habit he'd developed over years of visiting sale rooms and transporting antiques.

There was no sign of his ex wife, which suited him fine; in his present mood he really had little he wished to say to her. As he lifted up the last item, a Victorian mahogany plant stand, the back door of the premises swung open and she stood in the doorway, her arms folded across her chest and an accusing look on her face.

'I see you finally woke up then.' Dressed in a smart grey suit, she lounged against the doorframe, looking slim and businesslike.

'Yes thanks.' He mouthed the right words but they were hollow. He looked at his ex with a jaundiced eye, then remembered his vivid dream. She was still a very attractive woman, he had to concede that, and they had had a very passionate few years before it had all turned sour. He shook his head sadly.

Vickie spotted his mood and said pointedly. 'Too late feeling sorry now.'

'Who's sorry? I am enjoying the peace and quiet.'

She slammed the door shut, leaving him alone in the yard.

'Must be my bloody hormones! Just for a minute then, she looked very attractive to me. That testosterone stuff has a lot to answer for.' As he muttered to himself, a different female voice broke into his thoughts.

'This your van, Sir?'

Chris turned to see a traffic warden was eyeing his van, pad and pen poised in her hands.

'I'm loading, love.'

'From where I'm standing you're just day dreaming.'

'Just checking I've left nothing behind.' He lied. 'I'm on my way.'

The warden reluctantly closed her notepad and stood back to let him climb into the driver's seat.

'Bloody officious women!' He grunted to himself. 'The world's full of them.' Then an image of Sara, smiling at him from behind the bar of the Barrowick Arms, came into his mind; well, hopefully not all women were like that.

After he'd finished at his old shop, he drove the van to the Stamford sale rooms and viewed the items for sale that day. Most of them were modern furniture and books but there were one or two items left over from the previous antique sale, including a pair of longcase clocks. They were not desirable, early clocks, with elegant narrow trunks and long doors. They were a pair of Yorkshire clocks with wide cases and short doors. That style of clock became popular in the late Victorian period. They had large painted dials, sometimes as large as fourteen inches across, and very wide veneered cases to match. Clocks of that period seemed to have lost their elegance. He didn't like that type of longcase clock at all, but those two should sell at a profit if he got them at a bargain, price, and he badly needed the stock.

Chris toyed with the idea of leaving a bid with the auctioneer for the clocks but decided he'd have a coffee, stay for the sale and bid for them in person. He was pleased to see very few of the regular antique dealers had bothered to turn up for this general sale, so he ought to get the clocks cheaply, especially as they had been offered the previous week and hadn't sold then. That meant they would probably have a greatly reduced reserve on them , if they had one at all.

The pair of clocks were offered as one lot and came up for sale early in the auction. Chris waited until the auctioneer had reduced his asking price to a very low figure then put in a bid. The man took Chris's bid for one hundred pounds.

'One hundred pounds. I have one hundred pounds. Where's One Twenty?' The auctioneer worked the room. 'One Twenty. Where's One Fifty?'

Chris raised his hand again.

'I have One Fifty.' The auctioneer pointed to the back of the room. 'One Sixty.' Then he came back to Chris.

The dealer bid again.

'I have One Eighty. Any advance on One Eighty?'

The room was quiet and Chris thought for a minute he would get the clocks for that reasonable figure; he certainly didn't want to bid much more for them.

Suddenly a female voice piped up from the back of the room. 'Two Hundred.'

He looked around and saw a familiar figure in a smart grey suit. It was Vickie who was bidding against him!

'Two Twenty.' He called out.

'Two Fifty.' She topped his bid yet again. Vickie was not a clock enthusiast, so he knew she was outbidding him just for spite. Those clock would take some restoring and would cost a lot of money to make them saleable. She was just being bloody minded towards him.

He raised a hand and put in one last bid, and that was more than he had intended to spend.

'Two Hundred and Seventy.' The auctioneer called out.

'Three Hundred.' The familiar female voice called from the back of the room. Vickie knew he couldn't continue to match her bids.

He turned to face her and gave her a sickly grin. 'You win' He mouthed. He had some satisfaction in knowing she had paid well over the odds for those wrecks but he was mad that she should have been so mean towards him. As he left the sale room he couldn't resist a jibe as he passed close by. 'You paid far too much for those clocks, dear. It will cost you twice as much again to get them in working order.'

She smiled cattily at him and turned away to speak to a woman at her side.

Chris didn't drive directly back to Barrowick with his load of tired furniture but took the main road and travelled towards Oakham. As his van climbed the hill towards Barnsdale he glanced over Rutland Water towards Barrowick, which nestled on the far shore. It looked so peaceful but because of the stretch of mature woodland lining the foreshore, the village was barely visible. The only clue to the presence of the houses was the very tops of the chimneys and the spiral of smoke issuing from one of them. The only buildings clearly in view were the church with its crenellated sandstone tower, and part of the old stone vicarage nestling behind its barn. Unfortunately there was no sight of his antique shop. Even if travellers happened to glance over the water as they drove along the main road, as he had done, they would have no inkling his business was there. What he needed was a huge signboard, right at the water's edge but he knew there was no chance of that in an area noted for its natural beauty. Maybe he could persuade the new owners of the vicarage to put a billboard at the back of their premises. Fat chance of that either!

In Oakham, Chris struggled to find a space in one of the car parks but patience did eventually pay off. He walked into South Street and called at the Rutland Times office to place an advert in the newspaper to try to sell the pine grandfather clock. The girl at the desk was very helpful, she typed out the ad and handed it to him to check.

'Better add the name William to that. Make it 'William Aris of Uppingham.' There was a son of his called Thomas, who traded in Horn Lane, but that was a bit later. An older clock is more valuable.' He handed back the advert for correction and paid for two insertions.

After visiting the newspaper office he drove to the local auction room. It wasn't official viewing day but the auctioneer was always accommodating to the trade and let them have a look at the goods going into the next sale when they picked up their last purchases. Chris had left a bid on a bundle of damaged picture frame in the last sale. He knew it would mean a lot of work repairing the missing plaster and gold leaf if he'd managed to buy them, but he'd left a very low bid in the hope of getting a bargain. He did need some new stock and he was short of cash.

'Anything for me?' He asked at the office window.

The girl checked her files. 'Yes, Mr Doughty, some frames.'

Chris paid for his purchases and loaded them into the back of his van before he walked around the trestle tables to view the goods on show for the next sale.

'Hello, Chris.' The auctioneer came out of his office and greeted him. 'Picking up your frames?'

'Yes thanks. I'm amazed I got them at that price.'

'Well not everybody want's to be bothered to restore damaged goods like that even if they had the skill to do it.'

Or daft enough to spend the time, Chris thought. Business was so slow at Barrowick, he had all the time in the world. He changed the subject. 'I see the old vicarage up the road from me in Barrowick, has been sold at last. Any whispers of who's bought it?'

The auctioneer shook his head. 'I don't think it's a local, Chris. Someone did mention a professor or doctor of some sort, but I don't know anything definite.'

Chris raised his eyebrows at that snippet of gossip. A professor? Maybe some academic was retiring and wanted a challenge?

'That's not gospel. It's only something I heard this morning.' The auctioneer looked over the sale room at the stock laid out on the tables. 'Anything you fancy?'

'No, not this time.' He rarely found anything he fancied at the ordinary furniture sales but it was always worth checking in case there was a valuable sleeper that no one else had noticed.

The auctioneer continued. 'The sale after this one is an antiques and collectibles one. I'm fetching in a couple of early oak grandfather clocks from Braunston. They might interest you.'

Chris nodded. Good stock that was right and not a marriage, was hard to find. 'Are they right?'

'They've been in the same family for generations, so they might be. You'll have to view. I haven't seen them yet. I just got a call about them.'

Chris thanked him for the information and returned to his van. Most grandfather clocks that came onto the market had passed through the trade and had been messed about. Unscrupulous dealers thought nothing of fitting a replacement dial or movement into a nice case to get a better price for it. That was what the trade meant by a marriage, he thought. A bit like my marriage; not exactly made in heaven!  He arrived  back in Barrowick in time for a late lunch at his local pub.

## Chapter Five

After lunch, when he'd unloaded the contents of the van, Chris buffed the final beeswax coat on the pine clock case and moved it into the showroom. He was pleased with the restoration and hoped the advert in the Rutland Times would help to sell it. He brought the movement and dial down from his bedroom and fixed them in place. Once the weights and pendulum were fitted, he started the clock and adjusted the pendulum crutch to put it into tick. Satisfied with the even sound of the escapement he put the hands to the correct time and the date wheel to the correct date then started the clock.

It sounded good and it looked even better. He was confident it would sell and it would look good in a traditional farmhouse kitchen. He was more than pleased with the results of all his hard work, and sat on a chaise on the opposite side of the showroom, just to admire it. Getting that clock set up had taken his mind off the fiasco at the Stamford sale. His silly bitch of an ex had really excelled herself at that sale. Just because she thought he wanted those two wide clocks, she had to outbid him. That was her mistake. He would have had the clocks at the right price as he had the time and the expertise to restore them but she paid far too much for them. Now she had the problem of getting them restored and selling them for more than they cost her. There was some hopes of that.

Chris checked his work on the eight day pine clock. 'Well William Aris, I don't think you'll be here for long. Someone is going to like the look of you, I'm sure.' He addressed the clock like an old friend. Grandfather clocks had that effect on him. He felt he knew them personally, once he'd restored them and brought them back to useful life. It was a great pity he had to pass them on to make a living. Other antiques he bought and sold without a qualm but each longcase clock had its own personality and became something of a friend as he restored it.

With the work on William Aris completed, Chris came to a crossroad in his day. What to start next? There were the bits of furniture he'd picked up from the Stamford shop but he knew there was nothing inspiring among that lot because Vickie had made sure she kept the best pieces. There were the gilded picture frames he'd bought at the last Oakham auction, just waiting to be restored, but he'd no immediate need for them as he had no oil paintings or prints in stock that needed framing. Inevitably his thoughts returned to the bronze knife and chalice locked in the safe.

A witch's Athame and a drinking vessel lined with the top of a human skull. Those thoughts gave him the shivers. Where did a chalice maker get a human skull from? What did they put in the chalice during a Black Mass? With difficulty, he dismissed those disturbing images from his mind and concentrated on thoughts of the barn behind the old vicarage. That tantalizing glimpse of bun feet on the clock case in the barn was still exciting him. That night he must get a proper look at that case. As the vicarage had been sold, he knew that may be his last chance.

Chris passed the afternoon checking over the items he had acquired and noting what work was needed to make them saleable, a replacement handle here, a piece of new veneer there, a set of period brass handles to replace the plastic monstrosities someone had fitted to a Victorian chest of drawers. He made no attempt to start the restoration as his mind was filled with anticipation of the evening's work. He pottered about, passing the time until it went dusk. He had decided to return to the barn just after dark that night and not wait until the pub closing time, just in case the vicarage porch proved to be a regular haunt for courting couples. Chris lingered over his tea, reading every paragraph in the Antique Gazette several time, just willing the time to pass.

At last, at about half past nine in the evening, he judged the time was right. Main Street was deserted, the last fisherman had left the lake and any customers at the Barrowick Arms were busy drinking. He was glad to see there were no cars parked in front of the pub that evening. Gathering some tools he made his move.

Once again it was a fine evening. The moon was up but there was more cloud cover. The water fowl were all roosting. The sheep, which grazed the foreshore, were laying quietly under the hedges. The trees in the woodland rustled gently in the evening breeze. Overhead, the small bats flittered to and fro, catching the flies which hovered in thick clouds over the lake. A Barn Owl passed overhead, white and silent on velvety wings as it quartered the foreshore, only disclosing its presence with an eerie shriek. He was pleased to find all was peaceful and quiet; the only signs of people were on the far side of the lake where car headlights constantly lit up the main road between Oakham and Stamford. He made his way stealthily to the barn doors and hesitated there, listening intently to the sounds around him. There was nothing to be heard, no courting couples behind the vicarage, no one on Main Street and there was no light showing in the old vicarage. He breathed a sigh of relief and set about forcing the barn doors open.

The vicarage barn was well built. The doors resisted Chris's attempts for some time but gradually he managed to increase the gap between them until he could insert the crowbar properly and get a good purchase on them. He pulled on the crowbar with all his strength and the doors parted with a suddens resounding crack! The iron ring that held the lock had been torn out of the old wood. He stood stock still, letting his breathing settle and straining his ears to detect any unusual sounds about him. Thankfully nothing stirred. Chris was sure no one had been about to hear the sound of the door breaking but he needed to be certain. Finally, satisfied he was undetected, he slipped into the barn and stood just inside the doorway letting his eyes get used to the dark.

Once Chris got his bearings, he closed the barn door behind him and switched on his torch. He kept the beam on the ground so little stray light lit up the triangular slits, high in the barn walls. The long piece of furniture with the bun feet was clearly visible under a trestle table. He drew in a sharp breath as the torchlight confirmed the black box was indeed a small clock case, only about five feet tall. Dropping to his knees he took a closer look. It had four bun feet, a long narrow door in the trunk and a small, hood. The top was pointed like a house roof, it looked to be an example of an early, architectural style, longcase clock. Such clocks were produced in England very soon after the grandfather clock was first invented, in the second half of the 17$^{th}$ century. Unfortunately someone in the distant past had 'improved' this example by painting it brown and putting a false grain on it by dragging a comb over the wet paint. When he had overcome his disappointment, he shone the torch into the hood to check the dial and movement. He was to be even more disappointed. The clock works and face were missing. It seemed he had discovered just an empty case, which had probably suffered at the hands of some amateur restorer in Victorian times when they regularly 'improved' antique pieces of furniture by painting or carving them.

Chris played the torch beam all around the barn, hoping to be rewarded with a glimpse of a small square clock dial but there was nothing but dusty old furniture to be seen. Disappointed but not too down-hearted, because there were still ample places for the clock movement to be hidden, he turned his attention back to the clock hood. Placing the torch on the barn floor, he tried to open the glazed door on the front of the hood. To his delight the door didn't open towards him, like a regular cupboard door hung on hinges, the whole hood lifted up over the top of the case. This was exactly what he would have expected of a very early grandfather clock case.

Satisfied it had been worth his while breaking into the building, Chris turned his attention to the rest of the barn. Under layers of dust, dirt and cobwebs he could make out the shapes of chests of drawers, chairs and several stands. There were also many pieces of old timber, probably the partitions from the stable. Even though they were riddled with woodworm and useless, someone in the distant past, had thought it worth storing them. He ran his fingers over the top of one chest of drawers to remove the thick layer of dust and was delighted to see the rich colour and grain of dark Cuban mahogany. By the style of the brass handles it was late Georgian and would be well worth restoring.

By this time, he estimated he would fill his van four times over to remove all the barn contents, but how could he do that? People would certainly notice a van parked in the yard for it was in full view of the street and the pub. There was no way he could carry all that furniture along the lakeside path back to his shop. He was in a dilemma. He had been keen to see what was in the barn but now he knew what treasures lay there and realised there was no way they could be removed easily, he was bitterly disappointed. Thinking he could at least take the clock case, he knelt down under the table and eased the hood up from the trunk, intending to carry that home for a start and then find a way to collect the rest of it. He had just managed to remove the hood when there was a sound of gates opening and the bright beams of car headlights lit up the barn. There was a vehicle drawing into the vicarage yard!

'Damn!' Chris cursed aloud and switched off his torch. Voices came from the yard from the direction of the garage. Someone had parked a car there and was coming in his direction. He had to think quickly. Whoever had parked in the yard had done it openly and must have permission to be there, whereas he was an intruder. Maybe the new owners had turned up at this late hour to view their purchase? Not wishing to be caught in the barn with the evidence of a recently broken door, he sneaked out of the building and crept towards the back of the garden.

'Who's that?!' A man's voice rang out and a powerful torch beam cut the gloom, illuminating Chris in its light.

He decided to brazen it out rather than run. He did not know how many people there were in the yard, and they had by that time got a good look at him anyway. Surreptitiously, he dropped the crowbar against the wall into some long grass and stepped forward.

'I'm local. Who are you?' Chris held his hands up to shield his eyes from the bright beam.

The man ignored his question and asked in an educated voice. 'What are you doing here?'

'I happened to be walking by on the road and thought I saw some lights in here. I decided to investigate. I live at the top of the village and I know this house has been empty for years.'

Slowly the man approached Chris, keeping the light fixed on him. Finally, satisfied that he looked innocent enough, the man softened his approach. 'I'm the new owner of the vicarage. I suppose I should thank you for keeping an eye on it. Mr er...?'

Chris wiped his dusty hands on his trousers and shook hands with the new arrival. 'I'm Chris Doughty. I'm in business at the old butcher's shop on Main Street.'

'Oh! We have a butcher in the village as well as a pub. The place is not as backward as I thought.'

'No. Sorry to disappoint you. I run an antique business from the premises.'

'Oh! I see.'

The dealer had by that time regained his composure and began to take stock of the new arrival. The man was tall and slim; a good six inches taller than he was. It was impossible for the dealer to see his face with the torch beam trained on him, but he appeared to have a large shock of light grey hair. The man's shoes, which were clearly visible in the circle of light thrown by the torch, were of highly polished, black leather and looked very expensive. His voice was clear and cultivated. This could well be the professor Chris had heard about, being a man with such an educated accent.

'I'm Dr O'Conlan by the way. I'm sure we shall meet about the village.' The newcomer turned and went back to his car. Chris recovered the crowbar and hid it under his coat, then left the vicarage grounds by the front gate. That had been a close call. If he had been discovered inside the barn, it would have taken a lot more explaining. He glanced back at the car parked in the vicarage grounds just in time to see Dr O'Conlan arm in arm with a woman. They crossed the road and went into the Barrowick Arms.

# Chapter Six

The next morning Chris was busy in his workshop when he heard the sounds of workmen in the village. There was the noise of loud hammering coming from somewhere nearby. It was the unmistakable ring of mallet on wood; it sounded as if wooden posts were being hammered into the ground. Suspecting this activity might be at the old vicarage, he put down the veneering iron and ran upstairs to his balcony overlooking the main street. Sure enough, things were happening at the front of the vicarage.

From his high view point he could see three men standing in front of the building and erecting two stout posts overlooking Main Street. From the size and position of these posts, it was obvious a substantial sign was being placed there. He recognised one of the men from his appearance and the way he moved. The man was small with a slight limp and he had an untidy shock of black hair, which fell over his face. It had to be Dave Porter, a local antique dealer who frequented the auctions and car boot sales, always trying to do somebody down.

Chris hadn't a lot of time for Dave. He didn't trust him. Helping Dave erect the posts was a man he didn't recognise; he was probably a local carpenter or builder. The other figure was Dr O'Conlan who stood on the pavement, directing the operation with his arms folded over his chest. That was a strange pairing; O'Conlan, the educated professor and Dave Porter, the untrustworthy dealer. He wondered how that pair had come together.

Chris had little interest in the vicarage, except for the contents of the barn; which were probably lost to him now the new owner had arrived on the scene, but he took a better look at Dr. O'Conlan in the daylight. The previous night he had assumed the man's fair hair to be white but now he could see it was light auburn, knocking fifteen years off the previous estimate of the his age. He looked to be about fifty years old in the light of day. Chris watched as the tall thin figure directed the erecting of the sign. He seemed to be used to authority and obviously knew exactly what he wanted as he stood and supervised the work being done on his property.

All this activity intrigued the dealer. The sign they were erecting must be advertising something. Maybe the new owner was going to run a business from the house? Maybe a hotel or even a B&B? But he had to admit that O'Conlan didn't look like a typical businessman; certainly not a hotel keeper. Someone had mentioned the new owner was a professor.

He was certainly very well spoken and had an educated air about him. He was also a doctor. A doctor of what? Chris mused. What sort of business did a professor run? The dealer walked slowly down the stairs and back to his workshop, intrigued and heartened by the thought of more customers being attracted to Barrowick by the arrival of a new business venture in the village.

It was lunch time before Chris left the shop to walk down to the local pub for his mid-day meal. On the way he stopped at the vicarage and read the newly erected sign. 'The Psychic College' it announced in large gold capital letters. Under this title was the owner's details. It read, Principal Dr. Francis. O'Conlan MA, DD. then below this was a website address and phone number.

DD? Chris pondered on the letters. That must be Doctor of Divinity, a strange qualification for a teacher of the occult, but maybe the man had church connections. He was still considering this mystery and wondering what exactly a psychic college taught its students when he entered the bar at the Barrowick Arms.

'Hi Chris.' Sara greeted him cheerily. 'Your usual?'

He nodded and glanced around the bar. Seated in the far corner near the bay window was the new owner of the vicarage and beside him was a woman. Chris found a table behind the couple where he could face the woman but Dr O'Conlan's back was turned towards him. He was curious and wanted to observe them without being too obvious about it.

The woman was an interesting looking female; probably in her mid forties but very well preserved. She had red hair falling in tight curls to her shoulders. Her face was not pretty in the traditional sense, but attractive and strong, with high cheek bones and the most unusual green eyes. Her figure, what he could see of it as she was sitting down at table, was willowy but not too thin. She realised he was looking at her, caught his eye and gave him a knowing smile. He could feel himself colour up, a trifle embarrassed at being caught out. He lowered his gaze and concentrated on his lunch.

Dr. O'Conlan had an air of authority about him. He was very much at ease and teased Sara when she came to serve them drinks. She seemed taken with the compliments he gave her and blushed at his remarks. The dealer watched them with interest and was surprised to see Sara acting so girlishly. He realised he had never seen her blush before. Francis O'Conlan obviously had an easy manner with the ladies.

As Chris ate his meal, he watched his new neighbors out of the corner of his eye. They were engrossed in deep conversation, heads together and occasionally laughing. It was obvious they were on the same wavelength and very much at ease in each other's company.

After lunch Chris returned to the shop and started renovating some of the swept and gilded picture frames he had bought at the Oakham auction. When he eventually stopped for a coffee as the gesso dried on the frames, he decided to get his laptop and check online what the new Psychic College was offering in the way of courses. He was curious about this new business in the village and wondered how it might increase his own customer numbers.

Chris found the College offered numerous esoteric and occult subjects. It seemed many of these could be studied by distance learning. He found courses on telepathy, on dowsing, on mediumship, on Wicca and psychic development advertised on the website. The site also stated they planned to have in-house teaching available once the college had renovated its new premises and prepared its large lecture hall. Large lecture hall? That must be the barn, he thought. That large building would make an ideal lecture hall once it was renovated but they would need new lighting and heating in there. He read the blurb about the various courses and noticed there was a picture of the woman he had observed in the bar. She was tutoring the Tarot and Psychic Devlopment courses. Her name was Tanith O'Conlan, and her qualifications consisted of a cluster of letters he had never seen before. There was no doubt in his mind that she was Dr. O'Conlan's wife. It was a family business, but a strange one for a Doctor of Divinity to be involved in.

Chris was intrigued by Francis O'Conlon's wife's name. Tanith was an exotic and unusual name that he'd met only once before, in a science fiction story. He Googled the name and found Tanith was an early Phoenician deity, the goddess of love, fertility, the moon and the stars. He wondered if she had been given such an exotic name at birth or if she had adopted it to fit her persona as a mystic. Having checked the whole website, he closed his laptop and considered the situation. It couldn't be bad that a new venture was opening in the village. Maybe there would be more business for him once the residential courses got underway and more people were attracted to the area.

Chris's thoughts then turned to the vicarage barn and its contents. Obviously the new owners would soon want to empty that building so they could get on with converting it to a lecture hall. It might be worth his while suggesting he could do a clearance for them at a reasonable price. He had the van and the time and he was also close at hand in the village. He decided he'd take the first opportunity to offer them his services.

Chris's afternoon was taken up with restoring the old picture frames. He replaced the missing pieces with new gesso then sanded these areas and applied fresh gold leaf to them. It was painstaking work, which could not be hurried, and the time passed quickly enough. There were no interruptions from customers and no business to be had. Eventually he stopped when the daylight started to fail and the evening began to fall, had a shower and made himself a simple meal, then he sat in the light of the French windows in his flat and read the Antique Gazette. Finally he threw the trade paper down and poured himself a large Scotch as a nightcap.

Sitting in the half light, relaxing, his mind returned to the contents of the shop safe. The Athame and the chalice were safely locked away in there, but they kept playing on his mind. He felt that he must get rid of them to a collector as soon as he could. Where to advertise them? The Antique Gazette seemed the obvious place; the local newspaper would hardly be the place to advertise such exotic objects. He determined to write an advert the very next day and post it off to the Gazette. The sooner the better, as he found the presence of those witchcraft items strangely disturbing.

With no chance of getting into the barn again at the old vicarage, Chris went to bed early that night. It was with some relief, he gave up any ideas of stealing the antiques in the barn as the house was now occupied. He realised how desperate he had become contemplating such a crime, but with his business failing and money getting very short, he felt he had an excuse. He had often sailed close to the wind in his antique dealings but had never done anything outright criminal in the past. Perhaps it was a good thing he had been prevented from getting really involved in stealing by the timely arrival of the new owner of the vicarage. Looking at it from a distance, and sitting in a comfortable chair with a glass of whisky in his hand, he knew he would not have been happy if he had stolen the vicarage antiques. He could only think the lack of business had temporarily clouded his judgement. Maybe, O'Conlan turning up when he did, had been a blessing in disguise.

Chris sat musing about the dagger and the chalice until it grew dark then finished off the cheese and the last of a jar of pickled onions for his supper before he checked the shop door was locked then went up to bed.

During the night the wind sprang up and it rained hard. The old butcher's shop was far from draft proof with its old sash windows, ill fitting doors and French windows. The curtains in his bedroom billowed out from the window as a storm brewed over Barrowick. He buried his head under the pillow to cut out the noise of the wind and rain raging outside, and eventually drifted into a disturbed sleep.

At two o'clock in the morning he had a vivid nightmare. It wasn't at all like his normal dreams. He dreamed that someone or something had broken into the shop and was searching for the bronze knife and chalice that were locked in the safe. The presence was dark and menacing; there was an air of evil about it. He smelled the fumes from burning sulphur in his nostrils and experienced feelings of intense dread. Chris shook with fright and his body was wet with sweat. He had only partially woken up when he was shocked by a crashing sound from down in the shop.

The dealer sat up in his bed and peered into the darkness, temporarily unable to distinguish fact from the dream world he had just left. The bedroom curtains, billowing in the gale, which was still raging outside, looked for all the world like a tall figure silhouetted against the light of the window. Chris panicked and reached to turn on the reading light on his locker but it didn't work; the storm must have cut the electricity supply to the village. He fumbled in the drawer at his bedside, frantically feeling for the torch he kept there.

His bedside locker was a mess. The drawer was full of loose tissues, broken biscuits, dud batteries and other bits and pieces he'd stuffed in there and never bothered to sort out. In his haste he grabbed the first flat object his fingers fell upon. He held it up in his hand, searching for the switch with his fingers but he couldn't find it. When his fears finally subsided, he was surprised to feel it was a small hard-backed book. He held it close to his face to try to identify it but it was far too dark to see. Putting the book to one side, he searched again with both hands until his fingers felt the flat metal case of the torch. Chris turned the torch on and shone its beam across the room looking for the intruder. With intense relief he found there was no one there, only the disheveled curtains draped across the window panes.

Wet from sweat, he sank back on the bed and tried to relaxed. The sounds of his heart beating loudly in his ears and his heavy breathing only gradually lessened. It was then he realised the gale had stopped blowing. The lightning and the rain, which had been beating against the building, had abruptly stopped. All was peaceful and normal again.

That had been quite a squall. He guessed there would be some damage done; maybe a tree or two down in the village. He lay back, trying to relax and calm down, when suddenly from downstairs he heard a loud but familiar noise! He immediately realised it was the sound that had woken him up. It was the shop door banging!

Abruptly the bedside light came on as the electricity supply was reconnected. He put on his dressing gown and made his way downstairs and into the shop area. There he found the front door wide open and swinging in the breeze. With his bare feet he felt wet on the floor inside the doorway, where the rain had blown in. Chris shook his head in disbelief. He was sure he'd locked that door before he'd gone to bed, but decided he must have been mistaken and had obviously forgotten to make the shop secure. Maybe he'd better cut out the whisky night caps and the cheese and pickle suppers, if they were going to upset his sleep like that!

Thoroughly awake by this time, he made himself a warm milk drink and took it back up to bed. He adjusted the curtains at the bedroom window and peered out into the night, looking out over the sleeping village. He was not surprised to see the vicarage was ablaze with lights in every room. The gale must have disturbed their sleep as well. Back in bed, he punched his pillow to make it more comfortable and lay back. It was then he felt the small book he'd taken from the drawer in his panic. Intrigued by the find, which he couldn't remember ever putting in the drawer, he clicked on the bedside light again to look at it more closely. He was surprised to see it was a Gideon bible, a New Testament that he'd occasionally seen in hotel rooms where they were left by the side of beds so that a weary traveller might find solace in the text. How it got into the locker drawer he couldn't think. He'd certainly not put it there. When he thought more about it, he decided the book must have been hidden in the back of the drawer all the time. He'd bought the cabinet at the local auction when he moved into the old butcher's shop; it had come with other bits of second hand furniture.

It was years since Chris had read a bible; not since his early days in the army. He hadn't been interested in religion since his early childhood when he was sent to Sunday school to give his mother a peaceful hour or two on a Sunday afternoon. In spite of his lack of interest in religion, he found the little book comforting. He placed the bible on top of the bedside cabinet until the morning.

Next morning Chris was surprised to see there had been no damage in the village. There were still puddles of rain water in the road but no sign of any tree branches down. He was standing at the front of his shop taking in the morning when he noticed a man walking up the high street towards him. He immediately recognised the new owner of the vicarage.

Francis O'Conlan continued up the High Street until he arrived at the antique shop then he came inside. This was the first time Chris had had a chance to really size the man up at close quarters in the daylight. O'Conlan was tall and slim with an athletic figure for his age. His eyes were a piercing grey blue in colour, complimenting the sandy colour of his hair. He had the air of a self assured man, who was used to getting his own way.

'Morning' Chris smiled and greeted the newcomer.

'Good morning...Mr Doughty isn't it?' The doctor held out his hand and firmly shook the dealer's. 'You remember we met the other evening when you kindly checked on my premises.'

Chris nodded but didn't interrupt the man as he seemed to have more to say.

O'Conlan continued. 'You were right to suspect someone was lurking around the vicarage. We had a burglary only a few days ago.'

Chris frowned. 'That is unfortunate. Anything valuable stolen?'

'Yes actually, and that is what I want to talk to you about.'

The dealer was taken by surprise at this remark. 'I haven't seen anything suspicious since we last met but if there's anything you think I can do to help, I will.'

'Good. There were only two items stolen. Small things, but part of my collection and of some sentimental value to me.' The visitor reached into his pocket and took out a photograph, which he handed to Chris. 'You being in the antique trade, I wondered if anyone had offered you these items.'

Chris took the photograph and glanced at it. His heart missed a beat when he saw the picture was of the very same bronze knife and chalice he had locked in his safe. The shock must have shown on his face because his startled expression was immediately pounced on by the visitor.

'Ah! So you have seen them.'

The dealer could hardly deny the fact that he'd bought the items. He slowly nodded his head and looked even closer at the image on the photograph, hoping he'd got it wrong, but there was no doubt it was the same Athame and chalice. He went into the back shop, opened the safe, took out the bundle containing the stolen goods and took them in to the customer where he hastened to explain. 'I bought them thinking they were Victorian brass things of little value. I never suspected they were stolen.'

41

Francis O'Conlan beamed when he saw the bronze artifacts unwrapped and placed on the table.

'Brilliant! I knew you'd have them...' Quickly he added, '...I had a hunch you might have them You being the closest antique shop to my home.'

Chris frowned. This seemed too convenient an answer, and O'Conlan had been a bit too fast adding that last comment. The doubt must have shown on the dealer's face.

O'Conlan smiled and put his hands together as if he was about to pray. 'I must admit I did some research first before I approached you. I dowsed for the objects with a pendulum and was certain they were here in your shop.'

This explanation really did surprise Chris. He did not believe in such methods but said nothing as he remembered the man did run the Psychic College and was probably an expert on such things.

'I suppose you paid someone good money for these.' O'Conlan pointed to his items on the table.

'Yes, as a matter of fact I did...but I can't tell you who he was as I've never seen him before or since.' Chris lied to save Steve.

Ignoring the disclaimer about who sold the items, O'Conlan continued. 'I will reimburse you, of course.'

'That's very fair of you.' Chris was surprised at his generosity, knowing from past experience that if the stolen goods had been reported to the police, the rightful owner would eventually get them back and the dealer would be left out of pocket.

As if reading his mind O'Conlan said. 'I have not yet reported the theft to the authorities. As a serious collector of these artifacts I have several such items for my studies, but not everyone would understand my interest in the unusual. I would much prefer to buy the items off you and put them straight back into my collection, no questions asked.'

Chris nodded agreement, but he wasn't entirely convinced by the man's explanation.

'Now, as to the cost. If you bought them as Victorian items you can't be much out of pocket. What am I in your debt? £20? Or was it a little more?'

The antique dealer gulped; that was too much of a coincidence. To come straight to his shop to look for the items and then to offer exactly the amount he had paid for them. That was uncanny. He nodded . '£20 is exactly what I paid for them.'

Francis O'Conlan smiled a self satisfied smile. 'Good. I'm glad my psychic powers are working well today.' He took a twenty pound note from his pocket and handed it to Chris, then continued. 'Now to some other business. I see you have a van, Mr Doughty. I need someone to clear the barn at the vicarage as we must get on with our renovations in there. Would you be interested in clearing it for us?'

Chris was even more surprised at this request. The man must indeed be a mind reader the way he kept astonishing him with his insider knowledge. It had been in the dealer's mind to volunteer to clear the barn, in the hope of getting some of the antiques in there. Now he was being offered the job without even asking for it.

'Of course we'll pay you to take any rubbish to the local tip and anything valuable to the auction room, unless there's anything you would like to buy for your own business.' The man picked up the knife and bowl and made to leave the shop. At the door he turned and smiled. 'Many thanks for your help, Mr Doughty. I'm sure as neighbours, we will often see each other about the village.'

Chris nodded and followed the man to the door then watched him leave the shop and walk back to the vicarage. When he was alone again, Chris flopped into a chair and took a deep breath. That was some meeting! The Athame and chalice were gone and any hope of a good profit gone with them. Doctor O'Conlan seemed to know exactly what had happened and where to find his stolen goods. He knew, or made a very accurate guess at, the price paid for them, and he seemed to know that he was interested in the contents of the barn. Chris wondered if he had put two and two together when he found the barn door forced open. The events of the past half hour seemed more and more mysterious to him as he sat and pondered them. Not once had the man shown any interest in who had sold the stolen goods to him. There was no query about a name or even a description of the thief. He had never met anyone quite like Dr Francis O'Conlan and was very intrigued by him. He and his wife, Tanith, were proving to be an interesting and unusual couple.

## Chapter Seven

In the afternoon, after Francis O'Conlan had collected his bronze artefacts, the Reverend John Smyth called at the antique shop to buy the carved oak misericord. Chris was pleased to make a sale as money was getting very short.

'So, John, you decided to buy it after all.'

'Yes. I would have taken it on my last visit but I was sidetracked by your bronze knife and chalice. Tell me, have you destroyed them or sold them yet?'

'It seems they were stolen goods and I sold them back to their original owner.'

'Oh! I can't say whether that's good news or not. I would have preferred to see them destroyed, as you know.'

Chris nodded; he understood the vicar's interest in the occult items, especially as he was involved in exorcisms. 'You'll never guess who owned them. It was someone in the village.'

'Dr. Francis O'Conlan I presume.'

The dealer was a little surprised at this accurate guess. The day seemed to be full of such surprises. 'Why would you assume that?'

'It's not too difficult to work out. You've seen the sign outside the old vicarage. Francis O'Conlan dabbles in the dark arts. When I knew who had bought the vicarage, I put out a few feelers about the man. His name was already faintly familiar to me.'

Chris sat down and pointed to an empty chair, hoping the vicar would sit and talk. The new owner of the Psychic College intrigued him, especially after the meeting with him that very morning.

The vicar continued. 'I would not be breaking a confidence if I told you Francis O'Conlan was himself once a priest in the Church of England. He did the same job as I used to do. He was the Deliverance Priest in a North East diocese . Unfortunately he seems to have been badly influenced by his work. He took to delving into spirit possessions on his own account and was eventually asked to leave the priesthood.'

'Defrocked you mean?'

'No, he was asked to leave and he readily agreed. Whatever demons he dealt with in his ministry seem to have turned him away from the path of God.'

'So he's taken the left hand path, as they call it in the horror books?'

44

'Yes, in a manner of speaking. His teaching people to use the Tarot and other occult paraphernalia can only end in problems. I am very troubled and afraid for this village.' The Reverend Smyth started to get up to leave but Chris held up a restraining hand.

'Stop and have a cup of coffee with me John. I need to talk to you about Francis O'Conlan.

The Vicar sat back in his chair and looked concerned. 'I guess you have not told me everything about the knife and bowl, have you.'

Chris nodded vigorous agreement. 'I don't really know where to start. There have been some strange occurrences since we last spoke.'

The Reverend Smyth smiled encouragement and waited for the him to carry on.

'Well, there was a sudden storm last night. It hit the village in the small hours of the morning. It rained buckets and the wind howled and shook the building. It must have triggered a fault in our electricity substation because the lights were all off. I awoke from a nightmare and thought I had an intruder in my bedroom. I'm not usually given to panicking or superstition, but my nightmare was all about that knife and bowl. I woke up, or maybe I wasn't completely awake, anyway, I saw a tall dark figure in the room, framed by my bedroom window. It was obviously a bad dream but it was so very real.'

The vicar frowned. 'Those witchcraft items will have a bad aura about them. Who knows what devilish things they have raised. I am not surprised your subconscious picked up on their presence here.'

Christopher carried on. 'I panicked and searched through my bedside locker to find my torch. Instead, I found a Gideon Bible that I didn't even know was there. Thinking back to what happened next, I am sure when I held the bible up in the darkness, the wind and rain stopped and the figure vanished.'

The vicar nodded vigorously. 'That would be a very lucky find. Tell me, was that the end of the experience?'

'Well, no. Immediately after that I heard the front door banging. I came down and found it wide open.'

'The gale must have forced it open.'

'Yes, that's what I thought at first, but I'm sure I had locked and bolted it. I definitely recall doing it before I went upstairs to bed. And there was a puddle of rain on the floor just inside the shop." He pointed to the entrance to the room where they sat, to where the wet area had spread over the tiled floor the previous night.

The vicar shook his head and sighed. 'This must seem all very mysterious to you, but everything you have told me could just be a simple dream and a bad storm in the middle of the night.'

'There's more.' Chris licked his lips. 'I have been considering all morning what happened today. Dr O'Conlan came to see me and seemed to know I had the knife and chalice here in my shop. He even guessed the price I had paid for them and got it right first guess. He told me he thought they were here because he had dowsed for them with a pendulum and it directed him to these premises.'

The vicar folded his arms across his chest and frowned deeply. He seemed lost in thought. Finally he looked up and said. 'When I realised Francis O'Conlan had come to this village and so close to this particular church, I was filled with foreboding. What you have just told me only confirms my fears.'

It was Chris's turn to look worried. 'How come? What is so special about Barrowick church to make you think that way?'

'Barrowick is an ancient site. If you think about it, the church is built on a mound and that's where the village name originates. Barrow, meaning an ancient earthwork, and wick meaning a farm. This village was named after a farmstead built near an ancient barrow. I don't believe in them, but some authorities insist there are several Ley Lines crossing at this church site.'

Chris nodded to show he was following the explanation and waited for the vicar to continue.

'Ley Lines or not, man must have worshipped here long before Christianity was founded. There are even traces of the old religion here.'

The dealer raised his eyebrows in surprise at this comment. He was certainly learning a lot about his new home village; a lot he could never have suspected.

'There is a so called Shelagh stone set in the churchyard at the back of the church. These goddess stones are usually Roman in origin but ours is much older than that. It is without doubt a mother goddess carving. It could have been worshipped here long before Christ was born. I am of the opinion it dates from the Bronze Age.' The vicar hesitated then continued. 'There's also the witch's grave of course.'

Chris grinned at this last remark. 'A witch's grave? I don't believe it!'

'Believe it or not, in the 1500's a witch was buried here after they drowned her on a ducking stool. Her grave is still there in the churchyard. The vicar at the time, suggested she be buried close by the church to make sure she could do no more mischief after death. It's a well documented local event from the middle ages.'

Chris shook his head, intrigued by all the things he had just heard. 'And you think this psychic college will stir up problems from the past?'

'Not if I can help it, but the possibility is always there. Thank you for telling me your suspicions about our newcomers. I will go to the church and pray now for God's help to counteract any evil in our midst.' The vicar got up to leave.

'Hang on, Don't forget the misericord.' The dealer placed the carving in a carrier bag and held it out to the old man.

'I don't suppose you have time to come and pray with me in the church?' The Reverend Smyth looked Chris straight in the eyes, challenging him to help.

Chris was taken completely by surprise by this suggestion. He didn't regard himself as a religious man but he had to admit the events of the last twenty four hours had shaken him. He hesitated, trying to find an excuse to refuse to help, but finally he gave in for he felt he owed the old man something for his friendship and the way he had been taken into his confidence. 'Of course. I'm at a loose end here anyway. I'll carry the oak carving for you as it's rather heavy.'

They walked to the Barrowick Arms where the vicar called to pick up the key to the church. Sara's mother, who acted as caretaker for the church, kept the key in the village pub in case any visitors wished to see inside the old building.

'The door should be already open, vicar.' Mrs. Goodacre told him. 'Our new professor asked to have a look around there only half an hour ago.'

The vicar shot a worried glance at his companion, thanked Sara's mother for her help, then turned on his heels and marched quickly across the road to the church. Chris followed close behind him.

When they arrived at the old studded oak door of All Saint's Church they found it slightly ajar. Cannon Smyth held a finger up to his lips urging silence, then they both stepped quietly into the church.

Standing just in the doorway, they could see the entire body of the church and it seemed deserted. The dealer was about to say it looked as if

47

Francis O'Conlan had left the building, when the vicar raised a silencing finger once again. From the far end of the church, from the vicar's robing room, they could hear faint rustling sounds. The vestry door was slightly open and the shadow of someone moving about in there was clearly visible.

The Reverend Smyth tiptoed along the aisle and gently pushed open the door to the anteroom. Chris followed close behind him. Peering over John's shoulder, he could see a small, long haired, man with his back turned towards them. He was busily searching through a cupboard on the far side of the room.

John Smyth cleared his throat noisily. The intruder whipped around to face them, confusion and guilt showing on his face. Chris stood back and watched the two men face each other. The vicar made the sign of the cross in front of his chest then asked. 'What are you looking for?'

The dealer recognised the intruder as soon as he turned to face them. It was Dave Porter, the local antique runner with a bad reputation. Chris had often seen him at the sale rooms. Porter was a man he did not like. He was not a man to be trusted and had recently been banned from some of the local sale rooms for stealing small items on the viewing days.

Porter seemed to recover his composure almost immediately. 'I was hoping to find a leaflet or two on the history of this wonderful old building.' He smiled at Chris, recognising him from their contact in the auction rooms.

The vicar nodded and smiled. 'I'm sorry to disappoint you. We do usually have such leaflets but we are awaiting delivery of a new batch. When they arrive from the printers, copies will be just inside the doorway in the main body of the church.'

It was obvious from the way the man was holding his coat close to his body that he had something hidden under it. He made to leave but he had to pass the vicar and Chris to get out of the vestry. The vicar stood in the doorway and blocked it. He smiled at the man and held out his hand, inviting Porter to give him whatever he had hidden under his coat.

Dave Porter shrugged his shoulders and handed over a tin box he had taken, then he walked past the two men and left the church without a word of apology or a backward glance.

Chris frowned at his companion. 'What was that he'd taken?'

Cannon Smyth turned the key and opened the box to show it was empty except for a clean linen cloth. 'I think our visitor was hoping to find a store of the Host, the wafers we use during the communion. This is where I store them before I conduct that service.'

48

'Why on earth would he want those?'

'Possibly because Satanists use the wafers as part of a parody of the holy communion when they hold their own black mass.'

Chris was even more shocked at the matter of fact way the Reverend Smyth explained his suspicions.

'Surely not. You must be joking.' He just couldn't believe such things could happen in a quiet little village like Barrowick.

The vicar patted him reassuringly on the shoulder. 'When you have seen and experienced all that I have in my ministry you would never doubt me. Come, we must kneel at the altar and pray for God's guidance and for the protection of this church and village.'

The antique dealer followed the old man into the main area of the church and knelt beside him to pray.

When the prayers were over they left the church, securely locking the door behind them. Chris took the opportunity to ask a question he had been dying to ask. 'That ancient statue - a Shelagh you called it - can you show me where it is? I'm interested in anything antique or ancient.'

John Smyth led him to the back of the church where a large stained glass window overlooked the churchyard. At the back of the building he stopped and pointed out a large sandstone block leaning against the wall of the church. 'I know it's called a Shelagh or a Shela-n-gig by some people but those names really refer to a carving of the Roman or Medieval period. This one is considerably earlier.'

Chris scrutinised the carving. It was about five feet tall and as wide as a man. The carved head had grotesque features with thick eyebrows over bulbous eyes, which had hollows drilled into them to represent the pupils. The mouth was open, with a rudimentary tongue protruding from it. The lips were thick and turned down to give a fierce appearance. The nose was long but had the tip broken off. A small part of the top of the head was missing, broken off years before judging by the dark colour of the break, but the face was still mainly intact and discernible. The body had no arms, just shallow grooves cut into the sides of the sandstone to represent them. The breasts were large and had prominent nipples carved onto them, making it obvious this statue was a grotesque female form. The lower part of the body was hardly formed at all; there were no legs, just a groove cut in the middle of the stone, stopping about half way up it. Parts of the statue were obscured by a heavy growth of mosses and lichen but enough could be seen to leave no doubt it was a ritual object of some antiquity.

'Reminds me of some of the small stone carvings of mother goddesses found in continental stone age cave sites.' Chris said.

'Exactly. That's why experts have dated it as pre-Christian. It has probably stood here on this mound for five thousand years. It was found in the churchyard by a grave digger over one hundred years ago. He must have had quite a shock when he unearthed that body.'

'That's amazing!' Chris turned to look over the old grave stones and abruptly changed the subject. 'Where's this witch buried then?'

John Smyth pointed to a small gravestone a few feet away from where they were standing.

Chris walked a few paces and stood in front of the gravestone, to view it from the front He was rather surprised to see a cross carved deeply into it. 'A cross? A Christian symbol on a witch's grave? I'm a bit surprised at that. Mind you, I'm more than surprised they buried her here in consecrated ground in the first place.'

'It's well documented in the church records. The local vicar was sure such a burial would ensure she didn't terrorize the village after her death. The parish records show he was responsible for her burial here as he persuaded the superstitious locals her spirit would be at rest and contained here near the church and under the sign of a cross. That was a very Christian and enlightened attitude for his day. He must have been an exceptional man.'

Chris stared at the witch's grave. 'There's no name carved on the stone. Do we know her name?'

'Local legend has it she was called Molly Bent, and I have no reason to doubt that name. Whoever she was, I hope she has rested in peace all these years.' The vicar turned to go. His companion followed him to his car. As he opened the car door, John Smyth checked his wristwatch then handed the church key to Chris. 'Here. Be a good fellow and take the key back to Mrs Goodacre for me. I have another urgent appointment I must keep.'

'An exorcism?'

'No, an appointment with my dentist.' The portly cleergyman got into his car and drove out of the village.

Chris returned the key to the local pub and gave it to the landlady, who was polishing the wooden tops of the bar tables.

'Everything alright?' She asked.

'Yes. I think so. The Reverend Smyth seems to have everything under control.'

50

'Oh yes. He's a good man is John. We are lucky to have him.'

From the sudden warmth and enthusiasm in Mrs Goodacre's voice, Chris felt she had a soft spot for the old man. She even gave him a rare smile.

He was pleased with himself. Now he was in with the vicar, Sara's mother was not so antagonistic towards him. That had to be an improvement.

## Chapter Eight

Early next morning Chris Doughty drove his van down to the vicarage and parked it in the yard next to the barn. He had hardly jumped from the cab when Francis O'Conlan appeared from the house.

'Ah! You've come to empty the barn, Good man. The sooner it's emptied the sooner I can use it.'

'Yes, I'll get it done today. I wanted to confirm with you exactly what you want done with the things. I can take anything valuable to the auction room and the rubbish to the tip, but that will cost you a permit to dump such a lot of rubbish.'

O'Conlan nodded he understood and made to return to the house.

Chris called him back. 'Shall I tell the auctioneer not to bother with reserves on the things, just to let them go to the highest bidder?'

'Good idea. I must be rid of them so I can use the space in the barn. I certainly don't want them back again.'

'There are a few pieces of old timber and a damaged clock case that I can probably find a use for in my restoration work. Is it OK if I keep those.'

'Take what you like but get the barn cleared for me.' The doctor went into the vicarage and closed the door behind him, leaving Chris to his own devices.

The dealer worked hard all that morning taking three loads down to the auction room and a further two to the tip to be dumped. Gradually he emptied the barn of its contents, always keeping the early clock case to one side in the hope of finding the movement and the dial, but he was to be disappointed. There was no sign of any clock movement, weights or pendulum. He guessed they must have been thrown away years before. Years ago people placed no value on such things, they even chopped up old clock cases for firewood, which would be unheard of today. The thought reminded him of a past experience when a farmer had burned an old oak grandfather clock because he saw one or two woodworm holes in the case. On that occasion Chris heard of the clock too late to save it. He was devastated by that experience and never forgot it.

Each load delivered to the local auction room was carefully catalogued by the staff there and a copy given to Chris for his records. He folded them into his inside pocket to give to O'Conlan when the job was completed.

Francis O'Conlan looked into the barn occasionally to see what progress was being made but never stayed long. He cast a quick glance at the timber pieces and the painted clock case that the dealer had put to one side, but made no comment about them, seemingly satisfied with the way the work was progressing. Finally, with the last item removed from the site, Chris knocked on the vicarage door and presented the doctor with a list of the items entered into the next Oakham antique sale. 'I've entered this lot in your name Doctor O'Conlan. You will get a cheque in the post eventually from the saleroom when they've sold all the items.'

'Good man. Now what about your charges for the work?'

'I'll have to work out my time and the petrol costs. I'll drop the bill to you in the next day or so. By the way, I've kept those few bits of old timber that you saw, for my own use for restoration.'

'Good, that's fine. We have a party of our students coming tomorrow to help clean up the barn and get it ready for use. You have been a great help.'

Chris drove the van back to the shop and parked it at the front. He did not remove the clock case and the pieces of old timber, thinking it best to leave that task until after dark, when certain prying eyes would not see him. Chris was very aware that Dave Porter was a friend of the doctor's and he might just make trouble if he could. He washed and changed into some clean clothes and threw his work clothes into the washer to remove the grime and cobwebs of the morning's work.

Upstairs, when he was getting dressed, he glanced out of the window and noticed a police car and several officers down at the edge of the reservoir. Curious about what they could be doing, he watched them for a few minutes, but nothing appeared to be happening. Maybe a poacher or someone has been rustling the sheep that were left to graze the foreshore. Maybe some stray dogs had savaged the sheep. Suddenly an ambulance and a police van joined the other squad car and several policemen could be seen at the water's edge. Intrigued by what he'd seen, Chris decided to walk along the reservoir path to see what was happening, when he went to the Barrowick Arms for his lunch.

There was a narrow lane opposite the antique shop that led down to the woodland and the pathway skirting the reservoir. The dealer took that pathway through the trees until he'd passed the wooded area behind the church and the vicarage and found himself in open grassland where sheep were grazing beside the water's edge. Just ahead he could see the police had put wooden stakes and a tape around part of the foreshore to

53

keep people off the area.    It reminded him of crime scenes he'd seen on the TV news. Coming close  to the area, he stopped to look at what was happening.  There were two  police divers working in the water and they were towing something towards the shore. Recognising one of the young constables on duty, Chris asked, 'Got a problem?'

'A drowning. Two fishermen reported it earlier this morning.'

That was a surprise. He'd never heard of such an incident before at the reservoir. Perhaps someone had fallen from a boat when they were sailing single handed, or maybe it was a suicide. Whatever had happened it was a sad day for somebody's family. He was about to continue on his way to the pub when there was a shout from the frogmen as they pulled a body out of the water and laid it on the grass at the water's edge.

Chris was intrigued and  glanced over at them,  then he did a double take! The figure they had just pulled out of the water wore an old army coat and  blue trainers. It could only be Steve! Chris turned back and approached the policeman again.

'I believe I might recognise your dead man. I know  that coat and those shoes. I think he's local to the village.'

The constable shouted to his sergeant who came over to speak to them.

'This man's local, serg. He thinks he may have recognised the body from the clothes.'

'Right sir. Come with me.'

Chris ducked under the police tape and followed the sergeant to where the body was laid out at the water's edge. Even before he got up to the corpse, he was positive  it was  Steve. There was no mistaking that long hair and weather-beaten face. Poor sod! What a way to end his life

The police sergeant bent down and moved some strands of wet hair from Steve's face and closed his eyelids over his staring eyes. 'Do you recognise him?'

Chris nodded. 'It's Steve Mattock. He's local. He lives at the far end of the village in Honeysuckle Cottage.'

'Do you know if there's any next of kin?'

Chris shook his head. 'I can't say. He lives alone.' He thought for a second then added. 'His ex-wife lives in Oakham. She may be able to help you.'

The sergeant called over the young constable who had first spoken to Chris.    'Take down all the details from this gentleman and let me have

54

them. I'm going to call HQ for a detective. It looks like a suicide or an accidental drowning but we'd better let plain clothes make that decision.' He returned to his squad car and made his call.

'Right sir, what is his full name?'

'Steve..er..Steve Mattock as far as I know. I'm not sure if he had any other names.'

'That'll do to identify him. Honeysuckle Cottage you say? And that's on Main Sreet. Barrowick?'

'Yes.'

'How come you know the man?'

'Everybody in the village knows Steve. He's...er...er...he drinks rather a lot and sometimes makes a bit of a nuisance of himself at the local pub. He has been known to sleep it off at the roadside before now. He dropped into my shop here in Barrowick only a couple of days ago to sell me some antiques.'

'If he's regularly drunk, could be he fell in the reservoir in an inebriated state.' The constable suggested.

Chris shrugged his shoulders and nodded agreement. That was what he'd been thinking as well.

'Do you know his ex wife's name?'

'Molly...Molly Mattock...she's not remarried to my knowledge. She lives in Oakham, but I couldn't say exactly where.'

The young constable wrote down all the details then folded his notebook and put it away. 'You might have to come to the station and make a statement but we will try to see his ex wife first.'

'OK. Anything I can do to help.' Chris took a grubby business card from his inside pocket and gave it to the policeman. 'You can get me here most evenings, or you can leave a message on my phone.' As he turned to go, an unmarked car pulled up at the waterside and a tall, thickset, man got out and walked over to the police sergeant. He was not in police uniform but he looked official. The dealer was curious and asked the constable. 'Who's that?'

'That's DC Phillips. He won't bother to stay around once he knows it's just a suicide or an accident. Hang on a minute, I'd better tell him you saw the dead man only a couple of days ago. You might be the last person to have seen him alive.'

The detective came over at the constables call.

'This man's local. He knows the dead man. He served him in his shop only a couple of days ago.'

The detective turned to Chris. 'I gather he was a drunk. Was he sober when you last saw him?'

'No. Actually he could hardly stand up, and that was in the morning.'

Turning to the constable, Phillips said, 'Get full details. I might have to interview this chap.' Then he got into his car and drove back to the main road.

'I've got all your details, sir. You can go now.' The policeman thanked Chris for his help.

Having helped the police all he could, Chris left the scene and walked along the path to where it joined the main road, just up from the Barrowick Arms. He stopped where the lane left the reservoir and looked back at the police car just as they were lifting Steve's body into the back of an ambulance. He felt very sad for his old friend. He was a drunk and a nuisance but he didn't deserve to die like that. Because of the delay at the water side, Chris realised it might be a bit late in the day for lunch at the pub, but he hoped Sara could rustle up something tasty for him.

At the Barrowick Arms, Sara was busy serving drinks to a couple of men; fishermen by the looks of their clothes. She greeted Chris with a frown on her face. She was nothing like her usual cheery self.

He was pleased to see Sara was managing the bar on her own; her mother would probably have refused to serve him lunch so late in the afternoon. 'Can you manage me a late lunch, Sara. I've been too busy to stop for a bite until now.'

She pointed to an empty table and went into the kitchen to check what she had in the fridge. 'All we have left is some salad and cheese.'

'Lovely...and a pint of best bitter please, Sara.' He said cheerily. She didn't return his smile and went to fetch a plate of food and a glass of beer. It was obvious something was bothering the girl. Chris raised his eyebrows in a silent question. Sara just shook her head, looked pointedly over at the two fishermen who were finishing their drinks, oblivious to the silent conversation, then returned to the bar where she busied herself filling up the shelves with clean glasses.

Finally the two men finished their drinks and left the pub. Only then did Sara throw her glass cloth down and come over to Chris's table. She sat down heavily opposite to him and let out a deep sigh.

'What's up?' He pushed his empty plate away, but he already had his suspicions about what was bothering her.

'Awful news, Chris. I think Steve is dead.'

56

'I know he's dead. I've just identified his body.'

Sara looked shocked.

'I happened to be walking along the reservoir path when they fished him out of the water. What have you heard?'

'Those two fishermen found a man's body floating in the reservoir this morning. From their description of his clothes I just knew it had to be Steve. It's been all go here all morning. Policemen and divers calling for directions to the foreshore.'

'Do the police suspect foul play do you think?'

'I don't know what to think, but I know he could have been so drunk he fell into the water and drowned. I feel terribly guilty about it.'

'That's awful, but surely you aren't involved. Why the guilt trip?'

'They'll want to know if he drank here and did we serve him when he was too drunk to realise what he was doing.'

'You wouldn't do that, Sara.' He reached over the table and took her hand in his to reassure her. 'I've been in here many times when you've refused to serve him because he'd had enough.'

She nodded but still looked unhappy with the situation.

'Come on Sara, I can tell something else is eating you. What's the problem?'

'I did stop serving him last night because he'd had enough, but he produced a twenty pound note and demanded a bottle of spirit to take out.'

'Well, if he was going home to drink it, where was the harm in that?'

'That's what I felt, so I sold him a bottle of whisky to take out. I'm worried he may not have gone straight home. He may have taken that bottle down to the water's edge and drank it all. I feel so guilty about it!'

Chris tried once more to reassure her. 'If that's what happened, Sara, I might be as much to blame as you.'

'You! How?'

'Steve came to me a few days ago to sell me a couple of small antique items. They didn't look worth much but I gave him a twenty pound note for them. I might have guessed what he would do with that money. When he was reluctant to leave the shop I turfed him out and told him to go down to the reservoir to sleep it off.'

Sara just shook her head. His involvement seemed negligible compared to her own.

He tried again to reassure her. 'You know Steve. He was an accident waiting to happen. If this hadn't killed him, his liver soon would have done. Don't beat yourself up about it, Sara. There's nothing you can do and there was no blame in what you did.' He squeezed her hand again.

She looked down at the table. 'He's had a bottle of spirits many times to take out. He usually staggers home with it and drinks it there.'

'There you are then. You have nothing to blame yourself for. With his way of life this was almost inevitable. If he hadn't fallen in the water he would probably have fallen under someone's car and maybe even caused a fatal accident to somebody else.'

After the pub lunch, Chris unloaded the pieces of timber from his van, taking care to keep the clock case well hidden under a piece of old carpet and some blankets that he used to separate and protect pieces of antique furniture when he was transporting them. The loose timber was mainly old oak, which would prove useful for making replacement beadings and panels, but there was some Cuban mahogany pieces that must have come from a broken chest of drawers. Old wood like that was difficult to come by and would prove invaluable to him in his restoration work. Having removed everything except the clock case, he drove the van around to the yard at the back of the shop where he usually parked it, and locked the doors.

Sitting in the back shop and drinking a coffee, Chris's thoughts turned to Steve Mattock. It was very sad that he had drowned. The events of the past few days had been most unusual. Steve had sold him the bronze witchcraft artifacts, which must have been stolen from the old vicarage while no one was in residence, but after the furniture and effects had been delivered. Then Dr. Francis O'Conlan had turned up to claim his goods. That man was an enigma! How did he know where to look for the bronze knife and bowl, and the how did he guess the price paid for them? On mature consideration, the dealer discounted the dowsing explanation that the doctor had offered. In his limited experience dowsing might help find underground water but surely not stolen items?

O'Conlan coming straight to the shop was an almighty coincidence. One might even think the doctor had spoken to Steve and got the information from him. It will be interesting to see what the coroner's verdict will be on the cause of Steve's death.

After dark that night Chris unloaded the clock case from his van and put it into the workshop. Closer inspection confirmed his first impression that it was part of a very early grandfather clock. The style was quite simple and architectural. He scratched off some of the old brown paint and discovered under that grunge it had an oak carcass, which had been veneered with a fruitwood and stained black. Early clock cases were often ebonised like that. The oak case, which was smaller than the usual longcase clock, had its original bun feet but they were riddled with woodworm. That was no surprise as those early clocks usually stood on flagstone floors and their feet were regularly dowsed with water when the floors were washed. He estimated it probably dated from the mid 1600's when the first longcase clocks were made in England. He was more than satisfied with the find and looked forward to restoring it and looking out for an early movement and dial to complete it. If he did manage to restore it to working order he had every intention of keeping it and putting it in his living room where he could admire it every day.

After supper Chris calculated how much Francis O'Conlan owed him for the work clearing the barn, then he printed a copy of the account from his laptop and placed it on the table for delivery next morning.

## Chapter Nine

Next day, Chris Doughty delivered Dr O'Conlan's bill for the work he had done emptying the barn. He was just pushing the envelope through the vicarage letterbox when O'Conlam came around the corner of the building.

'Ah! Mr. Doughty. We have an army of volunteers cleaning and restoring the barn today. They will no doubt find some more rubbish to be taken to the tip. Could you oblige by picking it up?' He took the bill from Chris glanced at it then handed it back. 'You'd better add today's cost to this bill when you've finished the job.'

Chris was only too pleased to make a bit more money from the transaction. He stuffed the original account into his pocket and walked across the yard to the barn where work was already underway. Two young men had removed the damaged doors to the building and were working on a replacement. When he glanced into the barn to get some idea of how much more rubbish they might find for him to remove, he was surprised to see the electricians were there already, wiring lights and fitting heaters. Everyone seemed very busy. Several young women were scrubbing the flagstone floor and the stone walls with yard brushes and soapy water. Two others were painting the cleaned walls with white paint. There was a heap of old wood and rubbish standing in one corner, which he assumed he would have to collect and take to the local tip. He also saw three younger men were clearing a raised platform, which was built several meters above the floor at the far end of the building. He hadn't taken much notice of this hay loft when he'd originally emptied the barn but now he could see it was like a gallery, set near the roof with wooden steps leading up to it. The platform overlooked the main area of the barn and reminded him a little of a minstrels' gallery that overlooked a medieval hall. The men were throwing down a quantity of old pine boards that had been stored up there, creating clouds of dust and cobwebs. It was obvious he would have to call back much later in the day to pick up the rubbish when they had completed their restoration work.

As he looked around the group of volunteers, Chris noticed some of them were not young people. Many where middle aged men and women, which surprised him as he had assumed most students would be teenagers. There were as many older men and women working in the barn as there were youngsters. He realised then that O'Conlan's courses must appeal to a wide age group of students. While he was watching the work, Francis

O'Conlan and Tanith, came into the barn, closely followed by Dave Porter, the scruffy antique runner who had been in the church the previous day. They were checking on the work being done. Chris wondered what the connection could possible be between an educated, well spoken, professor like Francis O'Conlan, and a layabout like Porter, but he couldn't even guess at an answer. 'Nowt so queer as folk.' He smiled to himself as that apt Northern saying popped into his head.

It was at that point something else struck Chris as unusual; everyone except the O'Conlans and Porter, was wearing large face masks, which not only protected them from any dust but made it almost impossible to recognise them. He thought one man looked very much like the detective, DC Phillips, he had seen at the reservoir only the day before when the police were recovering Steve's body, but the man wore a full face mask and seemed to be keeping his back towards the door and avoiding the dealer's gaze, so he couldn't be sure if it was him.

Chris was trying to understand the policeman's actions, asking was the man deliberately avoiding him or had he just imagined it, when Dave Porter sidled up to him and started a conversation.

'Sorry about that misunderstanding in the church. I don't know why I picked up that biscuit tin. It was probably old habits. I wanted to see if it was a rare pattern and maybe valuable. I would have put it back before I left, you know.'

Chris nodded that he believed his story even though he didn't believe a word of it. 'No harm done, Dave. I'm sure the vicar understood.'

'You and the vicar, good friends are you?'

'Heavens no! He had just bought a heavy oak misericord from me and I carried it over to the church for him. You know me, I'm not the religious type.' He decided to play Dave at his own game. 'Tell me, how come you are helping Dr O'Conlan? Is he an old friend of yours?'

Dave seemed to hesitate at this direct question. He looked over his shoulder, checking where the O'Conlans were. Seeing they were too far away to hear the conversation, he replied. 'Actually I have been a student of the Psychic College for some months.'

'Oh! I thought it had only just opened here.'

'Yes that's right, but they've taught over the internet for some years. This place is a new venture and an expansion of their work.'

'What exactly are you studying, Dave?'

Porter took his time to answer. Again he hesitated and seemed uncertain. At last he said. 'This and that, you know. Dowsing using pendulums, and Telepathy. I'm hoping to locate buried treasure using my dowsing skills.'

Although Chris was far from convinced by this answer, he smiled reassuringly. 'I wish you luck with it. If you do locate anything antique, I might be interested in buying it.'

This last offer seemed to please Dave. 'Oh right! That's kind of you to say. I'll give you first refusal.' With that parting comment he went back into the barn to help with the clearing up.

As he left the barn, Chris stopped to speak to the two young carpenters who were working on the new door. They weren't very forthcoming either, but he did get a look at the plans for the doorway. Sensibly, they were going to fill in the huge doorway with a timber screen, and fit a smaller door into it. That would reduce any draughts and cut down on heat loss from the building.

As Chris left the area, he thought how lucky O'Conlan was to have so many skilled volunteers to restore his outbuilding for him. It also dawned on him that the professor hadn't worn a facemask. If there was some dust in the air, it obviously hadn't bothered him or his wife, yet everyone else wore one. Even the chippies who were working outside, had their faces covered. He speculated that they must be very keen on health and safety regulations, or on not being recognised!

'I'll be back later to pick up the rubbish when it's all sorted.' He told the carpenters, then climbed into his van and drove back to his shop.

The rest of that afternoon Chris spent checking the early clock case he'd taken from the barn. When he'd carried it from his van, he had noticed a metallic sound coming from somewhere inside the wooden case. This intrigued him as he could see no loose bits of metal. The iron door hinges, which were fitted on the long door of the trunk, were not loose, neither was the spring mechanism fixed to the back board, which controlled the raising and lowering of the hood. He picked up the case again and shook it gently. Sure enough, he heard something unusual; there was definitely the faint rattle of metal on wood coming from somewhere inside the trunk.

The dealer fetched the torch from his bedroom to search for the offending item. Eventually he located a small metal disc, loosely nailed to the backboard. A gentle tug with a pair of pliers pulled the object away from the pine board and revealed a blackened coin with a rusted, hand-made, nail driven through a hole drilled in its centre. Intrigued by this find, he took it to a window to check it properly in the daylight. Sometimes case makers did put a low value coin inside their cases to indicate the date of manufacture. He was pleasantly surprised when he rubbed the copper disc, to see it was not just a coin. It was a tradesman's token.

In the old days, the joiners who made the cases for grandfather clocks were usually anonymous. The signature on the clock dial was the movement makers, or in later clocks, the retailers. The humble craftsmen who produced the  beautiful wooden cases were not often identified.. This early case was an exception. The maker was proud of his work and had identified himself with that copper token. Chris rubbed the token with a wad of fine wire wool and polished it with a duster to reveal the legend stamped on it.    Round the perimeter was a name and address; it read  'Jos. Clifton. Bulls Head Yard. Cheapside. His halfpenny  1663.'

Chris was extremely excited at that find. From his study of longcase clocks he knew that Joseph Clifton was one of the few early case makers who ever identified his work, and he had made cases for some of the most famous London clock makers of the period; such famous craftsmen as Ahaseurus Fromanteel, reputedly the first clockmaker to produce a longcase clock in Britain. Chris was thrilled with this find. Even though he had no brass dial or movement  to go with the clock case, he knew he would enjoy restoring it and spend the next few years looking for a suitable clock works and dial to fit it. He was a clock enthusiast and was much more excited about owning such an early example than in the monetary value of it.

**Chapter Ten**

On Friday, the night the folk group were performing at the Barrowick Arms, Chris made an effort to look his best for Sara. After work, he showered and changed into clean jeans and a new sweater. Sara had specifically asked him to go to the gig and he didn't want to let her down. It had gone nine o'clock by the time he got to his local. The sounds of music were already audible as he walked the length of the village. From the type of tune being played he guessed it was a traditional folk line up.

Once inside the pub, Chris bought a pint of bitter and found an empty seat near the band. He was pleased to see the pub was already filling up with punters and the bar was busy. While Sara was involved singing with the band, the bar was being manned by a young man he didn't recognise. Mrs Goodacre, Sara's mother, was nowhere to be seen. As he sat down, Sara came over and greeted him. She was wearing a tight blue dress and high heeled shoes. The contrast with her usual uniform of jeans, a sweater and trainers, was stark, and he very much approved of the transformation..

'So glad you could make it. It's nice to see a friendly familiar face.'

'When are you performing?'

'Any minute now. The band has been warming up playing a few standards. Must go. I'm on now.' She walked to a raised platform in the corner of the bar and took the microphone. 'Welcome to the Barrowick Arms. This is our first folk night and hopefully the first of many.' She acknowledge the hoots and hand claps from some of the younger folk in the crowd. 'Now, let me introduce the band. There's Jim on drums, Penny on the violin; I nearly said on the fiddle, but as she works at Barclays Bank in town, that wouldn't be appropriate.'

The audience laughed, appreciating the local flavour of the joke.

Chris looked closer at the violinist. He hadn't recognised her even though she had served him in the bank many times. Usually Penny was anonymous in her dark blue uniform with her hair drawn back in a tight, businesslike bun, and her gold rimmed spectacles perched on her nose. Who would have thought this tall, slim girl in jeans and a floral blouse, and with no glasses on, was the same person?

Sara continued. 'Barry on guitar and me, singing and thumping the tambourine. I usually stand behind the bar pulling pints but just for tonight my cousin Richard has taken that job over.' She pointed to the barman and gave him a clap of appreciation.

The band members held up a hand and smiled as each one was introduced. The drummer gave them each a drum roll. Sara took the microphone off its stand and counted the band into her first number.

As he listened to her singing, Chris's eyes searched the room for any familiar faces. Most of the customers were not local to the village, probably from Stamford or Oakham. That couldn't be bad for the pub's trade as they might well like the atmosphere and call regularly. Sara was certainly trying to put the Barrowick Arms on the map. Full marks to her for trying. Over in the far corner, near the window, he spotted Dave Porter, the antique runner. He made a point of nodding at him in a friendly acknowledgement even though he didn't like the man. Near the bar, among a younger crowd of drinkers, stood two local farm workers that he recognised. That pair lived in the village. Apart from those few familiar faces, Chris knew no one in that audience.

Sara finished singing her first number, bowed and took the applause from the audience. He could see from her smile of relief and the flush on her cheeks, that first ice breaker had been an ordeal for her but she had enjoyed it. Her singing pleasantly surprised him. She had a light voice well suited to the folk songs she was performing.

After Sara's debut, the band went into an instrumental number where the fiddle player showed her virtuosity by playing a long solo part in the middle of it. The audience tapped their feet in time to her playing and really enjoyed it. There was obvious enthusiasm for the event.

Chris finished his first pint and went to the bar for a refill. Richard, the relief barman was being kept very busy pulling pints for the men, pouring wine for the ladies and supplying light bar snacks that Sara had prepared earlier.

'You could do with an extra pair of hands.' The dealer suggested as he waited patiently to be served. 'Where's Sara's mum when you need her?'

'She's at her WI meeting. I don't think she'd appreciate this crowd if she was here. Aunt Brenda likes a quiet, ordered, life. She leaves the busy times to Sara.'

Chris took his pint back to his seat and listened to Barry, the guitarist, playing and singing a solo version of one of Bob Dylan's hits. He had just sat down when Sara came over to speak to him again.

'What do you think?' She asked in a low voice not wanting to interrupt the singer. 'Are you enjoying it?'

Chris nodded. 'Very good, and you have a good audience turnout.' He glanced around the bar just in time to see Francis O'Conlan and his wife slip into seats at the back of the room.

Sara also noticed Francis and Tanith and raised a hand in greeting. It was nice that newcomers to the village made an effort to join in with local attractions. She made her way to them through the crowded bar and held a whispered conversation with them.

After Barry's solo, the guitarist was joined by Penny, the violinist, and the pair of them made a brave attempt at an arrangement of Duelling Guitars. The audience loudly clapped this last offering, appreciating the expertise shown and the willingness to try it.

Sara was soon back at the microphone singing some more gentle ballads. Chris was pleasantly surprised at her voice and how well she performed. It was an auspicious beginning for the new band and a successful night for the Barrowick Arms.

In the interval, when Chris had bought another pint of bitter and some crisps, Dave Porter made a point of coming over to speak to him.

'I wanted a word with you.' The runner explained. 'I did mention I had found a few church antiques and I wondered if you would be interested in buying them.'

Chris didn't like or trust the man, especially after the altercation in Barrowick church, but business was business and he would never turn down a bargain, even if he didn't like the seller. 'Bring them to the shop tomorrow, Dave. If I think I can sell them, I'll consider buying them from you.'

Satisfied with this promise, Porter left him to eat his crisps in peace and made his way to sit with the O'Conlans at the back of the room, where he was soon in animated conversation with them.

Chris noticed how friendly the professor and his wife seemed to be with Dave Porter and wondered how that had come about. They were an unlikely trio of friends.

At closing time, when Sara saw the last of the customers off the premises and locked the doors, she was still wide awake and hyperactive; her adrenaline was still in full flow. Her mother had already let herself in by the back door and gone up to bed. Sara paid her cousin for his help then went to lock the front door behind him as he left for home. Chris hung back before he made for his home, wishing to congratulate her on her efforts to bring more trade into the village.

'Don't go yet.' She placed a hand on his shoulder and held him back. 'Stop and have a drink with me. I deserve a nightcap and some supper after all that effort, and I'd appreciate your company.'

He sat at the bar while she went into the kitchen. He had no need to rush, living only a short distance away and answering to no one but himself.

Sara called from the kitchen. 'Could you eat a chicken sandwich and drink a coffee?'

'Please.' That would save him getting something later at home. He'd had four pints of beer during the evening and wouldn't go to bed without something solid in his stomach.

After a few minutes, Sara brought out two plates of sandwiches and two milky coffees which she placed on the bar top. She pulled up a bar stool and sat down close to Chris.

'What did you think of this evening?' She asked as she munched hungrily on her food.

'It was good. You are good. I didn't realise you were such a professional singer.'

She giggled at this description. 'I'm not, not really, but I suppose after tonight I could call myself a professional.'

'Sara, I've been to a few folk nights when I lived over in Stamford and yours was as good as any of them. I enjoyed it. Tell me, where did you meet the band?'

'I went to school with Jenny, the fiddler. She still lives locally. Barry is her boyfriend and Jim, the percussionist, is someone I met at night school.'

'Night school? Where you studying music then?'

She laughed. 'No! We were both doing pottery.'

Chris laughed with her. The study of ceramics was far removed from music. 'I'm surprised you get time for night school with a pub to run.'

'I make a point of having one night off a week. Mum goes to her WI on her night off and I used to go to pottery classes on mine.'

'Are you still studying pottery?'

'No. This year I'm looking for something a bit more challenging. Maybe something a bit nearer home as that ceramics course was in Stamford and it was a bind to get there. I would like to learn some new skills that might pay me eventually. I run this place with my mum but when she retires, I can't see me putting my name above the door and taking it over on my own.'

Chris nodded he understood but said nothing as his mouth was full of a delicious chicken sandwich. They both ate their suppers seated at the bar with just the dim light from the kitchen illuminating the empty pub. The atmosphere was intimate and relaxed. He was surprised to realise he hadn't been that contented for years, not since he first met and courted Vickie, his ex.

When it came time for him to leave the pub and make his way home, Sara saw him to the door and unlocked it. 'Thanks for coming, Chris. It was reassuring to have a friend in the audience.' She leaned over and quickly kissed him on the cheek. That friendly gesture took him completely by surprise. He couldn't wipe the grin off his face all the way back to his shop at the top of the village. Sara was an attractive girl, and she seemed to find him attractive too. Life in Barrowick was looking up.

# Chapter Eleven

Time passed slowly for Chris Doughty in Barrowick village but the pace of business did pick up a bit when some of his regular Stamford customers found where he was doing business and visited the new shop. It was hardly anything to shout about but things were ticking over and he was just scraping a living, unlike the new college in the village.

The Psychic College was getting extremely busy. The post was now delivered by special van as there was too much mail for the local postman to handle in his small vehicle. There were new faces seen daily in the village as clerical staff were taken on at the college to handle the new business. Chris found a few of these people seemed to be familiar and he suspected some of them were people he had seen helping the O'Conlans when they cleared the barn.

Some days and some evenings there was activity in the barn and lights could be seen shining through the high slits in the stone walls. The locals were pleased with those signs of life and assumed lectures and seminars were being held there.

Sara was a frequent visitor to the antique shop. Chris suspected she visited every day or two just to see him; she certainly didn't come to see new stock as his turnover was never that rapid. They became closer friends as time went by, and he grew fonder of the girl.

'You must let me take you out for a meal, Sara.' Chris plucked up his courage and suggested a date on one of her regular visits to the shop.

'I'd love that.' She seemed genuinely thrilled with the offer.

'When's your next night off?'

'Wednesday next week. And I'm free. I've nothing booked and nothing planned.'

They made a firm date to go for a meal in Stamford, to a restaurant where Chris knew the chef and trusted they would have a nice meal together.

Sara looked around the shop, admiring things she'd seen a dozen times before. Suddenly she stopped. 'Chris, I meant to tell you, Molly Mattock, Steve's ex, was in the pub last night. She mentioned she'd seen the coroner's report on him. It looks as if Steve's death was accidental. He had a terrific amount of alcohol in his blood stream and would probably have died of alcohol poisoning if he hadn't drowned first. He must have drunk far more spirit than that one bottle of whisky he bought from me.'

Chris nodded. 'I'm not surprised. I expected as much. Did she say when he's to be buried? I thought I might go along to his funeral as I've known him some years. I don't think there'll be many mourners. I don't think he had any family except Molly.'

'She said she would be at the funeral for old time's sake and she'd let me know the details when it was planned. It seems it will be a paupers' funeral, whatever that is?'

'That's when someone dies destitute and there are no relatives to foot the bill. Usually the local authority picks up the tab. Steve will probably get a simple funeral with a cardboard coffin, no flowers and no speeches. He'll be cremated at the rate payers' expense and his ashes scattered on the garden of remembrance at the crematorium. I think it's awful when there's no one there to say goodbye.'

Sara looked very sad at this description and smiled wanly as she told Chris. 'I notice his old cottage is being done up by the landlord. We'll have a new family in the village soon.'

'Lets hope they like the occasional drink and they like antiques.'

Their conversation was interrupted by the insistent ring of the telephone in the back shop.

'You'd better answer that, it might be a customer, and I'd better get back to the pub. We are expecting a delivery from the brewery.' Sara blew him a kiss and left the shop.

'Barrowick Antiques. Can I help?'

'I'm sure you can.'

He recognised the voice immediately. It was Vickie, his ex wife, and she sounded sugar sweet.

'Oh it's you! I was hoping it was some business.'

'Ah! But this is business.'

He grimaced even though she couldn't see his reaction, and shifted the phone to his other ear.

Vickie continued. 'I have two grandfather clocks in need of complete restoration. Are you interested in doing them for me?'

Chris guessed immediately she was talking about the two clocks she'd outbid him for at the Stamford sale room. He was about to tell her to go to hell and to find another restorer, when common sense prevailed. He could certainly do with some restoration work and Vickie must have the money to pay for it, knowing what she got out of their divorce! 'Bring them over and I'll look at them and give you a quote for the work. I will expect cash on collection from you. I can do with the readies.'

70

'Good. Thanks. I'll get a carrier to drop them off to you tomorrow as I'm far too busy to come myself. He's delivering a wardrobe to an Oakham address for me anyway.'

'I'll be here.' He put the phone down and went back into the shop. Vickie still rubbed him up the wrong way whenever she spoke to him.

The next day the carrier delivered the two longcase clocks. As Chris suspected, they were the two clocks she had bought when he was the under bidder. He didn't particularly like that style of clock, but there was a market for them at the right price. The cases were softwood, veneered with very thin mahogany and other exotic woods, but the animal glue used on them did not survive well in modern, centrally heated, houses. The cases always needed attention. The wide white dials made them look top heavy. They were made of iron, painted white and decorated with crudely painted country scenes. Some people thought they had charm but Chris didn't appreciate them. The movements were mass produced in Birmingham as were the dials. The names written on the clock faces were those of the retailers, who had no hand in the making of the clocks. As far as he was concerned, they were the dregs of the great British clock making industry and not very collectible.

'Bring it through to my workshop.' He carried one of the clocks through the shop and directed the carrier to follow him with the other one. 'Put it there by the wall. I don't want them in my way while they're waiting to be restored.'

'I've got the iron weights and the pendulums in the cab.' The driver said.

'Good. That's saved me supplying new ones.'

'Can you sign here for them, sir?' The driver got a signature for the delivery then went on his way.

Chris stood the clocks side by side against the workshop wall and looked them over. They had wide arched dials with country cottage scenes painted in the arches. The corners of the dials had further country scenes painted on them to replace the brass spandrels an older, brass faced, clock would have had. Just as he expected, they needed a lot of attention to the veneers and even more work on the movements. They were in a worse state than he remembered them from the sale room.

There were signs of woodworm in both of the cases, but that was not unusual in pine carcasses. Judging by the thick cobwebs inside them, they had not been ticking for years. Vickie never did appreciate good clocks. She bought these two monstrosities at auction and paid well over the

71

odds for them. By the time he'd restored them they would be very expensive, but they would look good. No serious clock collector would touch them. Still, he needed the work and Vickie's money was as good as anyone's.

Chris took the clock movements apart and put them into separate buckets of cleaning solution. The dials he cleaned with detergent and a soft cloth. The cases would need to be repaired before he could clean them. He checked each case and made a note of what replacement veneers he would need. Luckily he had quite a collection of old wood and knew he could produce the pieces of replacement mahogany veneer from some of the timber he'd acquired from the vicarage clearance.

The brass movements kept him busy all afternoon. Once they were degreased and polished he put them together and checked what repairs were needed. The condition was predictable. People usually ran grandfather clocks until they stopped, without thinking of having them cleaned or oiled professionally. The bearing holes in the brass plates were all too large and distorted from constant dry wear. 'You could drive a horse and cart through some of these!' he muttered to himself. He would have to replace most of the bushes. There was a problem with one of the strike mechanisms where a part had been lost. He checked his store of spare parts and found a replacement. The clocks needed a lot of work on them. It would be an expensive job he was undertaking for his ex. Served her right for buying such rubbish and for outbidding him on them. In some ways Chris felt he was getting the best of the deal. He hadn't paid for them and he wouldn't have to sell them, but he would charge Vickie plenty for the restoration work.

He worked on the clocks late into the evening. Listening to Rutland Radio on his portable radio, kept him entertained. By the time he stopped it was dark. He applied clamps to all the newly glued repairs and treated the wood worm, then made himself a sandwich and a coffee. It was a fine, moonlit night and he was tempted to take a walk by the reservoir just to get away from the shop; it was a good way to unwind after a long session of physical work. He picked up his binoculars and took the path opposite the shop, which led down to the woods and the water's edge.

Chris's eyes soon became accustomed to the failing light. The woods were alive with creatures feeding and settling down for the night. There were snuffles in the undergrowth from deer and badgers, foraging in the dark. He disturbed a family of geese that were sleeping near the lake's edge. The birds flew off with noisy cries of alarm and settled some way

72

across the water. As he neared the back of the churchyard, he saw a Barn Owl on the wing. The white bird silently quartered the graveyard listening for its prey. He thought they were beautiful birds. Their feathers were so soft they flew in absolute silence so their prey hadn't a clue they were coming. He was thrilled to see it. He knew there were Barn Owls in the area because he had frequently heard their screeching calls as he lay in bed at night. To see one quartering the churchyard and hunting was very special. He felt very lucky to live in such a wildlife rich area. The reservoir was a bird watcher's paradise. The Ospreys were breeding there in the summer and the Rutland Water Bird Fair was becoming one of the largest of such attractions in the country. Living in Barrowick did have some compensations for him.

## Chapter Twelve

Next morning Chris was woken up by the postman knocking loudly on the shop door. He peered through sleepy eyes at the bedside clock and was annoyed to see it had gone nine o'clock and he'd overslept. He pulled on his dressing gown and rushed down to open the front door.

'Morning, Sir. Parcel for you.'

He took the cardboard folder from the postman and signed for it. He had ordered a new book on early longcase clocks two days before and was hoping that was what was in the package.

'There's this other stuff as well.' The postman searched in his bag and took out a handful of envelopes. 'Probably only bills.' The man got into his van and drove up the main street away from the shop.

Chris looked through the envelopes and guessed the postman was right about most of them. Throwing the smaller post onto a table near the door, he took the book and the large plastic envelope containing the Antique Gazette, upstairs to his flat, pleased he would have something to look at while he ate breakfast. After a quick shower, he made himself some toast and a strong coffee. He dressed then sat in a chair by the window and opened the parcel containing the clock book. Flicking through the index he knew it was just what he needed to research the ebonised clock case he'd found in the vicarage barn. Chris put the book to one side to enjoy later when he would have plenty of uninterrupted time to read it, then he opened the Gazette.

The Antique Gazette, the weekly trade paper, carried the auction results so that dealers like himself could keep up with trends and prices, as well as find the details of forthcoming auctions and fairs. Near the back of that edition of the paper was a full page of photographs of stolen items that the police were investigating. From the pictures and accompanying details it was obvious there had been a spate of thefts from country churches across the midlands. Many village churches contain valuable old pieces like bible boxes, parish chests with old documents in them, even silver candle sticks. Valuable silverware, like communion cups and plates, was usually locked in a safe or stored in a bank vault, but some of the furnishings were too big for that. Historical oak artifacts that had been sitting in village churches for centuries, were now at risk of being stolen. It was a sad reflection on present day morals. Gone were the days when it was safe to leave the village churches open and unmanned all day for visitors to admire or for parishioners to go in to pray. It was a dishonest world. Chris's own

74

experience at the local church, when the vicar and he had disturbed Dave Porter in the vestry, only served to reinforce that message for him. It was while he was musing over the page of stolen ecclesiastical items the door to the shop opened and someone came in.

Down in the sales area, Chris found Dave Porter.

'Morning Dave. What can I do for you?'

'I've got a couple of those items I mentioned to you last night.'

The dealer creased his brow, trying to recall their conversation at the folk night.

'You remember. Church antiques I've picked up in the trade. There are one or two nice bits that would just suit you.'

Chris smiled as he remembered their conversation.

'There's an oak bible box and a pine pew. They're out in my car. They're too heavy to cart inside. You'd best come out to see them.'

Chris followed the runner as he limped out to his vehicle then inspected the stock in the back of his car. The pine pew was not in a good state. By the look of it, it had been left out in the weather and the rain had affected it.

'The pews a bit tatty, Dave. Where's it been?'

'It's fire damaged stock. This disused chapel in Birmingham burned down. Arsonists they suspect. The fire brigade pumped thousands of gallons of water over it. All the pews that weren't burnt were soaked in water and in the same state as this one. I thought, you being an experienced restorer, you could do something with it.'

Christopher looked closely at the pew and shook his head. 'It's not just spoiled the finish, it's warped the wood. I don't think I can do anything with it, Dave. It's not worth the effort to me.'

'What about this then?' Dave pulled a bundle wrapped in a grey woolen blanket from further inside the estate car. When he uncovered the item Chris could see it was an antique oak bible box. That was far more interesting. He lifted the box from the car and carried it into the shop where he could inspect it thoroughly.

When he'd placed it on the table near the window Chris could see the box was in good condition. It had that lovely dark colour that oak takes on after centuries of use and polish; a finish it's impossible to fake with modern wood stains and waxes. Genuine patina, the trade call it, and it's worth its weight in gold. There were some signs of wear where, over the centuries, fingers had grasped the lid of the desk to open it; signs completely compatible with it's legitimate use. The front edge of the oak

75

lid had a denticular decoration made with saw cuts to leave a row of tooth-like projections. One of the projection had been broken off but the damage was minimal and very old by the looks of it. That trivial damage was no problem and part of the piece's character and history.

'That's more like it, Dave.' Chris checked the box, opening and closing the lid to check the iron hinges and running his fingers lovingly over the patina on the wood. 'Where's this one from?'

Dave hesitated as if he was trying to remember. Finally he said. 'Same chapel...' Then realising there was no sign of water damage on the box he added hastily. '...Must have been in a more sheltered spot, which saved it from the fire hoses.'

Chris was immediately suspicious. There was something shifty about his visitor, nothing he could put his finger on, but he had a gut feeling, which told him to be wary of Dave Porter. He considered carefully what the runner had to sell. The pine pew was so obviously Victorian and had suffered from a soaking. The bible box was 17th century and had never been near any water. It didn't add up. Suddenly, he realised the box reminded him of one of the photographs of the stolen items featured in the Gazette.

'Hang on a minute I left my glue pot on the ring. I can smell it burning.' Making that excuse, he hurried into the back shop where he had left the Gazette, and checked the photographs of the stolen church items. Sure enough, there was no mistaking that bible box was one of the wanted items. The picture clearly showed the broken tooth on the front of the lid. That settled it. He went back into the shop and pretended to look the item over more thoroughly. Finally he shook his head.

'Sorry Dave. Neither item's for me.'

Dave was obviously disappointed but he knew Chris had only just set up the business in Barrowick and was probably very short of money.

'I'll carry it back to the car for you.' Chris wanted the stolen goods off his premises as soon as possible.

When he was carrying the box out of his shop he nearly collided with Dr and Mrs O'Conlan who were walking on the path outside the premises. The couple passed the time of day with the two dealers then crossed the road and took the lane to walk down to the reservoir.

Chris walked back into the shop, leaving Dave Porter to check the load was safe and lock the car's back door. When he heard the estate car drive away he fetched the Gazette and studied the photograph of the stolen bible box in more detail. There was no doubt in his mind that was the very box he had just been offered. He threw the paper down, went through to the workshop and leaned against the bench while he considered the implications of his suspicions. After some thought he decided he would not contact the police about the bible box. Dave Porter was a dislikable character but he couldn't report a fellow dealer. He gave the runner the benefit of the doubt; someone had probably taken advantage of him and sold him the stolen box. Anyone could handle stolen goods in the antique business without even knowing it. It was an occupational hazard.

His experience with Dave Porter and thoughts of the police, brought something else to his mind. Over the past days he had been thinking over the circumstances of Steve Mattocks' death and those funny coincidences in his dealings with Francis O'Conlan; the fact that the doctor knew where to look first for his stolen knife and chalice, and the fact that he guessed exactly the price that had been paid for them. In the cold light of day the explanation about dowsing for the items did seem very far fetched. Chris realised that a much simpler explanation would be if Steve had somehow told the professor where he had sold the items and for what price. That raised the question of why Steve would admit he had stolen the things, where he had sold them and how much he had charged for them. Then again, Steve was found drowned just after he'd sold the witchcraft items. Chris came to a conclusion; maybe he'd better share his suspicions about the man's death with the local police.

Later that morning Chris went into Oakham to get some groceries. He made a detour and called at the police station. The policeman on duty asked what he wanted.

'I need to talk to someone about a recent death at the reservoir.'

The man took out a note pad and made a note of his name and address.

'If you mean the drowning at Rutland Water, Sir, it's DC Phillips you need to speak to. He's in charge of the investigation.'

'That's the one. I'd better explain it to the DC then. When can I see him?'

'DC Phillips is over at the main police station in Leicester but I'll leave a message for him. He might phone you or even call on you. It might take a day or two as we are very busy.'

Chris thanked the officer and drove back to his shop.

Later in the morning as the dealer was altering the display in his shop window, a familiar car drew up outside. Immediately he recognised it.

It was the car he'd seen at the reservoir when Steve's body was dragged out of the water. DC Phillips sat at wheel for some minutes then he got out of the driving seat and came into the shop.

' Morning.' Chris greeted the detective cheerily.

Phillips smiled. 'I understand you may have some more information on the recent drowning?'

Chris signalled for the man to sit down, then collected his thoughts. 'Not exactly information, just some funny circumstances that may have a bearing on the death.'

'Right, fire away.' The detective took a notebook and pen from his pocket.

'Steve, that's the dead man, came in here and sold me two antique items two days before his body was discovered.'

Phillips nodded for the dealer to go on.

'I thought they were a couple of Victorian brass items but they proved to be medieval bronze witchcraft things.'

Phillips looked surprised. 'Witchcraft?'

'Yes. The local vicar assured me they were an Athame, that's a witch's dagger, and a chalice made from a human skull.'

The detective raised his eyebrows even higher.

Chris hesitated, searching for the best way to express his suspicions.

'Well?' Phillips prompted.

'The next day Dr Francis O'Conlan, the new man who's bought the vicarage in the village, came into my shop and asked if I'd got the items as they had been stolen from him.'

The DC nodded. 'You being the local antique dealer that seems to be a fair assumption to me. So what's your problem?'

'He also knew, or made a very informed guess, at the price I had given for the items. He said they were part of his collection. He bought them back from me. I find that very suspicious.'

The detective closed his notebook and frowned. 'What you're telling me has no bearing on the death, as far as I can see.'

'Don't you think it was suspicious, him knowing where the items were and knowing the price paid?'

'Did this man tell you the things were here?'

'No, not exactly. He asked me, as I was the nearest antique shop.'

'Well there you are. If you hadn't seen them he would have tried elsewhere.'

'But what about the price?'

'That was probably what he paid for them when he bought them for his collection. Anyway, as he collects these things I'd expect him to know the value.'

Phillips got up from his chair and moved towards the door. 'Is that all you have for me, Sir?'

Chris nodded.

'Well, thanks for the information. I will consider it along with the coroner's report.'

Chris had a sudden thought. He held up his hand to stop the man leaving. 'But what about the fact he didn't report the theft to the police?'

Phillips stopped in the doorway and turned. 'He solved the crime himself. I wish more people would do likewise. It would leave us free to get on with more serious business.' With that parting comment he left the shop, got into his car and drove out of the village.

Chris made himself a coffee and sat in the shop. Looking at it from the detective's point of view he could see his information was not very useful but he still had doubts about the events. He felt DC Phillips seemed all too willing to dismiss his suspicions and he had seen the same detective helping to clear the barn at the old vicarage. Phillips was obviously acquainted with the O'Conlans, and for that matter so was Dave Porter, who had tried to pass on some stolen goods only that morning. Things had been peaceful and quiet in Barrowick before the new Psychic College came to the village. The dealer was not sure he liked the changes.

Later, as he walked down to the Barrowick Arms for lunch, Chris met the O'Conlans again as they returned from their walk along the reservoir perimeter. The couple followed him into the pub. Sara was quite busy when he entered the bar. He found an empty table and sat reading a discarded newspaper until the girl came over to take his order.

'Hello Chris. What do you fancy today?'

'That would be telling...but for my lunch I'll have a ham salad and a pint of bitter as usual.'

Sara grinned at his cheeky reply.

Chris took his chance. 'While you're here, what about that meal out with me this Wednesday?'

'I'd love that.' She considered the offer for a minute then added. 'Who's going to drive? I don't really fancy getting dressed up then travelling in your old van. We can use my car if you don't mind.'

He nodded. 'Good idea, then I can have a drink with the meal.'

When Sara went to take the O'Conlan's order, Tanith O'Conlan kept her for some time in an animated conversation. They seemed to get on very well together.

Chris was curious what they were discussing. He could see from her reaction, Sara seemed quite pleased. She was still smiling when she went back into the kitchen to prepare the meals. After dinner he relaxed with a coffee and started to do the crossword in the newspaper. He knew he had the two Yorkshire clocks to tackle for his ex wife but he was in no hurry to please her. Once the mid day rush was over, Sara brought her lunch over to his table and sat opposite to him to eat it while her mother tidied up behind the bar.

'Have you finished it yet?' Sara pointed to the prize crossword.

'No, not yet.' He leaned over and asked in a low voice. 'Whatever was the professor's wife after? You looked very pleased with yourself when you left their table.'

'Ah! They have made a suggestion that could drum up some more business for us. The problem is, I might have trouble talking mother into it.'

Chris was intrigued. 'Go on then. Do tell. You can't leave it in the air like that.'

Sara grinned. 'Tanith is a psychic you know. She teaches the subject.'

He nodded and waited for her to explain more.

'She has suggested we hold a Psychic Night here at the pub.'

'A psychic night?' Even though he sounded incredulous, he had in fact seen such events advertised in the local paper. One of the pubs in Oakham had advertised such a night in the Rutland Times only the week before, but he didn't really know what it meant.

'Yes, a Psychic Night. You must have seen them advertised?'

He nodded.

'They usually offer to tell your fortune by reading your palm, or consulting the Tarot cards. Sometimes they have a psychic medium there. It's very popular, especially with the girls.'

'How will that pay you then?'

'We can charge an entry fee, then the customers pay the individual psychics for a reading, so we don't have to pay them. They tend to attract the lady customers and they drink a lot of wine at these events. We can put on food for them. It could be a winner for us.'

'I suppose the popularity of your folk night had something to do with this offer?'

'Yes. Tanith did say how much they enjoyed the folk night and how surprised she was at the turnout. They are building up their College business and we could benefit from that as well.'

'I can see Tanith might well be able to hold one of these events but you'd need more than one psychic. Is Dr O'Conlan taking part?'

Sara shook her head. 'I don't think so, he's far too serious for that. Tanith said she has several students locally who are already capable of mediumship. She seems quite keen. I suppose it might get them more students.' She chased the last prawn around her plate with her fork and smiled secretly to herself.

Chris got the impression she was pleased with herself about more than the offer of a psychic night at the pub. 'What's that sly little smile about? You look like the cat that got the cream.'

Sara grinned even more. 'I think I may have decided what night school I am doing this year.'

'Ceramics again?'

'No. Psychic studies. Tanith tells me they are holding some of their courses at the college in the evenings for people who work during the day. I could fancy being a psychic and it can pay very well. And it's very convenient, the course being just over the road here in the village.'

He was taken by surprise at this suggestion. Chris's doubts must have shown on his face.

'What's the problem?' Sara demanded.

He shrugged his shoulders. 'No problem, just surprised. You've never mentioned this before.'

'I've only just decided. Would you be interested in coming with me to an evening class?'

'You must be joking! I'm sure you'll enjoy it, but I'd find it a complete waste of time. Anyway, best of luck with it. You have a relaxed way with people and you could do well.' His endorsement was genuine but he had serious reservations about the subjects offered and about the O'Conlans. He felt that some of the people they kept company with, left a lot to be desired. He got up to go.

'I look forward to our date on Wednesday.' She said as they parted company.

81

## Chapter Thirteen

On Wednesday morning, Sara walked down to Chris's antique shop to confirm the arrangements for the dinner date they had planned for that night.

'It's my night off. I'll enjoy a meal out prepared by somebody else. It'll make a change from cooking for everybody else.'

He was thrilled she had agreed to go out with him that evening. 'I'll pick you up in my van about seven o'clock then.' He'd forgotten her earlier comments about their transport arrangements.

'Ah no! If we are going to Stamford we'll go in my car. No disrespect to your driving but I prefer my car to your old van.'

He couldn't help but smile at this. The girl was right. The van was hardly clean and she would no doubt be wearing some nice clothes. 'OK. You're right of course. I'll walk up to the pub at seven and we can go in your car.'

The rest of his day passed happily enough. With the promise of a night out with Sara and some clocks to work on, he was feeling good. When he joined Sara at the pub he could see she had made a big effort to look her best. She had on a green dress and a fake fur jacket, her long hair was combed up and her makeup was immaculate. He'd tidied himself up and made an effort but she made him feel a bit of a mess. He apologised to her. 'I didn't dress up, Sara. I've been too busy this afternoon.'

She let me off politely. 'You look fine. Don't mind me getting smartened up. I don't often get the chance to go out in the evening, so I've made an extra effort.'

Chris was thrilled she had made such an effort for him and wished he'd done the same for her.

'Where are we going?' Sara sat in the driving seat of her car and started the engine.

'I thought we could go over to Stamford. There's a little restaurant there, the Golden King, where I've eaten before. I know the chef and the manager well. They do a good meal. You'll enjoy it, I'm sure.'

Sara was only too pleased to fall in with this suggestion. She put the car into gear and drove out of the village towards Stamford.

The Golden King restaurant was not too busy. Mid week was a good time to have a meal there, unlike the weekends when they were invariably rushed. Chris had often had a meal there when he lived in

Stamford. The manager was an old friend and a business acquaintance, which was one reason he'd chosen to bring Sara to that particular eating house.

'Ah! Mr Doughty. It's nice to see you again.' The waiter greeted the pair and saw them to a corner table where he presented them with menus and left them to make up their minds what to order.

As they went to their table a tall young man came out of the toilets, recognised Chris and stopped to speak to him..

Chris apologised to Sara for the interruption. 'Sorry about this. It's probably business. You sit down and check the menu. I won't be a minute.'

'How's business at Barrowick?' The newcomer asked.

'Could be better. How are you doing at the antique centre in Deeping?'

'The same as you, but your ex doesn't seem to be doing too well without you.'

Chris shrugged his shoulders. Vickie had most of the good furniture, the Stamford premises and their contacts when they'd parted company, but he didn't know what had happened since.

'Vickie's owing a lot of money locally. She owes me for several items she's had from me. The furniture restorer at Deeping tells me she owes him a lot more. Her last cheque bounced so he wont deal with her again.'

Once again Chris shrugged his shoulders. He was no longer involved with Vickie and he certainly wasn't her keeper. However, the news did explain why she had brought some restoration work to him. In the days they were in business together he had done all the restoration work for their shop, now she had to farm it out to other people and she was getting a reputation as a poor payer. He slapped the young man on the shoulder and turned to Sara, who was sitting patiently at their table.

'Sorry about that, Sara. Business.'

Sara just nodded that she understood. She was reading the menu thoroughly as she had never been to that restaurant before. The meals offered where either Chinese or traditional English dishes; they tried to cater for all the local tastes. Chris knew exactly what he would have, he was never adventurous with meals and he knew what he liked. When the waiter returned, he ordered Sara's choice and his usual.

'My companion will have the sweet and sour pork. I'll have steak and chips with a side salad.'

'Wine, Sir?'

Chris looked at Sara and raised his eyebrows in question.

'Just a glass of house white. I am driving, after all.'

He ordered a half of beer for himself and they settled down to small talk while they waited.

'What do you make of our new college in the old vicarage? Is it going to bring more business into the village?' He asked, just to make conversation.

Sara nodded and put down her wine glass. 'We have already noticed a few new faces. We think they are people attending classes.'

When the waiter brought their meals to the table, the manager came over to speak to them. He spoke to Chris but couldn't take his eyes off Sara, obviously curious about his friend's new lady companion. 'Chris, lovely to see you again.' He smiled at Sara, including her in his greeting. Turning to the Chris again he said, 'That clock we had from you is still going fine.'

'Good, and how's your business?'

'Can't grumble. Stamford seems to be riding out the recession rather well.' With that brief exchange and a nod and a smile to Sara, he left them to get on with their meals.

As the evening wore on, a few more people came into the restaurant and the room began to fill up. Chris and Sara got on rather well together. The conversation never flagged. They found they had similar tastes and a similar sense of humour.

At about nine o'clock, when they were just finishing the meal, a noisy crowd of women tumbled into the room. There were six of them and they had obviously been celebrating as they were already a bit merry. It was a girls' night out. They commandeered a table on the far side of the room from Sara and Chris and immediately ordered more drinks. One of the group rose to visit the loo, tripped on the carpet and caused screams of laughter from her friends.

Chris had his back to them and didn't see who they were. Sara glanced up as they were making such a noise. Suddenly one of the women left her friends at their table and came over to their table. She stood behind Chris, placed her hands on his shoulders, dug in her thumbs hard and leaned over him. Then she spoke to Sara. 'Don't believe a word he tells you, love. He's full of shit!'

Chris recognised the voice immediately. It was Vickie, his divorced wife. He turned quickly to face her. 'You're still drinking too much I see. Get back to your friends and behave yourself.'

The manager, alerted to the noise in the dining room, came through from the kitchen and stood watching the scene. He wrung his hands and frowned. What was he to do when two people who were old friends and valued customers, squared up to each other? He stood ready to calm any problems but he was reluctant to interfere.

Chris was embarrassed, which was exactly what his ex wanted. She didn't want to be married to him but she was obviously jealous of anyone else he fancied and any success he made of his life without her.

Sara was dumbstruck. She looked up at the woman and back at Chris, several unanswered questions crossed her face, one after the other. He looked over at her and smiled wanly. It was just his bad luck to bump into Vickie on a night out.

The other women at Vickie's table shouted over to her. 'Come on, Vickie. Leave him alone. You need to order your meal.' She ruffled his hair and smiled very sweetly at Sara. 'Don't get too attached to him, dear. He's not reliable.' Then she retreated to her friends. Pleased that she had upset her ex-husband's night out.

Chris could see how embarrassed Sara was so he suggested they leave.

The manager sighed with relief and returned to the kitchen, pleased the altercation was over.

On the way home, Sara was very quiet. Chris could feel the atmosphere between them but wasn't sure what to say to make it right. Finally he broke the silence. 'That was my ex.'

'I guessed that.' Sara's answer was brief.

'She had been drinking. She's not usually so awkward.'

Sara didn't speak.

'My friend who you saw when we first went into the restaurant, tells me Vickie has money problems. That's probably why she's drinking too much, don't you think?'

Sara still didn't answer.

Chris was very unhappy about the turn of events that evening. What should have been a nice meal out to get to know Sara better, had turned into a complete nightmare. He didn't want Sara thinking he still carried a torch for his ex wife. He sighed deeply and tried to explain one more time.

'Sara, Vickie is my ex. She'll do anything to embarrass me when she's had a few. Don't take any notice of her. She's just a jealous girl and can't stomach me making a life for myself, especially with a good looking girl like you.'

In the dark, he felt Sara's left hand on his. She squeezed his hand, reassuring him she was alright about the evening, then put her hand back on the steering wheel and continued to drive home.

At the Barrowick Arms, there was still time for Chris to join Sara in a drink. They sat at one of the tables in silence. Finally Sara broke into a fit of giggles. He looked at her in amazement.

'It's not every night a girl gets warned off her escort by a stranger, is it. Your ex must still have a soft spot for you. You should be flattered.'

He shook his head and laughed with her, more in relief than at the events of that evening. Thank goodness Sara had realised the true situation and had not been put off. 'We must try another meal together sometime.' He suggested hopefully.

'Yes. Good idea, but I'll pick the venue next time. We can try one of the local Rutland pubs.'

Chris grinned sheepishly and agreed. 'You couldn't make a worse job of choosing than I did.'

The next afternoon. Chris drove into Lincolnshire to a farm auction. When a farm changed hands they often sold off all the implements and the contents of the house and yard. Sometimes the house contained old furniture that was worth restoring. This particular sale was a catalogued event so he had an inkling of what would come up. As he drew up in his van in the lane leading to the farm he saw most of the local dealers had already arrived. Dave Porter was parked near the gate and was stopping some dealers as they went into the farmyard, trying to sell them items from the back of his car. Chris nodded a greeting as he walked past but Dave was too busy to notice him as he was trying to sell the stolen oak bible box.

In the farm they had already sold the smaller items from the kitchen and the washroom. The auctioneer was just starting on the furniture, which is what most interested Chris. There was a lot of interest from the trade in the larger items like the Welsh Dresser and an old oak, 30 hr grandfather clock. He did not bid for these as they sold well above his price range. At last they came to a lot he was interested in; a set of three carver chairs, which were held aloft by the porters.

'How much am I bid for the chairs?' The auctioneer said. 'Should be three hundred, surely.'

Three hundred pounds was actually a very cheap price for such chairs, if they had been in good condition, but they weren't. Each one had rungs missing, rickety joints or some other minor damage.

Chris knew he had the expertise and the time to restore them so he was hoping for a bargain. 'One Hundred.' He offered a low bid.

The auctioneer took the bid .'That's cheap. Come on, who will bid One Twenty Five?' He looked around the room hoping for a further bid. 'They are here to be sold. There's no reserves at this sale.'

After some  minutes, which passed very slowly for Chris and seemed a lot longer, the chairs were knocked down to him. He was pleased to have got them with the maiden bid but he knew it was only because of the amount of work needed on them. Time was money, but he had plenty of the former and very little of the latter!

The auctioneer soon finished in the house and moved out to the farmyard and the outhouses. Chris paid for the Windsor chairs and loaded them into his van. As there was nothing in the yard or barns that interested him, he drove back up the farm track to the main road and made for home. On the way out, he noticed that Dave Porter's car was no longer at the road side, he had already left the sale. Chris wondered if he had managed to sell the stolen bible box. If so, some unsuspecting dealer had  bought himself a load of trouble.

## Chapter Fourteen

Chris didn't know how she did it, but Sara managed to persuade her mother to let her organise a Psychic Night at the Barrowick Arms. When she delivered a poster to him and asked him to display it in his shop window, she told him how difficult that persuading had been. 'It was only because a few of the other pubs in the area have tried it and have found it a success, that she allowed me to go ahead with it. And she had to admit a Folk Night paid handsomely.'

'When will you do it ? On her night off?'

'Of course. You know mother. Her religion wont let her get involved in things like fortune telling, even though it's only a bit of fun.' She unrolled the poster to show him. 'I hope I can persuade you to support me like you did on the folk night?'

He hesitated but he could see she was willing him to say yes.

'You'll not be charged an entry fee like the other customers. I could do with some moral support and you were the first person I thought of, you being such a good friend.'

He could see the pleading look in her eyes, and he was flattered she regarded him as such a good friend 'Of course, but don't expect me to get my fortune told. I think it's all rubbish just like the astrology predictions in the newspapers.'

Sara was delighted with his acceptance and gave him a hug.

On the night of the Psychic Fair, Chris made an effort to tidy himself up and walked down to the pub in the middle of the evening. He was surprised how busy it was. Sara had two helpers behind the bar but he still had to wait several minutes to get served. When he looked around the pub he was surprised to see he was the only man present, apart from the temporary barman. Sara had warned him this sort of event really appealed to the ladies. She was right, the room was full of women of various ages. Most of them were smartly dressed; obviously making a social event of it. The air was full of the sounds of female voices chattering happily to each other.

There were five female psychics, each one sitting at individual tables scattered around the bar. Every one was busy giving a reading to a client. Sometimes two girls were sharing the experience. Most of the psychics he had never seen before, but he immediately recognised Tanith. She looked striking with her curly red hair and her colourful dress. She seemed to be particularly busy with a queue of women waiting to see her. He guessed she must have a good reputation for this sort of event.

He sat at the bar and watched the proceedings with interest There were four psychics doing readings, two were doing palmistry and another one had a crystal ball placed on the centre of her table. In addition to those four, Tanith was seated in the centre of the room looking every inch the main attraction. She had tied back her red hair with a blue ribbon, which matched her dress, which was the colour of Lapis Lazuli. Chris loved that deep blue colour; Vickie, his ex, had sometimes bought Victorian Lapis jewelry for the Stamford shop. He watched Tanith with growing interest as she was using several different methods of divination. First she would ask for something the sitter wore or used regularly. Chris listened to her spiel, which she gave in a warm, West Country, accent. He hadn't realised she was from that part of the country but it was obvious that evening as she reverted to her childhood way of speaking when she was busy. He listened even more intently to try and locate the area she came from and decided it must be Hereford or Somerset.

Holding out her hand Tanith took a brooch from a girl who sat at her table. 'Ah! This belonged to an older woman. Your mother.' Her green eyes flashed as she looked up at the girl waiting for a reaction to her information.

The sitter nodded vigorously.

'She is no longer with us, my dear, but she's here this evening. She is a lovely lady. Her name is Edith.'

The girl was shocked at this revelation, She put her hand to her mouth and burst into tears.

Tanith patted her on the shoulder. 'Don't cry. You will see her again in the afterlife. She watches over you and your daughter. She thinks the child is beautiful. Your mother is pleased you named the girl after her. Your daughter looks just like your mother when she was a girl.'

'Oh! Thank you. That's exactly right. We have family photographs of them both as children and the resemblance is obvious.'

Chris was surprised how accurate Tanith seemed to be. On the face of it she was definitely psychic and good at what she did, but he was sceptical by nature and wondered how Tanith could have come by this information.

When the reading was over the girl came to the bar to buy a glass of white wine. She stood next to Chris, dabbing her eyes dry with her handkerchief.

'You're crying. Upset you, did she?' He asked.

'No. It was wonderful what she told me. I miss my mother awfully but she said she is looking over us.' As she spoke she involuntarily touched the gold brooch she had handed to Tanith.

He smiled and held out a hand for the brooch. 'Was this your mother's?'

'It was her favourite. Dad bought it for her. She always wore it. That's why I brought it here tonight.'

He had been listening to the girl's voice and detected a fen accent. 'You're not from around here, are you. Have you come far?'

'From Deeping, with my friend Deidre.' She looked over at a tall girl sitting and waiting for her turn for a reading, and gave her a small wave of her hand.

Chris turned the brooch over in his hand to admire it and check it out. It was made of 9 carat gold and was an Art Nouveau design. He looked to see if there was a name engraved on it, which would account for Tanith knowing the girl's mother was called Edith, but he found no clues on the jewelry. 'How come you've traveled all this way for a reading? Are you often in this area?'

'No. I've never been over here before. We saw the event advertised in the Mercury. It's sort of a girl's night out. I've left my husband looking after our daughter.'

Everything the girl said confirmed what Tanith had told her. He was intrigued. 'Would you recommend her.' He nodded towards Tanith who was busy doing a reading for the girl's friend.

'Oh yes. I've been to one or two psychics before and she is by far the best.' With that ringing endorsement, she took back the brooch and went over to join her friend at Tanith's table.

He looked at Tanith with increasing interest. She appeared to be the real deal. He was just considering whether to go back to his flat to escape from that girls' night out when Sara came over to him.

'Enjoying it?' She asked.

He smiled at her. 'Well I do feel like a fish out of water.'

She laughed at his attempt to politely tell her he was a bit embarrassed as the only male customer in the bar that evening. 'Don't go yet. I've been given two free tickets to have a reading with Tanith. One for me and one for mother, but of course, she's not here. She's not interested and she's gone to her WI meeting.'

Chris nodded that he understood. He was a bit surprised anyway that Sara had managed to talk her mother into allowing a Psychic Night at the pub.

'I am going to have a reading now and you can have the other ticket.' She pushed a card into his hand before he could object, and immediately went over to Tanith's vacant table.

He watched her sit at the table and have her reading. Sara and Tanith seemed to get on extremely well together. Immediately Sara sat down, Tanith made her feel at ease. There seemed to be a lot of laughter and warmth in their relationship. The medium certainly knew how to ingratiate herself with people. She had an easy charm that relaxed her sitters. He looked over at the barman and ordered another pint of bitter while he waited for Sara to return and report to him how she had found the experience.

Sara and Tanith lingered over the sitting, they seemed to be discussing other things than the reading itself. The hum of voices in the bar increased as more people turned up for the event and as more wine was consumed. The hubbub of voices grew to such an extent, Chris could not catch what Sara and Tanith were discussing. Finally Sara came away from the table with a beaming smile on her face.

'You seem pleased.'

'Yes, She's good and I have found out what I wanted to know.'

'Oh yes? What's that then?'

'I have decided to enroll in one of her classes. She told me I have the gift and could become a successful psychic with the proper training.'

He was about to question this when Tanith held up her hand and caught Sara's eye.

'Time for you to have your turn.' Sara pushed him forward.

He was not entirely reluctant to join the psychic at her table because he was intrigued to watch at close quarters how she worked. Anyway, he did find her rather attractive. She beamed at him and asked him to sit down opposite to her.

'Chris, isn't it? Sara told me she had given the ticket to you. She seems fond of you.' She took his hand in hers, turned up the palm and studied it for some time. 'I see a broken relationship here, Chris. Lots of anguish and anger. You must let it go. Your future will be happy if you give it time.'

He was a bit surprised at the accuracy of this reading but reminded himself that Sara had been talking at length to this woman and he had no idea what had been discussed. Maybe she had dropped some hints about him and his past.

Tanith took his other hand, cradled it in her hands and compared the two palms. She frowned deeply then said. 'You appear to be an agent of change. Great change. You will cause great upset to those around you.' She shook her head as if denying what she saw. Abruptly she let go of his hands and took out the Tarot pack.

Chris eyed her thoughtfully. She had told him nothing that she could not have gleaned locally and the talk of change was all vague and in the future, if it was ever to happen at all.

Tanith handed the tarot cards to him and asked him to shuffle them. As he made to hand them back to her she insisted he cut the deck and lay the top four cards out on the table between them. Chris looked at the cards as he laid them out and was immediately taken by them. He had seen the regular, mass produced, Tarot cards when they came up at auction, but this deck was very different. They were hand painted and consisted of designs he had never encountered before. They were a beautiful set of cards, definitely unusual and probably unique. As an antique dealer with an interest in art, engravings and maps, he would love to have owned them.

'Ah! Four cards and all of Major Arcana. That's unusual.' Tanith did not look up at him. She seemed to be talking to herself.

'What's that? The major what?' He queried.

'The Tarot are like a pack of ordinary playing cards. There are picture cards and number cards. The picture cards make up the Major Arcana, there are usually twenty two of them in a Tarot deck and they are the most important ones for telling someone's fortune. Like I said, this many picture cards turning up in a brief reading, is very unusual.' She looked down intently at the four cards.

He stayed silent while she concentrated on the spread. He had to admit the cards were beautifully painted. The first one was a jester stepping off the top of a cliff with a butterfly net in his hand. He was chasing a butterfly and not looking where he was going. Behind the jester was a little dog, which had bitten a hole in the seat of the man's trousers, trying to attract his attention. There was a lot going on in that design. Even he could see there would be many symbols to interpret.

Tanith touched the card and said 'The Fool. That's you.'

Chris sat back, not knowing whether he should be insulted by the comment.

From his body language and his reaction she realised what he was thinking. 'No no. You are not a fool, neither is this jester. The Fool is journeying through life ignoring what is happening about him but he is on a very important journey. Many things happen to him but he is oblivious to his surroundings.' She pointed to the next card and called out its name. 'The Tower.'

He could see the painting on the card was of a tall building being struck by lightning. Two figures were falling from the top of it along with a lot of pieces of dislodged masonry. The Bible story of the Tower of Babel sprang immediately to his mind.

'That is the destruction of something important. It needn't be a building it could be almost anything, but it is significant.' Her voice had dropped to a whisper; it was almost as if she was doing the reading for herself.

The third card bore the figure of a magician with a wand in his hand and conjuring tricks on a table beside him. There was a pentagram drawn on the table, which instantly reminded Chris of the Athame's hilt.

'The Magician, a mystical and powerful figure.' She fingered the card and lingered on it. Finally she came to the fourth card, which was 'Death.'

He saw the word 'Death' printed on the card and the skeleton depicted on it. The figure was leaning on a gravestone with a sickle in one hand and a glass sand timer in the other. It reminded him of illustrations of Old Father Time. He laughed. 'Is that predicting my death? I thought you psychics never let on when you saw someone was about to die? Isn't it against the rules to worry people with such dire predictions?'

Tanith shook her head vigorously. 'Modern interpreters of this card usually see it as the end of something. Not necessarily death. It is the end of something and maybe the beginning of something new.' She looked up at him, her green eyes flashing a challenge. Her West country accent thickened as she spoke more quickly.

He took all this with a pinch of salt and said. 'If anyone is going to die surely it must be the Magician? He's the one next to the Death card, not the Fool.'

Tanith quickly gathered up the cards and pushed them back into the pack. Without a word of explanation, she rose from the table and walked quickly to the Ladies' cloakroom. Realising his reading must be over, Sara came over to the table. 'Well? Wasn't she good.' It was more a statement than a question.

Not wishing to argue or upset her, he dutifully agreed.

'Is she OK?' Sara looked over at the empty table and glanced at the Ladies' loo door.

'I think she was taken short.' He grinned. Whatever he had said or she had seen in the cards had really upset her, but he had no intention of telling Sara that. Tanith soon returned from the toilets and carried on with her work but she kept looking over at Chris with a frown on her face. As soon as he'd finished his beer he made an excuse to leave the pub.

'You are managing fine without my help, Sara. I'm just a distraction for you on a busy night. I have a few business phone calls to make, so I'll make tracks for home.'

Sara was very busy keeping everybody happy while they waited for their readings. Chris gave her a quick peck on the cheek then walked to the door, but he couldn't help noticing that Tanith's eyes followed him all the way out. He made a point of turning and giving her a big smile as he got to the front door.

Back at his flat, Chris made himself a coffee and a couple of rounds of toast for supper. It had been an interesting and educational evening. He was surprised at how many gullible women turned up to one of those fortune telling nights. Sara had told him she charged twenty pounds entrance fee and each of the punters paid a further fiver for a reading. It didn't take a maths genius to add up the night's takings. Taking into account the amount of wine drunk by the punters while they waited for their readings, and the food eaten, that psychic night was a nice little earner. He sighed and spoke out loud in the empty kitchen. 'If only I could think up a few gigs like that, I'd have no more money worries.'

Later, as he sat in his bedroom listening to a late night music programme on Radio Rutland, his mind returned to the reading he had had from Tanith. That woman was certainly upset with him about something. He went over what had been said during the reading. The Death card seemed to be the main problem for her, and his comments about it. He was still very sceptical about psychic readings and he couldn't think the random selection of that particular card could have any significance whatsoever. He chuckled at her discomfort. The silly cow must believe some of her own mumbo jumbo! Then he remembered that Sara wanted to study the subject. 'Ah well, there's nowt so queer as folk! But I'd better not tell Sara that.'

He laughed out loud in the privacy of his flat.

# Chapter Fifteen

The arrival of the Psychic College in the village had certainly increased the number of people visiting Barrowick, although the antique shop did not benefit as Chris saw very few of them. The people arrived at the college, presumably for studies or seminars, and they tended to stay there. A few did walk across to the pub for a drink or a meal but the college was mostly self sufficient and the students did not mix with the villagers. This isolation was never more obvious than the night of the masked ball.

The first anyone in the village knew about the event on the evening of June 23rd was the arrival of scores of cars. The whole length of Main Street became one large car park as the vicarage grounds were already full.

Chris was surprised when he walked down to the pub for a drink after closing the shop. He was surprised not only at the number of vehicles arriving but at the number of expensive cars parked along the road. He had never seen so many Jaguars, BMW's and other luxury cars in the village at one time.

As he locked the shop, a Bentley drew up to the kerb at the front of his premises. Four middle aged people, two men and two women, got out of the car. They each took a small suitcase from the car boot and walked quickly down to the old vicarage. He followed them down the street, intrigued by what they could possibly have in their small cases and trying to guess why they were in Barrowick. Their clothes were ordinary day clothes, no evening dresses or dress suits as one would have expected at a social event held in the evening. Their small suitcases reminded him of the Freemasons, who he used to see going to their meetings when he lived in Stamford, but they were invariably men and this group was a mixture of men and women. It was indeed a puzzle. Dismissing these questions from his mind, he went into the bar of the Barrowick Arms and ordered a drink.

Sara and her mother were behind the bar. Mrs Goodacre left just as he arrived. Sara smiled at him and asked. 'Your usual, Chris?'

'Please, and a bag of crisps. I've been too busy to eat yet.'

Sara pulled a pint and placed it on the bar and commented, 'It's busy out there this evening but not in here.' She looked pointedly around the bar, at Chris and at the two fishermen drinking at a corner table. The lack of customers added weight to her comment. The empty pub contrasted sharply with the busy street outside.

'Aye, it's very busy out there.' He took a long draught of bitter, wiped his mouth on the back of his hand and grinned at the barmaid. 'Not one of them has visited my shop either. So you're not the only one missing out.'

Sara shook her head and frowned.

Chris continued. 'What's going on then?'

'I have no idea.'

'Oh! I thought you got on well with the professor and his wife. I thought they would have mentioned to you an event this big.'

'No, not a word, and there's been nothing in the Rutland Times.'

The pair slipped into a sociable silence. As he ate his crisps and drank his bitter, Sara polished the glasses and placed them under the counter.

It was a lovely evening. One or two locals drifted into the pub for a drink. Sara propped open the front doors as it was so warm. Chris stayed at the pub, seated at the bar, and chatted to her between customers. The bar was never full of people but there was a steady flow of drinkers as a few of the locals stopped on their evening stroll to have a sit down and a drink. From the noise of cars outside, it was obvious the event at the college was an ambitious affair. Eventually the whole of main street was filled with parked cars and new arrivals had to leave their cars on the lane leading to the main road. Strangers drifted past the pub and over to the college where they entered the stone barn. He guessed that large building was being used for some important event. Lights were visible inside the barn, shining through the high slits in the stone walls. Whatever they were planning at the college, they had a lovely evening for it.

Later in the evening the Reverend Smyth came into the pub. As soon as he spotted Chris at the bar he went over to join him.

'Lovely evening, Chris.'

'Sure is. Can I get you a drink?'

'Yes. Thanks. I'll have a half of bitter please.'

Sara, who was standing the other side of the bar near to them, poured the drink without being asked.

'Busy evening in the village.' John commented.

'Yes. We were wondering what was going on at the old vicarage.'

The vicar just nodded and frowned.

Chris turned to Sara and asked. 'Don't you know what's happening? I thought you were interested in taking one of their night school courses?'

She shook her head. 'I've no idea. Anyway I haven't started my course yet. I start next term.'

As they were talking, a couple of strangers came into the bar. The ladies were each carrying a small case; one had a suitcase the other a makeup case.

Chris leaned over to whisper to the vicar. 'I thought these visitors reminded me of Freemasons. I used to see them going to their lodge meetings in Stamford. They usually carried small suitcases, but they were always men.'

The two women found a table and ordered drinks.

'Two whiskies, please love.' They told Sara when she went over to take their orders.

Sara poured the drinks and took them over to the newcomers. As she reached the table one of the women stood up and accidentally dropped her makeup case off her lap. As it hit the ground, it sprang open and some of the contents fell onto the bar floor, spilling across the room and ending up at Chris's feet.

The sudden sound of the case hitting the wooden floor attracted everyone's attention. Chris bent down to retrieve the object that had rolled in front of him. He picked it up and was surprised to see it was a face mask. It wasn't an ordinary mask but an elaborate oval design like the ones he'd seen in pictures of the Venice festivals. It was silver coloured with raised golden patterns on it. It had a small moulded mouth with full, voluptuous, lips and two almond shaped eye slits. It was unmistakably a mask of a young female face. He turned it over and noticed two elastic ties attached to it, and a pair of small horns protruding from the forehead.

At the same time as the mask rolled across the room, a bundle of scarlet material fell out of the vanity case at the woman's feet. The two women leapt from their seats and quickly scrambled on the floor to retrieve the things. The cloth, which one of them quickly folded up, looked like a cloak made of thick red velvet.

Chris held out the mask to its owner. She took it from him without a word of thanks and put it back in her case along with the cloak, then the two women left the pub. They seemed flustered and were in a hurry to get away, leaving their drinks untouched on the table.

Chris looked at Sara, raised his eyebrows and shrugged his shoulders. She just shook her head, as surprised as he was at the customers' reactions. He considered the events of the evening; the number of visitors and cars and the strange way the two women acted. It struck him the

Psychic College must be holding a masked ball or something similar, probably for the students as a celebration. Maybe it was the end of a course and these were the successful students. It also struck him that the students of the college did seem to be very fond of face masks of one sort or another as all the people cleaning out the barn had been wearing them when he called to collect the rubbish. What had they got to hide?

The Reverend Smyth who had witnessed the mask and cloak falling onto the floor, frowned even deeper and shook his head. Chris got the impression that John was not entirely surprised at the episode. When the women had departed, Chris renewed his conversation with the vicar. 'We don't often see you here in the evening, John.'

'No.'

'It's a beautiful evening. I suppose, like me, you just fancied a beer.'

The vicar nodded noncommittedly. It was obvious he had other things on his mind.

As his companion was not more forthcoming, Chris ventured. 'A penny for your thoughts.'

John sighed a deep sigh, then answered. 'They're probably not worth a penny, Chris. But they could be, if what I suspect is happening.'

Now the dealer was intrigued and wouldn't let the subject drop. 'Come on. If it's not private, do share it with us.'

The vicar leaned over the bar and said in a low voice. 'Do you know what the date is?'

'June 23rd.' Sara answered perkily from behind the bar.

'That's correct. June 23rd. It's St John's eve.'

Chris was puzzled. 'What's the significance of that? Is it some obscure church festival that you've come to celebrate?'

'No. Not a church festival. It's one of the main dates in the witch's calendar. It is the night when covens traditionally meet to celebrate the black mass.'

Sara didn't take a lot of notice of these comments. They meant nothing to her. She busied herself behind the bar. Chris, on the other hand, had already had dealings with Francis O'Conlan over the Athame and the chalice and he'd been in the vestry when Dave Porter was caught searching for communion wafers. He frowned and looked questioningly at John. When Sara went further up the bar to serve another customer and was definitely out of earshot, he questioned the vicar further. 'Surely you don't think we have a black mass going on over the road?'

John nodded. 'That's why I've come tonight. I may be right, I hope I'm wrong, but I will hold a service in the church to counteract any possible evil. Will you join me?'

Chris was taken aback at this request but felt he had little choice. He was already deeply involved in the events leading up to the supposed mass. He tried to make light of the subject. 'It could just be a masked ball they are holding. You may be jumping to all sorts of wrong conclusions.'

'I sincerely hope so. Otherwise this village and the people in it are in grave danger.' John's grim expression left Chris in no doubt that the old man believed what he was suggesting.

When they had finished their drinks, the vicar and Chris made their excuses to Sara and left the pub. They walked across the road and stopped at the sign advertising the Psychic College. From that position they could see the barn with its lights showing through the slits high in the walls. They stood in silence and listened.

'Can you hear the dance music from your student ball?' John asked.

Chris hesitated and listened even harder. At last he was forced to admit there was no sound of music but he could hear a kind of chanting as several distant voices seemed to be repeating some kind of incantation. It looked more and more as if the vicar could be right.

'What will they be doing in there if it is a black mass they're celebrating?'

John did not answer immediately but ushered Chris into the church and away from public view. Finally, as they walked down the aisle of the church, he explained. 'The black mass is a travesty of the communion we hold in church. They will have an altar, possibly with a man or woman lying naked on it. They will use a chalice like the one you had in your shop. It will be filled with wine or even blood! It may well have hallucinatory drugs in it. Someone, well versed in black magic, will take the place of the celebrant and will lead the mass. A lapsed clergyman would be an ideal candidate.'

Chris recoiled at these comments. 'Blood and drugs?'

'Yes. Satanists have used human blood before now and strong drugs are commonplace these days.'

Chris shook his head in disbelief and waited for the vicar to continue.

'There will be drunken cavorting and much sexual intercourse. They will use real communion wafers in the mass, if they have managed to steal any. They sometimes defile the wafers by colouring them black and stabbing the Athame into them before consuming them.'

'What's the idea of it? Is it just to make fun of the church rituals?'

'No, not entirely. They will call on the devil to join them and they will hope to invoke his powers of evil.'

'But why? It seems a daft way for intelligent people to go on.'

'Why? It's because some people believe they can obtain power and influence that way and they can have a debauched night into the bargain. They are evil.'

'But surely they are just kidding themselves that their ceremonies mean anything?'

By this time the vicar had reached the altar. He turned and sadly shook his head. 'You are forgetting I have experience of exorcisms of some of the people embroiled in these ceremonies. I can assure you this is serious. At the very least some of them will suffer deep psychological problems because of it.' He fell to his knees on the steps in front of the altar and bowed his head in prayer.

Chris sat himself in a front pew and bowed his head. He didn't pray, but his mind was in turmoil. How could such a thing be happening in a quiet little Rutland village, in a backwater like Barrowick?

John started to recite aloud the Lord's Prayer. Remembering the words from his school days, Chris quietly joined in with him.

As midnight approached, the vicar took up a silver aspergillum and sprinkled holy water at the church entrance. He repeated the action at each of the windows while he recited some Latin prayers that his companion did not understand.

Chris felt as if the atmosphere inside the building was becoming heavy and dark. Several of the candles that the vicar had lit to illuminate the church began to splutter and smoke even though he could feel no draughts in the building.

John sprinkled the holy water at the base of each of the candle holders then returned to the altar and performed the Church of England communion service, giving Chris and himself the wine and wafers to fortify their souls.

Chris was torn between ridiculing the events and getting more worried as the atmosphere in the church seemed to get more turgid and heavy. He tried to stop his imagination running away with him as he saw the candle lights begin to fail; their wicks smoked, the flames died down and the church became suddenly darker. The shadowy recesses, behind the pillars and in the far corners, seemed to come alive. Out of the corners of his eyes he imagined he saw shadowy figures moving in those shaded areas, but nothing was there when he focused on them properly. The air in the church seemed to go stale, there was a putrid smell about the building that he hadn't notice earlier. He shivered involuntarily as the temperature in the building suddenly dropped. It's only a coincidence, he assured himself, it must be getting cooler as the night sets in, or maybe it was just his imagination working overtime.

The vicar renewed his prayers, reciting the words aloud and sprinkling more holy water from the aspergillum onto the font and the stone walls of the church.

Finally, at about one in the morning, the atmosphere suddenly seemed to lighten. The candles recovered, they stopped smoking and flamed anew; the cold retreated and the church became relatively warm again; the shadowy movements ceased and the church returned to its normal peaceful atmosphere. The vicar stopped his praying and sat down heavily on a pew beside Chris. John looked exhausted. 'I'm getting a bit too old for all this,' he said quietly.

Chris was still trying to understand what had happened that night. It was completely beyond his experience. He smiled wanly at the old clergyman hoping to reassure himself and asked, 'Is it finished?' Something totally inexplicable had been going on that night and it had just as suddenly stopped.

From outside in the dark that enveloped the village, they could hear the sound of cars starting up and driving onto the main road. Whatever had been going on at the college that night, was finished.

# Chapter Sixteen

One morning, several days after the events at Barrowick church on St John's Eve, Chris was in his back shop, applying French polish to one of the wide clock cases that his ex wife had bought. He had completed the repairs and had applied replacement veneers to the carcasses where bits had fallen off. The radio was playing and he was happily engrossed in the work. Suddenly, from the area of the front shop, there was a crash and the sound of glass shattering! He threw down his polishing brush and ran into the next room to see what was happening. The dealer was shocked at what he found; there were glass shards scattered all over the furniture and the floor from the broken front window.

In the very centre of the large display window he found a jagged hole. That large pane of glass was cracked and broken and pieces of glass were scattered onto the antiques displayed in the window space and those nearest to the window. He was dumbstruck. His first thought was that a large bird must have flown into the window. He knew there were hundreds of ducks and swans on the nearby Rutland Water and they sometimes flew into overhead wires. Maybe one had hit his window. He looked around the room for signs of an injured bird, but found nothing.

As he was clearing up the mess, gingerly picking pieces of glass off the antique furniture and sweeping them onto a shovel, he found the cause of the breakage. On the floor, hidden under a chest of drawers, was a brick. He picked it up and found a luggage label tied to it by a piece of white string. In disbelief he read the message written on it. It bore the single word 'Grass.'

Chris placed the missile on the floor in a corner and carried on clearing up the mess, but all the time his mind was searching for an explanation for the attack on his shop. Who bore him such a grudge they would throw a brick through his window? What did the word 'Grass' signify? He knew what it might mean but he certainly hadn't knowingly grassed on anybody. It was a complete mystery to him.

When he'd cleaned up the mess, he knew he would have to go into Oakham to get a wooden board large enough to nail over the whole front window and make the premises secure until he could get a glazier to replace the broken pane of glass. His problem was security. While he was away the vandal might return and loot the shop. Being a one man business had its disadvantages. He made a coffee while he considered his options but really he had very few choices. Sara was the only person who might be able to help. He finished his coffee then phoned her. Thank goodness the girl answered the telephone. He was relieved to hear her cheerful voice and not her mother's.

'Hi. It's Chris at the antique shop. I need a big favour, Sara.'

'Chris. What's your problem?'

'Some vandal has smashed my shop window. I must get some wood to board it up.'

'That's awful! What can I do to help?'

'Can you please keep an eye on the shop while I go into Oakham to get some chipboard to nail over the window? I'll be as quick as I can.'

He could hear Sara explaining to her mother what was happening. In the distance he heard Mrs Goodacre querying why her daughter should leave her jobs at the pub to help him.

'But mum, he's supported me at the open evenings we've had.'

Sara turned back to the telephone and  assured him. 'I'll be down in about fifteen minutes. I have to clear up here first.'

He put the phone down and let out a sigh of relief.

When he went back into the shop with a vacuum cleaner to sweep up the smallest bits of broken glass that had scattered everywhere, he took another look at the brick and the label on it but he didn't recognise the writing. He was still at a loss to understand what was behind the message.

'Grass!' Chris  repeated the word aloud as he removed the last slivers of glass from the showroom floor. 'Grass! Who would think I had grassed on them?'

As promised, Sara arrived at the shop to let him leave and drive to Oakham for the wood. She frowned when she saw the damage done to the window. 'They made a proper job of it. I can't understand who would  do it here in Barrowick. We never have any trouble at the pub like they do in town. Have you any ideas?'

He shook his head. 'There's one clue.' He handed her the brick with the cryptic message attached.

She frowned. 'Grass? What does that mean?'

'I think it means someone thinks I've grassed them up. Somebody feels I have got them into trouble by opening my mouth.'

'Who?' She frowned even deeper.

'I've no idea.   I haven't any enemies  as far  as I  know, and I haven't grassed on anybody.' He hesitated. 'Well, there's always my ex. We parted on bad terms, but I can't see Vickie coming all the way from Stamford to break the law like this.'

Sara grinned. 'I've heard of revenge, like cutting up the husband's clothes or giving away his best vintage wine, but this is ridiculous.'

Chris returned her grin. 'I was only kidding. Vickie wouldn't do that. Anyway she has asked me to restore some clocks for her, so there can't be too many hard feelings between us.'

With Sara installed in an arm chair in the shop, well fortified with a large mug of coffee and some Ginger biscuits, Chris drove his van into Oakham to the builder's yard to buy the chip board and to check about local glaziers to get the window repair underway. While he was at the building suppliers he called at the nearby sale room to see if he had been successful with bids he'd left for some old chairs.

The auctioneer was busy cataloguing the items for the next sale. He looked up when the dealer knocked on the office window.

'Ah Chris! Your name keeps cropping up this morning.'

'Why? Who's been maligning me?' He joked.

'That's it. You are not very popular in some quarters.'

Chris frowned. He hadn't a clue who he'd upset recently. 'Who's been talking about me then?'

'Dave Porter reckons you tipped off the police he was trying to sell stolen goods.'

Dave Porter! The name struck an immediate chord. Chris remembered the oak bible box he had turned down when he was offered it. So, Dave had a grudge. Maybe Dave felt upset enough to throw a brick at his window? He shrugged his shoulders. 'Beats me. I haven't a clue what he was on about. If I bump into him, I'll have to ask him.'

By the time he'd driven back to Barrowick, he was convinced he knew the culprit responsible for the broken window. Dave Porter was just the sort to hold a grudge and do something underhand like that.

When he arrived at the shop, Sara was still seated in the sale's area listening to Radio Rutland on the portable. She got up to leave immediately he reappeared. 'Got it sorted?'

Chris nodded.

'Good. I must get back to mother and start to prepare for the lunch time customers.' She left him, humming the latest pop tune as she went.

He unloaded the chip board from the van and went to screw it over the broken window. It completely altered the feel of the sales area, making it dark and drab. He decided to leave the lights on all day until he could get the glass replaced. Making the window secure took him the rest of that morning so he skipped lunch at the pub and snatched a quick sandwich while he caught up with the work on Vickie's clock cases. Those sandwiches and several mugs of strong coffee kept him going all afternoon. On one of his visits up to the flat to use the loo, he happened to look out of the window and noticed Dave Porter's car was parked in the drive of the vicarage. This was his opportunity to tackle the dealer about the broken window. If Dave had thrown that brick, Chris felt he would soon find out. He locked the shop and walked down to the college.

As he arrived at the parked car, Dave came out of the barn and walked towards him. It was obvious he hadn't noticed Chris at first because he stopped immediately he saw him and started to turn back.

'Hang on.' Chris sprinted to Dave's side and stopped his escape.

Dave smiled nervously at the him. 'What can I do for you, Chris?'

'What do you know about my broken window? I hear you have some idea I grassed on you to the police about some stolen antiques. I just wondered if that made you write a note and attach it to a brick.?'

Dave coloured deep red. He looked everywhere but at his accuser's face.

Chris continued. 'I didn't tell the cops about that stolen Bible box. It was probably someone who saw it when you tried to offload it at the farm auction the other day. It was reported stolen in the Antique Gazette, along with a photograph of it, so a lot of dealers would recognise it. '

'I don't know anything about your window. Honestly, I wouldn't do that.'

Chris said nothing but stared his adversary straight in the eyes. From the way the man squirmed he was sure he was the culprit. He was about to push the accusations even further when O'Conlan came out of the barn.

'Hello Mr Doughty.' Then seeing the tense stand off, he added 'Is everything alright?'

'Everything is fine, thanks. I was just asking Dave here what he knew about some stolen antiques and about my broken shop window.'

O'Conlan frowned and directed his gaze at Dave Porter. Chris could see the look of censure on the doctor's face. Under that searching gaze, Dave Porter cringed even more and looked down at his feet.

Sensing O'Conlan was not happy with what he had learned and that Porter was frightened of the man, Chris pushed home his advantage. 'I suppose it would be an embarrassment having the police coming to your new college and asking questions about one of your helpers?'

O'Conlan turned and without another word went back into the barn.

Dave Porter sighed deeply and looked hurt. 'What did you have to tell him about it? It's non of his business. Anyway, I didn't do it.'

Chris shook his head slowly, not taking his eyes off the man's guilty face. 'The window's broken now and I think you did it. If I catch you near my shop again I'll break your legs. Do you understand?'

Dave Porter hurriedly pushed past him and dived into his car, locking the doors once he was safely inside.

## Chapter Seventeen

Chris completed the restoration of the two grandfather clocks that his ex wife had brought to him. He was satisfied with the results of his work but relieved he hadn't bought them to sell. She'd bought them by outbidding him for them. At the inflated price she'd paid, she was welcome to them. They looked OK, but he still thought they were wide monstrosities. He phone Vickie to tell her to collect them.

'Morning Vickie. Your clocks are finished. When can you collect them?'

She seemed pleased to have some new stock for the shop. 'Oh good. I have to deliver a chair to a customer in Empingham tomorrow morning. I'll collect them then.'

'Make sure you bring cash for them. I can't afford to do jobs on tick these days.' He remembered the conversation he'd had in the Stamford restaurant with one of his old contacts when he learned that Vickie was short of money and she was getting a reputation for being a bad payer.

'Will a cheque do?'

'No. Cash on the nail. I can't be doing with cheques.'

His ex hesitated, then said. 'I'll get cash when I deliver the chair. How much do I owe you?'

'Two hundred for each clock. There was a lot of work.'

Again she hesitated; finally she said 'I'll see you tomorrow morning then.'

He put down the phone and frowned. From her reaction he suspected she hadn't enough money to pay for the work. He would have to be firm with her; no cash, no clocks.

Next morning Vickie drew up outside the old butcher's shop in a hired van. She came into the antique shop and interrupted Chris at work; he was busy wax polishing an oak refectory table in the front show room.

'Ah. There you are. Now where's my clocks?'

He showed her through to the back room where he did the restoration, and uncovered the two Yorkshire clocks; they had been covered in dustsheets to keep them pristine while they were stored in his dusty work room.

Vickie nodded her approval. 'Lovely job. They will look good in my shop window. Will you take them out to the van for me?'

He stood his ground. 'After you've paid me, Vickie.'

She looked down at her feet but said nothing.

Chris was doubtful 'I suppose you can afford to pay me?'

'I got cash for the chair I've just delivered but it's not quite enough.'

He shook his head in despair. 'I told you on the phone. No cash no clocks. I can't afford to deal any other way these days.'

She looked very thoughtful then suggested, 'I can pay for one now.' She took a roll of notes from her bag and gave him all of it. 'There's two hundred pounds there. I'll have to think of another way to pay for the other one.'

Chris took the money and grunted his thanks. 'Which clock do you want?'

She pointed to the one nearest the door. He lifted off the hood and carried the clock case containing the movement and dial, through the front shop and out to her van. As he went through the front door to the pavement outside she shouted after him. 'I'll just go upstairs and use your loo.'

It was when he was loading the clock hood into the van, he spotted Sara walking very slowly along the pavement towards him. She had her head down and she hadn't noticed him. She seemed very engrossed in what she was doing. He stood and watched her as she walked steadily and deliberately along the path, her arms held in front of her with a piece of bent wire clutched in each hand. Suddenly she stopped, the wires had moved in her hands and crossed over each other.

He grinned to himself. She was dowsing by the looks of it.

When she stopped and readjusted her pieces of wire, Sara glanced up and saw Chris smiling at her. She smiled broadly and quickened her step, joining him at the van.

'Dowsing are you?'

'Yes. I had my first lesson last evening and I am trying out what I learned.'

Chris took the two pieces of wire from her hands and inspected them. It was obvious they were cut down, wire coat hangers, bent into an L shape and loosely mounted in wooden handles so they would swing freely.

'Where did you get these beauties?'

'Tanith loaned me them until I could get some of my own.'

Chris shook his head in disbelief and asked. 'What are you dowsing for exactly. I though it was usually done to find water.'

'No, not only water. You mentally ask the rods to seek what you are looking for. I am dowsing for Ley Lines. The vicar mentioned to me and mum that the church is built on a cross road of Ley Lines.'

'Ah yes! He told me that as well. Did you find any?'

'Yes, I think so. You saw me hesitate just up the path there. The wires crossed for me. I think that was one of the lines.'

Chris laughed aloud. 'You've only got to tilt your hands a bit and the wires will cross for you anyway. It may be nothing to do with those imaginary lines.'

Sara wasn't pleased that he made fun of her. 'Here.' She handed the dowsing wires to him. 'You have a go.'

Realising he may have upset her by making fun of her, he took the wires and walked slowly back along the pavement the way she had come. To his complete astonishment, the wires crossed over at exactly the same spot they had moved for Sara. He stopped in surprise.

Sara laughed aloud at him. 'Now who's making fun of my dowsing?'

Chris gave her back the wires and shook his head in amazement. This was too much.

Sara pushed the wires into her pocket. 'I need a pendulum for map dowsing. If you see one in your travels will you get it for me please.'

He held open the door and invited her into the shop. 'I have dozens of old pendulums from broken clocks. You can take your pick.' He led her into the back shop and took down a box of old clock parts from the spares shelves.

Sara glanced into the box, saw dozens of clock pendulums with stiff rods and shook her head. 'Not that sort of pendulum. I need a small plumb bob to suspend on a string. Doesn't matter what it's made of. As long as it swings freely it will do.'

He was about to make another suggestion when his ex wife came down from the flat above and stopped in the doorway at the bottom of the stairs. Chris turned and looked at her when her footsteps came to a halt on the bottom step. He was surprised to see she was wearing his white toweling dressing gown. His mouth fell open. Maybe she had spilled something on her clothes? Why else would she be wearing his dressing gown?

'I've thought of a way to pay you for the other clock. Come and join me upstairs.' Vickie smiled broadly and opened the dressing gown to reveal she was completely naked beneath it. She posed brazenly in the doorway, arms held out at her sides, the gown open wide, revealing all of her charms.

Sara gasped aloud, threw the pendulum she was holding, back into the box and ran out of the shop. Chris started to follow her, but realising she was too far ahead of him, turned and shook his fist at his ex.

Vickie was defiant. 'You wouldn't have refused me when we were married. What's the difference now?'

'Get dressed and get out!' He shouted at her. 'If you want that other clock you'll pay cash for it like any other punter.'

Vickie pulled a face at him and started to mount the stairs then she stopped, turned and smiled sweetly. 'Your little friend's gone off in a huff, has she? I didn't like the look of her when I saw you together in Stamford the other evening.' She made no effort to wrap the dressing gown around her body. Instead, she flipped up the back hem and flashed her naked bottom at him.

Chris turned on his heels and marched out of the shop. He stood on the pavement looking for Sara but she was nowhere in sight; Vickie had really upset her. He was seething when he returned to his workroom but he knew he couldn't leave the shop until Vickie had gone. He didn't trust her enough to do that. She'd probably take the other clock without paying for it.

Finally Vickie came down the stairs. This time she was fully dressed. He glared at her.

'You're boring. Can't you take a joke these days?' With that parting shot she sauntered out of the shop and drove her van out of the village.

He wasn't sure what to do to put things right with Sara. He knew she had been very upset and probably suspected he was still seeing Vickie. He had to admit, Vickie had really put him in Sara's bad books. How could he ever explain to Sara that he had no idea what Vickie was doing naked in his flat.

## Chapter Eighteen

For the next few days, Chris stayed away from the Barrowick Arms. He ate lunch alone in his workshop, not wanting to face Sara after the experience with Vickie. On the Monday he went to an antique sale at a nearby farmhouse. The entire contents of the farm house and the yard were to be sold as the farmer had died and the tenancy was changing hands.

Chris arrived after the sale had started but he wasn't interested in the contents of the yard and barns as they were mainly old farm implements. He was taking his opportunity to view the items inside the house when he bumped into Dave Porter. They eyed each other warily but kept a good distance from each other. It was while he was waiting for Dave to move to another room, Chris chanced upon an old workbox full of odds and ends. There were broken strings of beads, buttons of every colour and shape and lots of small sewing items like thimbles and hooks and eyes. At the bottom of the box he spied a large green pendant bead and he realised it could serve Sara as a pendulum bob. When he'd viewed every room he knew there was very little else at the sale that interested him. The large pieces of furniture, like the dresser and the long oak refectory table would be too expensive for him to buy. He found a porter who he knew from previous sales, and left a small bid with him for the workbox and contents.

When he returned to his shop he parked the van at the back of the premises, walked around the building to the front door and went through to his workroom. As he had no other jobs awaiting his attention, he decided to start work on the early ebonised clock case he'd collected from the Psychic College barn.

The case was made of fruit wood. He knew it was probably Pear tree wood because it had few knots and it had taken a black stain very well. There were bits missing; mainly some small pieces of beading, which would have to be made. His first task was to strip off all the old paint and get back to the original 17th century finish. He applied paint stripper and waited for it to work.

By mid day he had the entire case stripped of paint and was ready to make the missing beadings. He went to the back door to unlock it to search in the outside wood store for some suitable pieces of old fruit wood and was surprised to find the back door was already unlocked. He thought back to when he'd left to go to the farm sale and was sure he had locked it. He definitely recalled locking that door before he left for the sale view and he hadn't used that entrance since. It wasn't like him to forget security.

112

Anyway, everything in the building seemed to be as he'd left it, so no harm had been done by his forgetfulness. He was busy sorting through his collection of bits of seasoned fruit wood when the phone rang.

'It's the sale room. You bought that old workbox and contents. It's here at the Oakham sale room waiting for you to pay for it and collect it.'

'Thanks. I'll be over later this afternoon. How much do I owe?'

'A fiver.'

He'd almost forgotten he had left a bid in for the items but was thrilled he'd acquired them as he was sure the bead he'd seen at the bottom of the box, would be useful to Sara. Maybe, with that as a peace offering, he could go to the pub and speak to her. It would provide him with a good excuse to explain about Vickie.

When he'd collected the workbox, he took it back to the shop and tipped the contents out onto some old newspaper. There was very little of interest to show for his five pound investment but there on the top of the pile was the pear shaped green bead he had spotted at the farm house. He took it over to the window and rubbed the dirt off it. He was thrilled to find it was a green jade pendant, three inches long and drilled at the top for fixing to the bottom of a necklace. It would have been the largest piece on a jade necklace, hanging from the very centre of it. It was quite weighty and felt as if it would make an excellent pendulum bob if it was fixed onto a piece of fine thread. When he'd threaded it, he held up the pendulum and let the jade bead swing freely. It felt just right. He was congratulating himself on finding it for Sara when he suddenly went quite dizzy and felt a sharp stabbing pain in his back. The room revolved around him. He clutched at the table and waited for the strange feelings to pass.

'I need a coffee with plenty of sugar in it.' He mumbled .'Must have been neglecting myself this morning.' He left the sewing bits and pieces on the table and went up to the flat to get a sweet drink and some biscuits. After a time, when he felt better, Chris went down to his workshop and continued sorting through the old workbox. The rest of the contents, apart from a small solid silver thimble, were of no value; they were just the remnants of odds and sods that a housewife had collected over a lifetime, in the hope they might one day prove useful to her; they had never been needed and he had no use for them. He put them straight into the dustbin. The thimble he put in a safe place; it would probably pay back the five pounds he had spent.

That evening Chris went early to his local pub. He was the only customer at that early hour. Sara was behind the bar, polishing glasses and putting them away. She gave him a quick glance when he arrived but she carried on working without a word of greeting.

Chris went and stood in front of her so she couldn't really ignore him. She looked up without a glimmer of a smile.

'I have come to apologise for my ex's behaviour, Sara. But why I'm apologising I don't know. She took me by surprise as much as she surprised you. She came to pick up a clock I had restored for her. She hadn't enough money to pay me and thought she could settle the bill in bed. That funny business was entirely her idea.'

Sara sniffed and asked. 'Do you want to order anything?'

Chris couldn't resist a small grin. 'You do look angry. But it suits you.'

Sara shrugged her shoulders and a fleeting smile crossed her face. She couldn't keep up the pretence she was mad at him now he had explained what had happened.

'She's a problem is your  Vickie. That's the second time she's caused us trouble.'

'Don't I know it! Anyway she's no longer my Vickie and I have a small present for you to apologise for her behaviour.'

'You needn't have bothered.' But her face belied her words and showed she wanted to know what he'd bought for her.

'Here.' He gave her the green jade pendulum.

'Oh Chris!' She held the string and let the bead swing over the top of the bar. 'That's exactly what I wanted. You must be psychic. It's jade and precious stones make ideal pendulum bobs. No one else in the class will have one like this.' She took him completely by surprise when she leaned over the bar and kissed him full on his mouth.

Chris sat at the bar on a stool and drank his beer watching her swing the pendulum over  the  drip mat on the bar top. She seemed to know what she was doing.

'Explain to me how it works.' He suggested

'You let the pendulum swing back and forth and then ask it for a positive answer. You needn't ask out loud, just think the question to yourself.'  She demonstrated the action as she spoke.  'The pendulum will change its swing from back and forth and start to move in a circle.' The pendulum bob did exactly that as she explained. It began to rotate in a clockwise direction.

'What does that tell you?' He put down his beer and tried to make the question sound as if he was genuinely interested.

'Clockwise means 'yes'. If I ask the pendulum a question and it changes to a clockwise swing the answer is yes.' She stopped the pendulum swinging and then started it again in its back and forth swinging. 'This time I'm asking it for a negative response.'

At first he could see no change in the jade bead's travel but finally it settled into an anticlockwise swing.

'There you are.' Sara said triumphantly. 'That means no!'

He shrugged his shoulders. So what? What possible use could there be for a pendulum that randomly said yes or no. Foolishly, he voiced his doubts. 'That's fine, and you seem thrilled with it but what possible use is it?'

Sara gave him a look that said he must be thick. 'I'll show you.' She took a 5p coin from the till and handed it to him. Pointing to the four beer mats lined up on the top of the bar she said. 'You hide this coin under one of them. I'll not look.' She left the bar and went into the kitchen.

He played it very cool. He lifted each of the mats in turn, just in case she could detect which mat had been moved, and left the coin under one of them.

'Sara. You can come back now.'

She came back to the bar and started her search. She held the pendulum over each of the mats in turn and started it swinging back and forth. As she did this she asked aloud 'Is the coin under this mat?'

He watched her, fascinated by her earnest expression. It was obvious she really did expect the pendulum to provide her with the correct answer. Each time the pendulum swing slowly changed to a circular motion and each time it was anticlockwise to signify a negative response, until she came to the last mat. Finally the jade bead rotated in a clockwise direction.

'There you are. It's under here.' She took up the mat to reveal the coin.

He was surprised at her success and intrigued by it. 'Lets try again.' He was eager to see how often she could get it right.

This time, when Sara went into the kitchen, he was crafty. He pretended to put the coin under one of the mats but actually slipped it into his pocket.

Sara went through her pendulum routine once again but got a negative response at every one of the mats. She was exasperated by this failure and tried again, but got the same negative responses.

Finally she took up all the mats to check where the coin was hidden.

He held up his hands and apologised. 'I'm sorry. I put it in my pocket that time. I was sure you'd be fooled into picking the wrong mat.' He placed the coin on the counter.

Sara was mad at this ruse but thrilled with her success. She felt vindicated that he had played a trick on her, but the pendulum had got it right. 'Why don't you try it.' She held the pendulum out to him.

'There's no way I'm psychic like you.' Chris held up his hands in protest.

'That's not what Tanith says about you.'

He frowned at this remark. 'Tanith? what's she got to say about me?'

'She asked me about you when I went to her class on dowsing. You must have said or done something at the psychic night when she read your cards because she thinks you are psychic.'

He frowned even more and tried to recall what had been said. 'I only suggested she had read the cards wrong. I was being facetious and suggested an alternative reading for her.'

'Well she must have been impressed because she asked me if you had any previous psychic experience.'

'Oh dear! I doubt if I have a single psychic bone in my body. You couldn't find a bigger sceptic anywhere.'

She ignored his protests. 'Right. Let's see if you can use the pendulum.'

'Do I have to?'

'Just to please me.' She smiled her sweetest smile and held the pendulum out to him. He couldn't refuse her.

The experiment had surprising results. Chris managed to get a Yes and a No response from the jade pendulum and found the hidden coin six times out of six. He was pleased with this result but totally baffled by it. Six successes out of six was way above his expectations and much more than mere chance would dictate.

'I'm flabbergasted, Sara. That's quite a party trick you have there. Six out of six is way above what you would expect from a random guess.'

Sara held her finger up to scold him. 'Dowsing is no party trick. Men have discovered water in parched farm land and oil under the desert by using it. They've even found lost children by dowsing maps.'

He shrugged his shoulders. He had to admit he had read about such discoveries but had never given the reports a lot of credence.

Maybe there was something to this psychic business. Anyway, he had dowsing to thank for getting him back into Sara's good books. That fact alone made it special to him.

Back at his flat, Chris made himself a strong coffee and savoured the feeling of being back in favour with Sara. The girl had become important to him and he didn't want to lose her friendship. He sipped his coffee and stared out of the window at the tree tops around the reservoir. The evening shadows darkened and lengthened. Water birds flew onto the safety of the lake, silhouetted against the darkening sky as night began to fall. He went over his conversation with Sara and remembered her comments from Tanith and the suggestion he must be psychic. He couldn't explain the success with the dowsing pendulum but there was no way he could accept he might have psychic gifts. Finally he got up to close the curtains and to stretch his legs and promptly felt a sharp pain between his shoulder blades. The dealer gasped for breath from the severity of it. He felt suddenly faint and almost fell over. Clutching at the arm of a chair for support, he sat down again heavily. It felt like a knife was stuck in his back. It took him several minutes of shallow breathing to bring the pain under control then it faded as quickly as it had come.

When the weird feelings had passed, Chris considered the implications. That was the second time that day he'd felt ill. He must have been overdoing it. If this carried on he would have to go to see a doctor and that was a rare occurrence for him as he was never that normally ill.

## Chapter Nineteen

The pain in his back and the dizzy spells continued to occur over the following days. Chris was reluctant to contact a doctor, partly because he very rarely went to see one and partly because he had moved to the area only recently and had not bothered to register with the local practice. It seemed too much trouble to drive over to Stamford to see his old doctor.

During the day when he was out and about at sales, when he was shopping or delivering antiques to punters, he never felt a twinge, even if that involved heavy lifting. The pain seemed to strike him when he was relaxed and always when he was at home. When these facts dawned on him, he was even more baffled by the condition.

One afternoon Sara came up to the shop to see what new stock he had, and to pass the time of day with him. He invited her up to the flat to have coffee and a chat. She was full of praise for her psychic course. The dowsing studies were going well. She was getting very proficient at it and had even found an underground spring for a local farmer who was wanting to drill a well to water his stock.

'Marvellous! You really have the knack of this dowsing.' He laid on the praise.

'You could be just as good from what I saw you do at the pub.'

He had started to laugh and deny her suggestion when the acute back pain suddenly hit him. He wrapped his arms around his chest and gasped.

'What's the matter?' Sara jumped up from her chair and rushed over to his side.

'Pain..' He gasped. '.. Sharp pain in my back and chest.'

She panicked. 'Are you having a heart attack?'

He breathed shallowly and slowly recovered. Finally he could speak properly. 'No. I keep getting a very sharp pain between my shoulders and I feel dizzy with it. It only seems to happen when I'm relaxed and in the flat. If it was my heart surely it would come on when I'm doing something more physical. I can shift heavy furniture at the sale rooms and never get a twinge.'

Sara shook her head and frowned deeply. 'You need to see a doctor.'

'I know, but I'm not registered here yet.'

118

'That doesn't matter. I'll ring the surgery now and get you to see the emergency doctor.' In spite of his protests, she went down to the shop and used his telephone to make him an appointment. 'You are booked in for an appointment in one hour. I'll drive you down to the surgery.'

Chris had to admit that Sara was talking sense. He had ignored the problem for too long already. He wasn't used to being ill and hadn't visited a doctor for years, but the pain in his back was getting unbearable.

At the surgery the duty doctor gave him a thorough examination but could find nothing wrong with him. He went over the symptoms in detail, asked when they occurred, but came to no conclusions.

'Stand up and touch your toes.' The doctor put him through a rigorous physical test, which he completed with no problems, then he used his stethoscope to sound out his chest.

'We'll have an ECG and a blood test. You'd better book in to see the nurse as soon as possible. Meanwhile I'll give you some strong pain killers and something for the inflammation. See if they help.' The doctor wrote out a prescription and handed it to him. 'You are a mystery Mr Doughty. Let's hope we can come up with an answer.'

Chris called at the surgery the very next day and underwent the tests, but nothing untoward was detected. The doctor checked the results and told him all seemed well. 'Nothing showing in these test results. Have you suffered the pains again since I last saw you.?'

He was reluctant to confirm that he'd had two more episodes of back pain but he told the doctor what had happened. 'It seems to be when I'm relaxed. I get no problems all day until I get home. I relax in my armchair in my flat then the pain strikes.'

The doctor shook his head and looked puzzled. 'Are the painkillers helping?'

'No. I don't need them all day and when the pain comes on it's too damn late!'

'If it carries on I will have to refer you to the hospital for more tests. There's nothing physically wrong with you that I can see You are a mystery, Mr Doughty.'

As it was lunchtime, Chris called at the pub on his way home from that examination. Sara greeted him as soon as he appeared.

'Well? What's the doctor say?'

'Nothing. I'm a mystery it seems. He says he can find nothing physically wrong with me. He hesitated. 'Maybe It's not physical.

119

Maybe it's mental! Maybe it's all in my imagination. What do they call it, psychosomatic? Anyway give me a beer and a ham salad. I mustn't starve the inner man.'

Sara went to the kitchen and prepared some food. When she came back she said. 'If it's not physical but mental as you suggested, maybe my pendulum could help.'

He looked at her askance. He had only been joking about a mental problem but he decided to humour her. 'How could your dowsing possibly help me?'

'Last lesson we were using the pendulums to pinpoint disease states in different parts of the body.'

Chris didn't know what to say. He had some mystery condition, which the doctor couldn't diagnose, now Sara was suggesting a psychic answer. Finally he said 'I'm not imagining it you know. I'm not going mad.'

Sara laughed at this. 'You're definitely not insane, Chris. A bit weird maybe, but not mad.' She laughed even louder at her own joke.

He smiled and decided to go along with her suggestion. 'Why not use your dowsing. Medical science can't seem to help me. Why not try mumbo jumbo like the witch doctors use.'

Sara ignored his jibe about witch doctors and left him to eat his lunch while she served the other customers who were coming into the bar.

Later that afternoon, when he was in his workshop, French polishing a small table, Sara called to see him. She had brought her dowsing pendulum with her.

'Lie on the floor' She ordered him. Chris lay down on the dusty workshop floor with his arms at his sides just to humour her. She stood over him and worked her way along his body holding the pendulum above him, letting it swing freely in her fingers. Eventually she told him to get on his feet again.

'Well doctor? Anything to report?'

'Not really. The pendulum behaved normally wherever I used it on you.'

'Just as I expected.'

Sara left him working in the back shop and returned to the pub. She seemed as mystified as the doctor had been but said she was determined to give the problem some more thought.

When he called at the pub later that evening Sara called him over to her. 'I've had an idea about your pains.'

120

He raised his eyebrows and grinned. Maybe she was going to suggest a massage.

'You did say you only get them when you are in the flat or the shop?'

'Yes'

'Maybe its something to do with that building? There are Ley lines running all over this village.'

He looked at her in amazement. 'What the devil has that got to do with anything? Nobody else in the village is suffering from these Ley lines, are they?'

She shook her head. 'Not that I've heard. But you may be very sensitive to them. What do you think?'

He sat down heavily on a bar stool and sighed. This constant pain was getting him down but he could well do without hair-brained suggestions like that. He didn't reply but sipped his beer in silence.

'I am going to dowse a map of the village and ask the pendulum to tell me if there is a problem for you in any part of it.'

He just shrugged his shoulders and decided to go along with her suggestion.

Between customers, Sara took down an old map of the village from the bar wall and placed it on the counter top. She used her pendulum and worked her way along the village street pausing over each house marked on the map. She got no positive response until finally she came to the end house, which was the site of the antique shop. It was clearly labelled Butcher's Shop on the old map and must have been used for that trade for some years.

'Look!' She called over to him. 'I've got a positive response at last. The trouble is in the old butcher's premises.'

He frowned. 'Tell me something I don't already know. I told you I tend to get the pain when I'm at home.' Those remarks deflated her enthusiasm but she wouldn't let the problem rest.

'I just know there is a problem with your shop and flat. I will have to think of a way to solve it.' She retreated along the bar and served two new customers who had just arrived.

Chris sat and drank his beer. All this talk of his problem being something to do with the flat and the shop was disconcerting. He had no choice but to carry on doing business there. He decided to make that drink last as he was in no rush to go home. At closing time, Chris was still at the pub and still relatively sober but was thankful he'd had no sign of a return of the back pain.

Sara locked the doors when the last customers had finished their drinks and left. She joined Chris at the bar and sat down on a stool next to him.

'You not ready to go home yet?'

'Yes... I mean no... I am a bit apprehensive about this pain business, but I do only seem to get it when I relax at home.' He made to get off the bar stool and leave. 'I suppose I'd better go now. I can't stay here all night just worrying about something that may not happen.'

'Hang on a minute. I've just had another idea.' She went into the kitchen and came back with a pencil and a sheet of paper, which she placed on the bar in front of him. 'Draw me a plan of your shop premises.'

He decided to go along with her schemes yet again, and drew a floor plan of the shop area and another of the upstairs flat.

Sara fetched her dowsing pendulum and held it above each room in turn. There was no response until she came to the bedroom. The pendulum gave a very positive response there. She tried it several times and got the same result each time.

'Interesting.' She murmured. 'There's definitely a problem of some sort with the upstairs flat and it seems to be concentrated in your bedroom. Have you noticed anything different in there?'

He was taken by surprise at her comments. 'I have been having vivid nightmares the last few nights. In fact last night I made myself a drink at two in the morning and fell asleep in the chair in my kitchen.'

'Did you get a better night in there?'

'Funnily enough, yes I did.'

Sara looked pleased with herself. 'Tomorrow I will bring my pendulum down to your place and dowse every room. If there is a Ley line or any other psychic reason for your illness, I'll find it for you.'

He wasn't convinced by her reasoning but he held his tongue and agreed to her investigation. That night he had another terrible nightmare and the pain in his back struck again. He finished up falling asleep in the kitchen chair with the Gideon Bible in his hand. He remembered the previous nightmare he'd had, when he saw a dark shadow in his bedroom. He also recalled the calming effect the bible seemed to have on that occasion. He wouldn't admit he was a superstitious man, but he reasoned anything was worth a try. The recent events at the church and his talks with the Reverend Smyth had opened his eyes to a lot of strange possibilities.

## Chapter Twenty

The pain and discomfort Chris was suffering, made him very wary of sleeping in his bed at the flat. The following day Sara was too busy to come to the shop to dowse the rooms because her mother was away and it was the day the brewery delivered the drinks. She was tied up with business all day.

Chris became more nervous as night approached and decided to get out of the flat and take a walk around the reservoir to wind down before bedtime. He took his binoculars with him to do some bird watching for he had frequently heard the calls of a pair of Tawny Owls in the evenings in the woodland that separated the village from Rutland Water. He took a torch in his jacket pocket just in case he needed some light on his walk. He set out as it was getting dark and a full moon rose over the water, its silvery light reflecting on the water's surface, illuminating the sleeping swans that roosted there. The birds floated peacefully on the lake making only occasional quiet sounds as they rested.

Once he'd entered the wood, he followed the path that wound its way through the trees, veering towards the water's edge and back again into the depths of the woodland. The owls could be heard calling and answering each other in the darkness. Occasionally, birds flew away from him in panic as he disturbed their sleep. Their alarm calls echoed through the woods as they fled from the disturbance, then the woodland settled down again to the gentle sounds of the rustle of wind in the trees.

As he approached the area behind the church, he could just make out the shadow of the church tower looming in the darkness. He hesitated on his walk and looked over the churchyard towards the Barrowick Arms, which was by then closed and in total darkness. There was not a single light showing in any of the houses in the village. It was a peaceful and pleasant walk. He felt very relaxed and ready to return home for a restful night's sleep.

Suddenly, as he glanced towards the church tower, he noticed a glimmer of light among the gravestones. As he walked along, the light went on and off as the grave stones obstructed his view and the light came into his sight and just as quickly vanished again. He stood absolutely still and listened to the sounds of the night. From somewhere in the direction of the church he thought he could hear the murmur of a distant voice. He couldn't discern what was being said but from the rhythm of it, the rise and fall of the speech, he suspected it was some kind of recitation. Intrigued by this, Chris decided to investigate. Using the training he had learned in his service years in the paras he worked his way silently towards the sounds.

As he crept nearer to the church wall, he could see there were people standing in the churchyard near the tower. He knew from their position they would not be visible from the road. They could only be seen from the reservoir path where he was standing. At that time of night he suspected someone was up to no good. At first he thought it may be thieves stealing the lead from the church roof, but as he watched them he saw they were not moving, but standing in the same position among the grave stones. He climbed over the dry stone wall, which separated the church yard from the woodland, and crept silently towards the people, using the gravestones for cover.

When he was about twenty metres from the sounds of that chanting voice, he peered over the top of a gravestone and used his binoculars to see what was going on. There were two figures, both clothed in long dark cloaks with hoods over there heads, looking like monks. They were standing together facing the tower near the ancient carved figure. Unfortunately it was too dark to make out exactly what was happening.

Perhaps they're stealing the carving, he thought. But it suddenly dawned on him they were actually standing in front of the witch's grave! The tallest of the pair was holding a book in his hands and a small torch. That was the light that had first attracted Chris to the scene. The man, it was definitely a man by his deep voice and silhouette, was reciting some kind of prayer or incantation. Most of the words were unintelligible and sounded like the Latin prayers that he'd heard the vicar use, but occasionally a name was spoken. He strained to hear the words and suddenly realised the speaker was calling on Molly Bent, the witch who was buried in the church yard. Chris sat behind the grave stone and considered his options. He knew some kind of ceremony was being conducted in Barrowick churchyard. He was sure it was something clandestine and suspect at that time of night so he decided to creep nearer to the people to hear more clearly what was being said and to see if he recognised either of them.

The man's voice rang out across the graveyard, in English this time. 'Come from the grave Molly Bent.' He spoke the words in a clear educated voice. 'In the name of the ancient gods, of Persephone, Thoth, Hermes...' Chris couldn't catch the other names that were used but he did understand the final words when the speaker commanded. 'We order you to join us here and do our bidding.'

By this time the dealer's eyes were getting more used to the darkness in the churchyard but he still couldn't identify the two figures standing close together near the witch's gravestone. He sat back in his hiding place and considered his position. He was not fearful of the people in the graveyard but he was outnumbered and they could be armed. Finally he decided to retreat the way he'd come and return to the woods. He crept back in the dark, feeling his way towards the back wall of the churchyard, unfortunately he missed his way. He stepped forward and lost his footing in a deep hole in the ground and fell heavily. He was so surprised to be falling that he let out an involuntary sound as the breath was knocked out of him and he hit a gravestone with his shoulder.

Chris lay panting on the grass not daring to move in case the people he had been watching came looking for him. After a few minutes of silence, apart from a flurry of bird noises as some pigeons roosting in the trees just over the stone wall, took to the air frightened by his cry, he dared to rise from the ground and peep over the gravestone. He looked towards the church and saw the people had gone. They must have been disturbed by his fall and the commotion he'd made. He looked all around the graveyard , as far as he could in the poor light, but there was no sign of the monk-like figures. They had vanished into thin air. With no need to creep about anymore, he climbed over the dry stone wall and went back into the woodland surrounding the lake. As he walked home, he grinned to himself; if he'd made such a basic mistake as he'd made that evening, when he'd been training in the paras, he'd have been put on a charge. He decided the very next morning he would contact the vicar and tell him what he'd witnessed.

When the dealer got back to his flat he was tired and ready for bed but he slept only fitfully. His dreams were filled with dark robed figures who were crowding around his grave. He woke up in the small hours of the morning with a dull ache in his bruised shoulder and a sharp pain in his back, the same pain he had experienced a few times; the same pain he had described to the doctor. It was no use trying to fall asleep again in bed, laying down seemed to exacerbate the problem. Chris got up, made himself a cup of tea and sat in an armchair with his dressing gown wrapped around him to keep himself warm.

As he sat in the kitchen, watching the daylight increase as the dawn approached, he thought about what he'd seen and heard the previous night in the churchyard. He was not familiar with witchcraft practices but from what he'd read in occult novels, he knew some fictional characters did try and raise the dead from their graves. Whether that was a real possibility he wasn't sure, but there had been records of that actually happening in the past. The whole idea seemed to be to raise a ghost of a dead person and to order it to help in some diabolical scheme. He couldn't get back to sleep for the pain in his back and the thoughts of what he'd witnessed. The sooner he could contact the Reverend Smyth and tell him what he'd seen and heard, the better he would feel.

As soon as he'd eaten breakfast, Chris was on the phone to the vicar. 'John, It's Chris Doughty the antique dealer from Barrowick.'

'Chris. What's the problem? I guess this is far too early for a social call.'

'Sorry vicar. I need some advice. It's about the churchyard.'

'Hang on, Chris. I'll put down my tea and toast. Now, what's the problem?'

'I was walking in the woods behind the church very late last night and saw some figures in the graveyard.'

'Oh dear! Not after the lead again, I hope.'

'No. They seemed to be holding some sort of ceremony near the witch's grave and the old stone statue.'

There was a long silence on the phone.

'Are you still there, John? Is everything OK?'

The vicar finally answered. 'I will come down to see you. I must get the details from you first hand. Give me about half an hour and I'll see you then.' He put the phone down, leaving Chris in no doubt he took the news seriously and was disturbed by it.

By the time the vicar walked into his shop, Chris was busy working in the back work room. He put down the bottle of button polish he was using and went to answer the door to see who was calling. He was surprised to see the vicar was at the shop already.

'John. That didn't take you long.'

The vicar looked very serious. 'Now, tell me exactly what happened last night. Every detail, mind you.'

'OK. I have been having a lot of pain in my back when I go to bed so I tried to relax by taking a walk along the path that skirts the reservoir and goes through the woods.'

'What time was this?'

'Must have been after midnight I suppose. It was dark and the pub was closed.'

'Go on.'

'I was walking along the stretch that skirts the churchyard wall when I saw a faint light in the graveyard. It came from the area immediately behind the tower.'

The vicar nodded he understood and signaled for him to continue.

'I thought of burglars and the lead on the roof. We've had a spate of such thefts in the county lately, but these people weren't moving about. They were standing in the graveyard and not on the roof.'

The Reverend Smyth nodded once more to encourage him to continue.

'I decided to creep up on them to see what they were up to. I hid behind one of the gravestones and watched and listened.'

'What did you see?'

'There were two of them. They were dressed in dark clothes like monks with hoods over their heads. One of them was holding a book and a small torch. That must have been the light I saw from the path.' Chris hesitated while he gathered his thoughts, then he continued. 'They were standing close together, and the tallest one, a man by his voice, was reciting some kind of prayer or incantation.'

'Did you recognise either of them?'

'No. It was too dark and I wasn't that near. I did hear some of the words he was using.'

'Ah! That could be useful.'

'He was calling on that witch by name, asking her to do his bidding. Molly Bent, he called her, and he used other names but I couldn't catch them properly. They sounded a bit like the names of some of the old Greek gods that you read about in legends.'

John nodded again and frowned. 'Probably demons names. Sometimes necromancy spells include such names.'

'Necro what?'

'Necromancy, the art of raising the dead or getting a ghost to do your will. Warlocks and witches have used such spells for hundreds of years. They try to get the dead to come back and predict the future or give them certain powers. Tell me, did you see anything you couldn't explain?'

'Like what?'

'Like a ghost or some mist forming over the grave.'

'No' Chris was most emphatic. 'Mind you, I didn't hang about too long. There were two of them and I was on his own. They might have been armed.'

'You were wise to get away unseen. People who do such things would not like to be observed.'

'So what do we do now?' Chris changed the subject abruptly.

'I am going to inspect the churchyard. I don't expect you to come, so don't get worried.'

'Of course I'm coming with you. I can show you exactly where they were standing.'

They didn't go direct to the church but walked the waterside path that the dealer had taken the previous evening. When they came to where he had first seen the torch light, he stopped and pointed out the place to his companion.

'There. That's where I climbed the dry stone wall and entered the church yard.'

They stood close to the wall and looked towards the tower.

'That's where they were standing. Just in front of the tower.'

Chris and the vicar walked back to the road then went to the church, entered by the front gate and walked around the building to the graveyard behind it. When they stopped behind the tower it was immediately obvious that something unusual had been going on in that area.

'See that circle marked in the grass?' John pointed to the marks on the ground, which described a circle about eight feet in diameter and encircled the witch's grave. 'And here.' He pointed to some small burn marks in the turf. 'That's where incense burners would have been placed around the circle to prevent the ghost from escaping.'

Chris peered at the area. 'There seems to be some other marks in the ground.'

'There will be secret signs that are made to protect the practitioners in the circle. Look over there. There's another circle with a pentagram marked in it. While they stayed within that magic circle they would think they were safe from any evil they managed to raise.'

'Safe from a ghost?' Chris asked incredulously.

'Safe from anything they raise. It could be a ghost or it may be an evil spirit or demon. These things don't perform to order.'

In the cold light of day, Chris was beginning to feel a bit silly considering such possibilities but the seriousness that the vicar brought to

128

the situation prevented him from expressing his doubts out loud. Surely those men in the churchyard were just misguided individuals playing at witchcraft and probably frightening themselves silly while they were at it.

John guessed what his companion was thinking.. 'Don't dismiss it as some prank, Chris. I've seen all of this before and I've tackled the damage that such ceremonies can do to vulnerable individuals.'

'Does that mean you need to consecrate the graveyard again?'

'No. I will bless it, but consecration is a legal procedure and can only be done by the bishop.'

Chris kept quiet; John was the expert on these matters after all.

As they left the churchyard by the front gate, Mrs Goodacre happened to be at the front door of the pub. She held up her hand in greeting and called to the vicar. 'Everything alright, John?'

The vicar shot a warning glance at Chris and whispered. 'Not a word about this. I don't want to alarm people unnecessarily.'

They both walked over to the landlady. 'No, Brenda. Chris here saw some strangers in the churchyard very late last night. He rang me this morning in case we'd had thieves after the lead on the roof. Thank goodness nothing was taken. I don't suppose you or Sara saw anything suspicious?'

'What time was that?'

Chris answered her. ' It was well after midnight.'

'No. We were both tucked up in our beds and fast asleep by then. Anyway we sleep at the back.'

'Well. If you do see anything suspicious do call the police.'

By this time Sara had come to see what was going on. She smiled at the vicar and at Chris. 'Can I help?'

Mrs Goodacre answered for them. 'No, love. Chris saw some strangers acting suspicious behind the church very late last night. They were asking if we saw anything but we were tucked up in our beds by that time. John thinks they may have been looking for lead, but nothing was taken.' She smiled again at the vicar and went back into the pub leaving Sara talking to the men.

'Well, I must be off. I've got a wedding to prepare for. I am interviewing the couple later this morning.' John took his leave of them and walked back to the antique shop where he had left his car.

Sara looked at Chris and raised her eyebrows. 'What were you doing out in the small hours of the morning?'

'I couldn't sleep.'

'Still getting those pains in your back?'

He nodded.

'I intended to come and dowse your home but I've been too busy here. Will you be in later this morning?'

'Yes. I'm busy doing some restoration so I'm not going anywhere. I'll see you later then.'

## Chapter Twenty One

Just after eleven that morning, Sara went to the antique shop. Her arrival was announced noisily by the old school bell that Chris had recently fixed on the shop door.

'I like the sound of that.' She pointed to the brass bell.

'It takes me back a bit to the school playground. We were always called into class by a teacher wielding one of those. When it came up at a sale recently I couldn't resist it.'

'I suppose it lets you know someone's come in when you're engrossed in work out the back.'

He washed the French polish off his hands with methylated sprit then removed the meths with soapy water.

Sara took the Jade pendulum from her pocket and held it up for him to see. 'I'm thrilled with this. I took it to my last class and now everyone wants one.'

'Bad luck for them. I only managed to find one.'

Sara nodded happily. 'I wouldn't want anyone else to have one like mine. It's special.'

'How are the classes going?'

'Well. I am thinking of enrolling in a Wicca class as well as the dowsing.'

'Wicca? Do they teach basket weaving as well as psychic subjects?'

Sara laughed out loud. 'Wicca is white magic. It's nothing to do with weaving.'

Chris frowned. 'White magic as opposed to black magic, I suppose?'

'Yes. They teach you spells and things to bring good luck.'

'Does your mother know what you want to study?'

Sara shook her head. 'No way, and don't you mention it to her. She's very religious and very closed minded. I will make my own mind up what subjects I want to study.'

He could see he'd hit on a bit of a raw nerve, but he could understand her mother's attitude; he was not too sure he approved of her studying magic spells. The recent events in the churchyard and the vicar's views on the subject, had made him very wary of it. Chris changed the subject. 'Now, what about a bit of dowsing, if you think it will tell us anything?'

131

Sara took the pendulum cord between her fingers and swung the jade bob to and fro. She asked the question. 'Is there anything in this room to cause Chris harm?'

The bob began to rotate anticlockwise, which she interpreted as being a negative answer. He followed her and watched as she dowsed each room in the building. The answer was the same in his workshop, upstairs in the kitchen and in the bathroom. Finally, Sara used her pendulum and asked the same question in his bedroom.

'Look! It's rotating clockwise. There's something here, Chris, that's causing your back pains.'

He sighed. 'Yes, I know. It seems to be my bed. I'm getting the pain regularly when I try and sleep in it. It's not just the mattress, that's practically new, and the pain is not your usual throbbing back ache, it's an acute pain like a knife being pushed between my shoulder blades.'

Sara looked closely at the bed but could see nothing unusual about it. It was a double bed with a wooden bed head and it had a base with drawers to store bedding. It was the sort of bed most people had. She scratched her head and tried the pendulum again.

'Look. Exactly the same result.' She was mystified. Suddenly she had an idea. 'The pendulum isn't specific enough but my rods will point to the exact spot where the problem lies. I'll go and get them. I wont be long.' She put away her pendulum and ran down the stairs. By the time he had followed her, she was out of the shop door and walking swiftly towards the pub, leaving the new door bell jangling in her wake.

Chris waited in the workshop until he heard the girl return. She certainly had hurried, taking only ten minutes to get home, pick up her divining rods and rush back to him.

'What kept you?' He asked sarcastically.

Sara ignored the comment and went straight up the stairs to his bedroom. She calmed herself by breathing deeply, then took up the two rods and walked slowly up and down the room. He watched her from the doorway, not sure what to expect.

Suddenly the rods crossed and she stopped in her tracks. 'There! What did I tell you. The rods are more specific.'

He frowned. Sara had stopped with her arms outstretched over the bed. He went over to her and pulled back the covers to reveal the bare mattress. 'Nothing there. I've looked several times already, I got so desperate for an answer.'

Sara looked at the bed closely then dropped the rods on the bed and pulled out the drawer, which was directly underneath the spot where the rods crossed.

He was a bit embarrassed at this. He used that drawer to store his dirty clothes until he had enough to fill the washer. 'I'll look in there. It's not the best place for you to dig around in.'

She stepped aside and let him pull the drawer right out.

'It's only my dirty washing.' He explained as he pulled out the soiled shirts, socks and underwear. He had almost emptied the drawer contents onto the bedroom floor when he felt something small and hard hidden among the few remaining clothes. He took it out, held up the object and frowned deeply. 'What the hell is this?'

Sara took the object from him and turned it over in her hands. 'It's some kind of doll, a manikin or something.' She looked questioningly at him.

'Don't look at me! I've never seen it before.' He took it from her and turned it over. It was a wax figure with a hat pin stuck into its back!

'Voodoo!' Sara exclaimed.

'Voodoo? What the hell does that mean?'

'It's a wax effigy used to harm someone.'

'Someone being me?'

'It certainly looks like it.'

Chris sat on the edge of the bed and examined the effigy closely. It was a crude figure of a man with some human hairs pushed into the wax of the head. He pulled out one of the hairs. 'I suppose these are my hairs. Whoever put this doll here must have been in the bathroom and taken them from my comb on the washbasin.'

Sara shook her head in disbelief. 'How? How could anyone get in here without you knowing?'

The dealer thought back to who had been in the flat. At first he drew a blank, then suddenly remembered that his ex wife, Vickie, had been in the flat when she had come to collect a grandfather clock and had undressed to seduce him. Vickie? He couldn't see her having the imagination to leave a voodoo doll in his bedroom. She wouldn't have a clue.    But did she know someone who dabbled in these things? No way! He couldn't bring himself to believe she was at the bottom of this strange business. Anyway, she had been quite friendly on that occasion when she called on him, so why would she come prepared with a harmful wax effigy? Still there was a lingering doubt in his mind.    The hairs on the doll's head could have come from his comb in the bathroom at the flat or maybe they were from the bathroom in Stamford that he used to share with Vickie? The thoughts were upsetting. 'Sara, I haven't a clue.' He lied.

Thinking back, he suddenly realised the only other clue to an unauthorised entry was the unlocked back door he'd found when he returned from a recent sale. He was sure he'd locked that door when he'd left home but had finally put the omission down to his absentmindedness. Chris thumped the bed hard. 'I think I know when it happened, but who? That's the million dollar question. Who wishes me harm enough to go to these lengths?'

Sara took the doll from his hands and gingerly withdrew the hatpin from the figure.

'Do you think that will solve it? Will the pain go away now we've found the cause and you've removed the pin?'

She seemed uncertain and out of her depth. 'I don't know, but I think I know who will. I wont take a chance on it. I'll contact John Smyth.'

'Ah! The vicar. He's experienced in these things. Good idea.'

Chris took the pin and the figure from her and studied them even closer. Suddenly he found a clue to their origins. 'Look Sara. There's a thumb print in the wax. Whoever made this doll has left his or her calling card. It must have been impressed there when it was soft wax being moulded in their hands. If we could identify that print we'd have the culprit.'

She peered closely at the mark and agreed it was a clear print pressed into the figure.

When Sara returned to open the pub for the lunchtime trade, the dealer telephoned the vicar again but the number was unavailable and messages were being taken by the BT answer service. He left a message for John to contact him urgently.

It was nearly tea time by the time John Smyth answered his call. The vicar hadn't bothered to telephone him but came straight over to Barrowick to the shop. After the events of the morning he thought that Chris had something more to tell him about the necromancy.

The dealer heard the door bell ring and went into the show room. He was relieved to see it was the Reverend Smyth. 'Thanks for coming.'

'I guess you've something new to tell me about the other night's escapade.'

'No. I wanted your advice on this.' He handed the wax effigy to John.

'Oh! Well I never! Where did you get this?'

'It was under my bed.'

John frowned. 'You do know what it is?'

'Yes. I believe it's some kind of voodoo doll. This pin was thrust into its back. Bit of a coincidence that I have been suffering severe back pains in the same area for days now.'

The vicar's expression turned very serious. His mouth tightened and he shook his head. 'Whoever made this meant you harm, Chris. Someone with a grudge and a knowledge of witchcraft has tried to harm you.'

'What do I do with it now, John?'

'Burn it.'

'I'd rather not. You see, there's a thumb print on the doll that may help identify the culprit.'

John turned the figure over and checked it thoroughly. 'Yes. I see what you mean.'

'Can't you counteract the evil in it? You tried something similar in the church the other evening.'

The vicar thought for a minute then agreed. 'We'll take this over to the church and I will bless it and dowse it in holy water. That should do it.'

As they walked over to the church, Chris queried his companion. 'I've been having terrible back pains, just where that pin was thrust. The doctor was mystified and couldn't find a cause for it. Do you think that doll was the problem?'

'Yes I do. I've seen some unbelievable things in my ministry since I became a Deliverance Priest.'

'But surely these voodoo things only work if the victim is aware of them? Doesn't the effect only happen if it plays on the victim's mind?'

'That's certainly the accepted wisdom, but in your case, and in many others I've seen, it's proved otherwise.'

Chris fell silent and considered who could be behind this psychic attack.

At the church, John did as he had promised and prayed over the doll, finally completely immersing it in holy water. He held the wet doll up in his hands. 'What do you want to do with it now, Chris?'

'I'm going to store it safely hidden away and keep that thumb print intact. You never know, I might get to the bottom of this business one day, match that print and find the culprit.'

'Well, if you must keep this effigy I will give you a bottle of holy water that I've blessed. It might give you some peace as you seem to be at the centre of so much of these strange happenings in the village.' The vicar went into the vestry and returned with a glass bottle full of water. 'Here, keep it handy. If anything else strange occurs try using it and don't hesitate to contact me.'

Chris thanked him for the gift and put it in his pocket as they walked to the church gate. "What happens now?" He asked.

'You go home and take the wax effigy with you. I am going to bless the churchyard where it was desecrated. This village seems to have become a focus for evil and for some reason, you are definitely caught up in it. The Athame and chalice, the necromancy in our churchyard, now this voodoo doll. It all seems to have happened since the Psychic College opened next door.'

Chris watched the vicar as he turned and went into the church. A few minutes later he returned dressed in his church robes. He made an imposing figure in his green chasuble with a large gold cross embroidered on the front.

'I'll go now and bless the graveyard, Chris. You mind how you go. If you need me again don't hesitate to call me.'

The dealer knew Barrowick churchyard had been desecrated and the vicar had to bless it to repair the damage. There was nothing more for him to do so he turned and walked back to his shop, while John went into the graveyard to pray.

## Chapter Twenty Two

When he went to lock the wax doll securely in the shop safe, Chris decided to take no chances and put some of the holy water in there with it. He felt he may be getting a bit paranoid about things, but reasoned it was better to be safe than sorry. Even if there was nothing to this psychic business, he would be no worse off treating it seriously. If there was something to it, and the experience with the wax doll had shaken his scepticism, he would treat the holy water as some kind of insurance policy. He poured half of the water into a Victorian silver hip flask that he had in stock, and put that into his jacket pocket, intending to keep it on his person at all times to ward off any problems. The remainder of the water in the bottle, went into the safe with the voodoo doll.

Life continued much as usual in Barrowick. Chris bought and restored antiques, and slowly built up contacts who bought from him. Sara and he continued to enjoy each other's company, although he was not ready for a more serious relationship and she seemed quite happy to continue being just very good friends. Vickie dropped off his radar until one morning she telephone him about the remaining Yorkshire clock, which had stayed under wraps in his workshop waiting for her to pay for the restoration work, when she could afford it.

'Chris.'

He recognised the voice immediately from the way she said his name.

'Chris, I want that other clock when you can deliver it.'

He could do with the money for that restoration so he didn't balk at the thought of delivering it, if he had reason to be in Stamford. 'OK. As long as you pay cash for the work. I'll bring it over next time I'm that way.'

Vickie continued. 'We have an antique sale here next Saturday. I thought maybe you'd come and view and buy here. You could bring it over then.'

She was right. He had noticed the sale advertised in the Gazette and there were one or two items that interested him. 'OK. I will bring it over on Friday morning on my way to the sale view. Make sure you are there to pay me and take delivery. Cash only, don't forget.'

'I'll be here. Now the business is a one woman affair I can't afford to leave the shop on a Friday. It's market day, as you know, and hopefully there will be some business for me.'

He knew full well she would be finding it inconvenient being on her own in the shop. When they were together she got away with any excuse to leave him in charge. 'Right, see you Friday. Cash on delivery, don't forget.'

When Friday came, Chris drove to Stamford and parked the van at the back of the shop. There was no sign of a traffic warden but he left the back doors open and the longcase clock sticking out of it to prove he was delivering. Vickie met him at the back door and invited him into the back shop for a coffee. He had to admit it was a relief to be on reasonable civilised terms with her after the recent arguments they had had.

'Sit down and drink your coffee, Chris' She insisted. 'We can keep an eye on the van from here in case the traffic warden appears.

Warily he sat opposite to her at the table. He knew Vickie of old and was suspicious of her welcoming manner. She soon changed the subject.

'I'm sorry I upset things the other day when I suggested we could make love again. I didn't realise you had a girlfriend there.'

'Sara's not my girlfriend. She runs the local pub where I eat my lunch and she occasionally buys antiques from me.'

'Sorry, Chris. You must admit she reacted badly to my presence in your flat.'

He suspected where this conversation was leading but said nothing.

Vickie leaned over the table, revealing rather a lot of cleavage in a very low cut jumper. 'If she's not your girlfriend there was no problem then. What's wrong with you and me renewing our acquaintance. It wouldn't be the first time a divorced couple have decided they made a mistake parting.'

He rose from his seat. 'Vickie, I know what you are doing. We divorced and I'm pleased we did. You can forget getting me into your bed again just to pay for that clock.' He turned to leave.

'What about my clock?' She asked, frustration welling up in her voice.

'What about it? Can you pay cash for it?'

'Of course I can pay. Not in cash, but you can have a cheque as I've had no time to get to the bank. Doing business on my own is very restricting when it comes to getting to the bank.'

He was tired of her games and decided to give her the benefit of the doubt. 'OK then. Write me a cheque for the other two hundred. I'll bring the clock in.' To be honest, he was fed up with storing her clock. It took up valuable space in his workshop and was just collecting dust. He waited until she fetched her cheque book and stared to write the cheque then went out to the van and carried the clock into her shop.

'Here.' She threw the cheque onto the table.

'Good.' He made sure it was dated and signed then folded it away in his pocket. 'Now I must get to the sale room and view.' He left without another word and went on to the local sale.

At the viewing he was looking for some interesting items that he'd seen online in the catalogue. The auctioneers had recently taken delivery of some pharmacy antiques, which Chris knew were very collectible. There was a run of drug drawers with cut glass knobs and glass covered labels on each one, detailing what had been kept in it. He knew that would fetch a lot of money. People bought those drug runs and used them in their farmhouse style kitchens... He decided he'd leave a bid on the drawers but didn't hold out much hope of getting them. He guessed they would make top money.

The other items that interested him were three boxes of drug bottles. People call the old chemists' stock bottles, shop rounds. They are becoming rarer as chemist shops are updated and obsolete items are thrown out. He knew those shop rounds often finished up in the dustbin in the old days but now they were getting scarce and people seemed more in tune with their value. He picked the bottles out one by one to check the state of them. The box with half a dozen cobalt blue glass bottles interested him the most. That box contained syrup bottles with gilded and recessed glass labels reading Syr. Marrub., Syr. Zingib., and other equally exotic names. All of the bottles had ground pontils in their bases proving they were hand blown and not modern copies. The pontil mark is where the glass blower fixed his metal rod to the bottle when he was making it. Five of the bottles were perfect but the sixth had a large chip on the neck. He decided to leave a small bid on that selection. He had found only a few items of interest at the viewing so he was happy to leave bids on them with the office staff rather than waste a whole morning bidding in person.

On his way home from the sale room, he called at the bank and deposited Vickie's cheque into his business account. The sooner that was honoured the happier he would be. It was lunch time by the time he returned to Barrowick so he parked the van at the front of his shop and walked to the pub for a meal.

Sara was busy serving customers but she made time to acknowledge him with a smile. Eventually she was free to serve him.

'Hi, Chris. Your usual?'

He nodded and picked up the local newspaper from the bar. The Rutland Times often had items for sale in its classified columns. He usually glanced down them but seldom found any antiques there.

'Your salad.' Sara placed the plate in front of him. 'Beer?' She asked.

'Please.'

'Had a busy morning, Chris?'

'Yes and no. I've been over to Stamford to the sale room.'

'Ah! To the antique sale?'

'It's viewing today. I also had to deliver a clock to my ex.' As soon as he'd uttered those words, he regretted them. Sara looked away and frowned. Her expression said it all; she had not forgotten the last time Vickie was on the scene.

'I had to take it over, Sara. I need the money for the work I've done on it.'

Sara busied herself polishing glasses and ignored his explanation. He could have kicked himself for ever mentioning Vickie. He finished his meal in silence and left the pub to return to the work at the shop.

Five days after the visit to Stamford, he received a letter from the bank enclosing Vickie's cheque. It had 'Insufficient Funds' stamped right across it. It had bounced! He tried to telephone her several times but the phone was continually on an answer system or engaged. He wondered how many other disgruntled people were trying to get in touch with her. She was obviously in a financial mess and the business was failing.

After two days of trying to contact Vickie, Chris felt he needed to take matters further and see if he could sue her for the money she owed him. A visit to the Citizens Advice bureau in Oakham soon put him right. He was told he could use a private debt collection service or take his grievance to the small claims court. As it was under five thousand pounds the small claims route would probably be the cheapest way to try to get the bill paid but it would take weeks to get any action. He decided to prepare the court papers but write to Vickie and tell her he intended to take his claim to the small claims court of she didn't get in touch and pay up. He hoped the threat alone might make her pay. He heard nothing for three days then early one morning the phone rang

'Barrowick Antiques.' He answered the phone cheerily never expecting it to be Vickie.

'You shit!' She shouted down the phone. 'You would take me to court over that clock bill?'

'Yes. How else would I get paid? Your cheque bounced as you knew it would.'

She fumed and swore down the phone but finally burst into tears and stopped shouting abuse.

'Can't we come to some arrangement, Chris. I have half of Stamford chasing me for money. What if I give you the clock back to settle the debt? Will that satisfy you?'

He considered the offer. That clock was a pot boiler. It was not his choice of stock, but he had bid on it at the auction and would have bought it at a very cheap price if Vickie hadn't run the price up. Now he'd done all the work on it, it was in good order and a much more saleable proposition. If he accepted the clock for the two hundred pound debt, he would certainly make a small profit on it even if he had to sell it in the trade.

'OK. I will accept your offer. I am coming over to Stamford for a sale view on Friday. Be there so I can pick up that clock.'

She accepted his terms and rang off. He only hoped she was as good as her word this time and she would be at the shop to let him pick up the clock. He decided he would still keep the papers he'd prepared for the court, just in case she changed her mind.

When he called at his old shop in Stamford it was in chaos. Vickie stood in the sales area surrounded by young men who were moving stock out of the front door and into a van. Chris recognised one of the lads immediately as one of the local bailiffs. He turned to Vickie. 'What's going on?' Although it was painfully obvious what was happening.

'The bailiffs are taking my stock to settle my business debts. You better get your clock before it vanishes as well.'

He turned just in time to see a young lad lift the Yorkshire clock onto his shoulder and start for the door.

'Hey up! You can leave that one mate. It's not her stock. it's mine.'

The chap put the clock down but didn't let go of it. 'Who says?'

'I do and I have court papers to prove it.'

The head bailiff, who Chris had recognised, came over to them. 'Trouble mate?'

'No. That clock doesn't belong to Vickie. It's mine and I've just come to collect it.'

'You're her ex, aint you mate?'

'Yes. And that clock's mine. It just happens to be stored here temporarily.'

The bailiff scratched his head, took a look at the court papers that Chris had prepared then told his men to hand the clock over.

'Sorry mate. Only doing our job. '

Chris thanked him and loaded the clock into his van. It was a good thing he'd arrived when he had, otherwise he would have come away with nothing because there was no way Vickie could pay him; she was over her head in debt. He left her standing in the empty shop and wiping away her tears. In some ways he felt sorry for her, but recalling the grief she'd given him in the past, he hardened his heart towards her.

# Chapter Twenty Three

When Chris called at the Barrowick Arms for his lunch next day, he was surprised to see Dave Porter and a companion eating at one of the tables. He was even more surprised when he went to the bar and got a better look at the pair. Porter was deep in conversation with DC Phillips from the local police force.

That figures, Chris thought, they both seemed to be involved with the Psychic College. They were both there when the barn was cleaned out. Thinking more about it, he remembered that DC Phillips had never taken seriously his information about Steve's death. There had been the occasion when he told the policeman about the Athame and the fact that Dr O'Conlan seemed to know more about the events than was normal. Chris had toyed with the idea of reporting the business with the wax doll to the local police. At the very least someone had entered his premises illegally, but the thought that D.C. Phillips would be involved had put him off.

Sara broke his train of thought when she asked. 'Your usual for lunch?' She poured his usual pint of beer without being asked. She looked over at the policeman and the dealer sitting at the far side of the bar and leaned over to speak quietly to Chris. 'That little dark fellow isn't exactly a fan of yours.'

Chris raised his eyebrows, feigning surprise.

Sara continued. 'When he first came in he was alone. I chatted to him over the bar. He tells me he's an antique dealer, like you. I mentioned your name in passing. I just made a comment that he might know you. He was downright rude about you.'

Chris nodded. 'I would expect no less. Dave Porter and I have form from the past. He's known for handling stolen antiques and he tried to pass some off on me recently.'

Sara looked over at the two diners again. Chris's remarks had aroused her interest. 'That would explain it.'

Chris sat at the bar and ate his lunch and enjoyed a pint of beer. D.C.Phillips and Dave Porter were so engrossed in their conversation and their meals they didn't notice him until the detective got up to leave. Only then, Dave Porter looked around the room and spotted Chris seated at the bar. He got up immediately to follow the detective, but the dealer jumped off his stool and barred his way.

'I gather you've been bad mouthing me, Dave. What's your problem?'

'You know full well what the problem is. You're a grass! How else did the police know about that bible box?'

Chris shook his head. 'I told you, I have never mentioned it to anyone. You tried to pass that stolen item off on several other people. Why blame me? I'm sure most dealers read the Antique Gazette and the box was pictured there for all to see.'

Dave Porter didn't answer but tried to step around Chris and leave the pub.

Chris grabbed him by his collar. 'Not so fast. I want a word about something else.'

Porter recoiled and looked frightened, but he said nothing.

'What do you know about a wax effigy with pins in it, which was left in my flat? '

The dealer's face and neck coloured blood red but he still didn't speak.

'Someone left a voodoo doll under my bed. Someone must have broken into my flat to do that. It was someone with a large grudge. Any ideas who that could be?'

'Honest. It wasn't me' Dave shook his head emphatically.

'Honest? Since when have you been honest? You do understand why I suspect you? You bear me a grudge, you are involved with the Psychic College and no doubt have access to information on such weird things as voodoo dolls.'

Dave squirmed in the dealer's grip but he was held too tightly and he couldn't break free.

Chris continued. 'Whatever idiot made that wax doll left a beautiful clue to their identity on it.'

Porter stopped struggling and paid attention.

'Whoever modeled that wax doll left a very clear thumb print on it. Warm wax takes a good impression you know. It was a beauty. Very clear and not at all smudged.'

Porter collapsed into the nearest chair all the stuffing knocked out of him, but Chris still held firmly to his collar. 'I will take it to the police; not the local police mind you. That local DC and you seem far too friendly for that. He probably wouldn't take it seriously, would he? No, I will take it to the main police station in Leicester. If they have that thumb print on their records they will know who to call in for questioning.'

144

Porter buried his face in his hands.

Chris was thoroughly enjoying myself by then. He continued. 'It's no good you breaking in again and looking for the doll at my flat, It's been hidden elsewhere. If it was your thumb print, with your past criminal record, the police will definitely have your details on file because you've been involved with them before.'

Dave Porter was almost in tears by then. 'I don't know nothing about it, honestly. Maybe someone was playing a joke on you.'

'A joke! Well, breaking into my flat was no joke was it.' Chris let go of his collar, stepped aside and let the crooked little dealer leave the pub. He hoped he had put the frighteners on the man and warned him off any other ideas he had on taking revenge.

Dave scuttled out of the bar as fast as his damaged leg could carry him.

Sara, who had been pretending to clean the glasses during this conversation, waited until Dave Porter left the pub then she turned to her friend.

'Do you really think he was behind that wax doll business?'

'Without a doubt. You saw his face. He had guilt written all over it.'

'Will you take it to the police?'

'I don't think so. Can you imagine them taking a wax voodoo doll seriously? There was nothing taken and no damage done, so they won't be interested. But if anything else occurs I will contact them, and Dave Porter now knows it.'

'He's a funny little man. He spoke to me after my dowsing class last week and asked if I was interested in taking more classes. He was very friendly then.'

Chris frowned but said nothing.

'I think he's taking some classes as well. I often see him over there. I'm going to ask Tanith for a full syllabus and see what else they have to offer.'

Chris still said nothing. He didn't trust the O'Conlans and he definitely didn't trust Dave Porter or his detective friend. But Sara was a grown woman and head strong. She must do what she felt she wanted to do, but he had mixed feelings about her further involvement with the Psychic College.

## Chapter Twenty Four

A few days after his argument with Dave Porter, Chris was drinking late at night at his local. He had been out of the village to a sale in Bristol and had arrived back late in the evening, too late to get a meal but in time to have a pint and a bag of crisps before they closed. At a quarter past eleven he said goodnight to Sara and started to walk home. As he left the pub a car sped round the corner from the main road and parked in the vicarage yard. That wouldn't have normally attracted his attention but he recognised the vehicle; it was Dave Porter's car. He was certainly a late caller at the vicarage.

Back at his shop the dealer made a coffee and took it along with some paperwork up to his flat. It was late, well after midnight by the time he'd caught up with the paperwork, but he wasn't at all tired; it had been a stressful day and the motorway home had been very busy, so his adrenaline was still flowing and he knew he wouldn't sleep if he turned in for the night. It was a fine starlit night with a new moon. He opened the French windows and stepped out into the night, listening to the sounds from the lake and letting his eyes get used to the poor light. Suddenly two swans took off from the water with loud alarm calls. He guessed there must be a fox out there or someone disturbing their rest. He looked over the village, which was in darkness except for the vicarage, where the lights were on in several rooms. Dave Porter's car could still be seen parked in the driveway; he was obviously staying late with the O'Conlans.

While he stood staring at the vicarage, Chris noticed some shadowy figures leave the vicarage grounds and walk into the church yard by the gate in the stone wall between the two premises. That did arouse his interest. Why would anyone want to be in the churchyard that late at night? He wondered whether he should telephone the vicar but a glance at the time persuaded him not to bother. It was well after midnight and John Smyth would most probably be asleep. He decided to walk down to the church and take a look for himself.

Chris's experience in the parachute regiment came in very useful on occasions like that. He changed into some dark coloured trousers and an army camouflage jacket he'd kept for sentimental reasons. He went down to his workshop and smeared some dark brown wax polish on his face, just as he would have done when he was seeing action in the forces. He intended to approach the churchyard by the back wall, as he had previously but this time he would be very careful not to fall into any holes.

146

As a last thought, Chris placed the hip flask of Holy Water into his jacket pocket. Thus suitably prepared, he made his way through the woods to the back of the churchyard.

When he was through the woods and standing close to the stone wall that surrounded the graveyard, Chris stopped and listened. In the distance he could hear a voice chanting in the churchyard. As his eyes became more accustomed to the dark shadows surrounding the church, he made out the silhouettes of two robed figures standing exactly where he had seen them before. They were positioned in front of the witch's gravestone. It looked as if someone was attempting necromancy once again!

Chris climbed over the church wall and crept up on the people, making sure this time he gave them no clue they were being observed. As he got nearer to the robed figures one of them switched on a torch and opened a book. In the faint light of that torch Chris could just make out the features of Francis O'Conlan and Dave Porter! So, they were the culprits; they were the vandals who had disturbed the graveyard on the previous occasion. He sat behind a large gravestone and considered what to do. He realised he could still have crept away and telephoned the Reverend Smyth, but that would take ages and it would take even longer for the vicar to arrive at the church as he had to come from Oakham. Chris decided to keep watch on the pair of robed figures and wait to see what happened.

From where he was kneeling, looking over a gravestone, Chris watched Dave Porter draw a circle in the grass surrounding the witch's grave. O'Conlan held in his hand the Athame, which he used to draw another circle about ten feet away from the first one and closer to the dealer's hiding place. The man seemed to be making extra marks in the turf all around that circle then he placed some small bowls at intervals on the circumference of it. He put something into those containers then lit the contents with a cigarette lighter. Chris could see smoke curling up from the circle and eventually detected an aromatic scent as the herbs burned in them. The two men were taking an awful lot of trouble and seemed very engrossed in their preparations. Finally, they must have completed their work because they retreated to the second circle they had scribed, stood close together in the centre of the smoking bowls and began reciting again from the book.

Chris couldn't make out the actual words O'Conlan was reciting. He was sure the man wasn't using English but speaking in some foreign language. He recalled Jon Smyth telling him many incantations were written in Latin, which was the official language of the Catholic church for

147

centuries past.   As far as he could see, nothing was happening in the graveyard except the drone of O'Conlan's voice and the occasional chorus from Dave Porter. He began to get cramp in his legs, crouched as he was behind the gravestone. He decided to move nearer to them to get a better look at what was happening.  He crawled slowly along on his stomach  to avoid detection.

The dealer managed to get within a few yards of the ceremony and hid himself behind a large slate Victorian gravestone that afforded ample cover for him.  Now he could clearly hear every word that O'Conlan was saying. He still couldn't understand any of it, but assumed it was some sort of witchcraft spell. Dave Porter stood close by his companion and held the book open for him to read.  Every so often the doctor held up his arms almost as if he was calling on some unseen power above him, then he would point to the circle enclosing the witch's grave.

As far as Chris could make out nothing was happening. It seemed to be a futile exercise. He watched them for some time before he decided they were achieving nothing with their clandestine ceremony. They were not actually doing much harm to the churchyard either. If they had been overturning gravestones or stealing the lead from the roof, he would have shouted at them and  frightened them off, but they were just reciting Latin verses.  He thought the pair were misguided and wasting their time. He felt he was certainly wasting his. He would be better going home to his bed.

As nothing was happening, Chris prepared  to creep back the way he'd come and return home, but then something strange began to occur in the graveyard. He rubbed his  eyes to be sure he wasn't seeing things  when he noticed a strange white mist swirling close to the ground over the witch's grave. Slowly the mist formed into a column about the height of a small person. He watched fascinated as the manifestation  solidified into the shape of a human figure!  It was not actually standing on the turf but hovering just above it. From the shape of the apparition it  looked as if there was a sheet wound around it.  As the features became clearer he could make out the colourless face of a female corpse!  He was shocked and apprehensive.

O'Conlan spoke to the spectre in a loud commanding voice. This time he used English and Chris could hear him clearly. 'Molly Bent, I command you to tell me the secrets of the Black Mass.' He pointed at his book then at the ghost.

Chris recoiled in horror. In  his  years as a soldier he thought he'd seen enough horror, from  bodies blown apart to  captives decapitated by terrorists, but this was entirely different; this was beyond his experience.

The spectre let out an unearthly howl and tried to approach the two robed figures but it seemed to be confined in the circle, which they had formed around it. Dave Porter crouched down and hid his face but Dr O'Conlan didn't seem to be phased by the witch. He carried on demanding information from her.

'By all the demons at my command, I order you to tell me the deepest secrets of the Black Mass. Tell me how to order your master, Beelzebub, to bend to my will.'

By this time the spectre had somehow broken free from the circle around her grave. She approached the two robed figures. Dave Porter dropped to his knees and sobbed in fear. The doctor stood his ground and faced her fearlessly. It seemed to Chris, the incense and the occult spells O'Conlan had scribed around his circle were working and keeping her from getting to them even though the circle around the grave had failed to contain her. Slowly the witch's ghost wafted around the magic circle seeking a weak point to enter it and attack her tormentors.

Chris watched in horror. Lying behind a gravestone only a few yards away from them, he had no magic protection. Suddenly he sneezed! It was involuntary and he tried to stifle it by nipping his nose, but he couldn't stop it . The sneeze sounded so loud in that quiet dark churchyard. He froze and held his breath not knowing what to expect next.

Francis O'Conlan immediately turned towards the unexpected sound. He was obviously worried by this unexpected interruption. Chris could see the fear etched on his face. Dave Porter curled up on the ground, put his hands over his ears and started to sob even louder. The ghost hesitated in its constant circling of the two robed figures and turned towards the dealer's hiding place.

Chris realised his cover was blown. He stood up. From O'Conlan's reaction it was obvious the man did not recognise him as human, camouflaged as he was. He stopped his chanting and put his hands up to his face, hiding his eyes. With a blood curdling scream the apparition moved towards the slate gravestone.

Chris's years of combat training took over. He pulled the flask of Holy Water from his pocket and threw the contents at the spectre. There was a blinding flash of light then the stench of decay. Chris dropped to his knees behind the gravestone to gather his senses. He was certainly not physically afraid of Porter or O'Conlan'; he had been trained to deal with flesh and blood foes, but ghosts were an entirely different matter. He needn't have worried. When he looked over the top of the gravestone again the spectre had completely vanished and the graveyard was still and empty.

Chris heard a distant scuffle and turned to see Porter and O'Conlan running towards the dry stone wall, which separated the vicarage from the churchyard. They ran as if Old Nick himself was after them. The two men did not stop to open the gate but tumbled over the wall, dislodging several stones in their hurry to escape. Chris glanced back at the witch's grave, praying he'd see nothing unusual there, but he needn't have worried.; everything appeared to be back to normal, there was no mist in the air, just the lingering smell of incense and faint traces of smoke curling up from the bowls O'Conlan had placed around the circle. Chris walked over and kicked the bowls over making sure the magic circle was destroyed.

The dealer returned home the way he had come, through the woodland and along the lakeside pathway. He didn't bother to contact John Smyth that night. The vicar wouldn't have thanked him for interrupting his sleep, especially as he had managed to put a stop to the necromancy ceremony all by himself. Considering the events of that night as he got ready for bed, he decided Dr O'Conlan and Dave Porter would not have a clue who or what had disturbed them in the graveyard. He would brazen it out next time he contacted either of them and deny any knowledge of the events if questioned, but he doubted they even saw him let alone recognised him. He was well camouflaged and they were shocked by the ghostly apparition and his unexpected intervention. They must have thought they'd raised a different spectre from another grave. No wonder they ran. He placed the Gideon Bible on his bedside locker for reassurance. He was feeling very tired, either from the long drive home, or the totally weird events in the graveyard. He slept soundly until the morning.

Next morning Chris couldn't believe his memories of what had happened the previous night. He thought at first he'd had another nightmare until he looked in the bathroom mirror and saw his face was still smeared with brown wax polish. He rushed to get his camouflage jacket and took the hip flask from his pocket. When he shook it and unscrewed the top, he confirmed it was empty. After breakfast he telephoned John Smyth to let him know what had happened.

It was mid morning before the Reverend Smyth arrived at the antique shop. Chris had just stopped work to make a coffee when he heard the shop doorbell ring. He went straight through to the sales area hoping it would be the vicar. It was indeed the Reverend Smyth, looking very concerned.

'Chris, are you alright? Sorry I couldn't come earlier, I had an appointment with a young couple hoping to marry in Barrowick church.'

'Thanks for coming, but you needn't have worried. I think your holy water sorted out the problems last night. Thank you for that protection.' Chris signalled for him to follow him up to the flat where he had more comfortable chairs.

'Tell me exactly what happened last night, Chris. I've already been into the churchyard and seen the mess the idiots left behind them. Can you identify the perpetrators, by the way?'

Chris smiled at John's description of Porter and O'Conlan; calling them idiots! He couldn't have put it better himself, but they were dangerous idiots.

'Yes. It was Francis O'Conlan and his sidekick Dave Porter. He's the man who I suspect placed that wax doll in my bedroom.' He put down his coffee and explained the night's events to John in detail. 'I suspected something was going on when I saw a car arrive at the vicarage very late last night. I recognised the car immediately. It was Dave Porter's.'

John Smyth nodded he understood and asked Chris to continue.

'Much later, when I was looking over the village from my flat, I saw two dark figures go into the churchyard. I was immediately suspicious after the last time. I went to investigate. I took the woodland path and approached the church from the back just as I did before, but this time I was more careful.'

'Did you see what they were doing?'

'Yes. I crept up on them and watched. They drew a circle around the witch's grave and then another circle next to it. They set bowls of incense around the second circle and stood inside it.'

'That sounds exactly what I would expect. What about the witch? You did say they managed to raise her ghost.'

'Yes. They raised a spectre from her grave. I must admit I couldn't believe my eyes at first, but when it turned on me I threw that holy water at it.'

'Good. That's the best thing you could have done. There's no guarantee it was the witch herself; it could well have been a demon taking advantage of them.'

'The circle they made around the grave didn't seem to contain the ghost. It came for me when it realised I was hiding behind a gravestone.'

'You were at risk. You didn't have the protection of their magic circle.  Thank God I gave you that holy water and thank God you used it.

151

If the spectre escaped the first circle, it may well have breached the second one. Our two necromancers had a lucky escape as well, thanks to your quick action. Tell me, did you hear what they wanted with the witch?'

'O'Conlan wanted to know how to command Beelzebub to do his will. He mentioned a Black Mass'

The vicar frowned and shook his head. 'This is very serious, Chris. They are hell bent on raising the Devil and gaining power from him. I just hope this fright has put them off such a dangerous undertaking. This village is in grave danger if they continue with their mad plans.'

The vicar left soon after they had spoken and Chris made himself another coffee and sat in the shop considering what had been said. He was worried about the effects the psychic college was having on the village and especially concerned for Sara as she seemed so keen on studying there.

## Chapter Twenty Five

Later that morning, Chris had a surprise visitor. When he heard the door bell ring and went into the shop he was confronted with a tearful figure.

'Vickie! What the devil are you doing here?' He couldn't contain his irritation at his ex wife turning up unannounced. He still had the clock she had used to pay her debt to him; maybe she thought she could persuade him to give it back to her. He was about to say something sarcastic to her when she burst into uncontrollable sobs and threw her arms around his neck.

'Hang on, Vickie. Whatever's the matter, girl?' He hadn't the heart to be nasty to her when she was so obviously upset. He helped her to a chair and sat her down. 'Come on now. This is not like you. Whatever has upset you can't be that bad, surely.'

Vickie searched in her bag and brought out a packet of tissues, which she used to dry her eyes and dab the tears from her face.

Chris waited patiently for her to recover and tell him what the problem was. Finally she spoke.

'I've been thrown out of the shop and the flat. I owe so much rent the landlord has sent in the bailiffs and changed the locks.' She started sobbing again uncontrollably.

Chris stood and watched her, unsure what to do. She was no longer his wife but they had enjoyed a short marriage together and he was concerned for her. He recalled the sarcastic comments and the tricks she had pulled on him since they had parted; the scene when he had taken Sara to dinner, the bidding against him at the Stamford auction, and he realised it was all bravado to hide the real problems she was having. That was typical of Vickie. He stood by her chair, put his arm around her shoulders and pulled her to him. She buried her face in his jumper and sobbed against his chest. Finally she stopped crying and dried her eyes again.

'What am I to do, Chris? Where can I sleep tonight? Can you put me up here for a night?'

Chris was taken completely by surprise at these questions. He sympathised with her predicament but had not reckoned on becoming personally involved in it. He backed off and considered his options.

'For old time's sake? Surely you wouldn't see me on the street?' As she pleaded with him, tears began to run down her cheeks again.

Chris had to make a snap decision. He wasn't completely heartless about his ex, but he didn't want to become involved with her again. 'By the looks of you, you aren't capable of sorting yourself out today. Go upstairs and tidy yourself up then we can talk about your problems and try to find a way out of them.'

She kissed his hand in gratitude and went up to the flat.

Chris carried on working in the back shop restoring more of the picture frames he had bought at the Oakham sale. The original examples he had restored and gilded had sold for a small profit. The remainder, which were the more damaged ones, he was working on that day.

At lunch time Chris decided not to go to the local pub. He knew if he did turn up with his ex wife, Sara would be wondering what was going on, and he didn't want that to happen. His friendship with Sara was going along quite nicely and Vickie's appearance would almost certainly put a stop to that. Sara had already jumped to the wrong conclusions when Vickie tried to seduce him to pay for the repairs to her grandfather clocks. He knew another scene like that would put an end to his friendship with Sara for good. Vickie cooked a meal for them both and they ate in silence upstairs in his flat.

After lunch Chris broached the subject uppermost in his mind. 'Well, what plans have you made to sort out your accommodation? Don't any of your friends have a spare bed for you?'

Vickie was evasive. 'I have tried a few of them and have been half promised a room but nothing positive.'

'Well you can't stay here. I have one bed and I sleep in it. Dammit Vickie! We are divorced and we didn't part company on very friendly terms.'

She started to cry again. 'I know...I was horrible to you...' She blew her nose loudly on a tissue and sniffed the tears back. 'I have no right to ask you, but I'm desperate.'

Chris frowned. He felt cornered, but he tried one last ploy. 'OK. You can stay just this one night. Then you must make other arrangements. You can sleep in the bed and I'll make up an easy chair downstairs.'

For the remainder of the day Chris saw very little of his ex wife. She stayed up in the flat while he worked downstairs, restoring the picture frames and manning the shop when the occasional customer came in. He was unsettled by the presence of Vickie in his flat and in his life again but there was little he could do about it at that moment.

After lunch Sara came from the pub to see Chris. She had missed his company at dinner time and wondered if he was alright. She was already standing in the front shop when he went to answer the door bell. 'Are you OK Chris? I missed you at lunch time. I thought I'd take a walk and check if you needed anything.'

Chris felt uneasy with his ex upstairs in the flat while Sara was talking in the shop. He almost explained the situation to his visitor but thought better of it. He reasoned that Vickie would be gone the very next day and Sara wouldn't need to know anything about her presence there. Luckily, while the girl was visiting the shop, there was no noise from the upstairs flat and Vickie had not come down the stairs and put in an appearance.

Sara seemed in no hurry to return to the pub and looked around the new stock that he'd bought since her last visit. 'I do like this little workbox.' She opened the lid of a Victorian Walnut sewing box on a tripod stand. 'How much is it, Chris?'

'I've only had it a few days and I've just finished restoring it. As it's you, I can let you have it at cost.' He was more concerned about preventing the two girls from meeting than he was about his profit margins.

Sara was thrilled with the price he quoted her. 'I will get you cash from the bank in a day or two. You can put a sold sign on that one. I love it!'

Chris put a red sticker on the box lid to declare it sold. 'There you are. I'm pleased you've found a work box at last. I know you've been looking for months.'

She threw her arms around his neck and kissed him, which quite took him by surprise. 'I must be off now. I left mother filling up the shelves with clean glasses. She'll be missing me. Thanks for the sewing box, it's lovely.' With that cheery farewell, Sara left the antique shop with a broad smile on her face.

Chris let out a deep sigh of relief when he had finally closed the door after her. That had gone well considering the possibility for confrontation between Sara and his ex. He took the sewing box into the workshop to give it a final polish. The atmosphere at the antique shop was a little strained for the rest of that day. Vickie came downstairs after they had eaten lunch together and sat in the workshop watching Chris work on his latest acquisitions. He had bought a cheap pine dresser base and a set of antique wall shelves that more or less matched for material, size and date. The trouble was they were coated in thick layers of paint. Pine was a cheap wood that was rarely used plain in the old days. Showing the grain

155

was considered poor taste and the furniture was nearly always painted. He stripped off the many layers of old paint with caustic soda solution, taking care not to get burned by it. Elbow length rubber gloves and a rubber apron were his protection when he did that sort of work. Once the paint was removed the wood was washed down with copious amounts of clean water to remove the alkaline soda. When the bare wood was dry, he sanded it smooth then stained it a warm honey shade to bring out the grain.

'That looks good.' Vickie admired the work. 'It should sell quickly once its finished. It's a pity I didn't learn from you how to restore furniture, while I had the chance. You could have taught me a lot, then perhaps I wouldn't be in the financial mess I'm in now.'

Chris remained silent and tightlipped. When Vickie and he were in business together she never got her hands dirty. She always left the hard graft to him and preferred playing at being the knowledgeable antique dealer, an act she wasn't well qualified to do. He let the stain dry then applied a wax coating. The general public liked to think the wax finish was beeswax as this was regarded as the traditional way to finish furniture, but cheap pine was too absorbent for a beeswax finish and would have taken dozens of coats and scores of hours of work to achieve anything approaching a good patina.

As most restorers, Chris used coffin wax to treat pine furniture. That wax built up a patina on pine faster than any other polish. He buffed up the final coat and stood back to check the work.

'Looks good.' Vickie said, a slight hint of jealousy in her voice.

'It should. I've worked up quite a sweat producing that finish.'

Chris moved the dresser base into the shop display area and stood it against one wall, then he placed the shelf unit on top of it. Because the pine Victorian units were more or less of contemporary manufacture, and he had stained them to match, they looked as if they had always been together. He stood back to admire his work.

Vickie, followed him into the shop and watched him set up the dresser. 'Here.' She took a Royal Dalton vase he had set on a side table, and placed it centrally on the pine shelves. 'There. That's looks much better.'

Chris frowned and looked at her under lowered eyebrows. She was playing happy families and he wasn't having any of it. 'Hadn't you better get phoning around your friends to get yourself a permanent place to stay? Don't forget, I said you could stay only the one night.'

His ex shot him a mean glance. 'Oh, don't worry. I won't outstay my welcome.' She flounced out of the sales area and went back up to the flat. Chris could hear her using his telephone and making several calls.

That night Vickie slept in Chris's bed as he had suggested. He moved an Edwardian chaise from the workshop into the kitchen and made up a temporary bed for himself. It wasn't the most comfortable place to sleep as it had several loose springs, which created hard lumps in the middle of the seat. Chris had bought the chaise cheaply because it needed completely reupholstering and it would pay him to restore it. The frame was mahogany but had seen better days; the joints were loose and needed taking apart, cleaning and regluing. He made the best of a bad job and put a layer of pillows and cushions on top of the base before he made up his temporary bed.

When the time came to turn in for the night, Chris made himself a warm drink and flopped onto the chaise. Vickie flitted about the kitchen in a thin nightie preparing a night drink and a glass of water for herself. Finally she said goodnight.

Chris turned out the kitchen light and tried to get some sleep. The chaise was really too small for him and there was no room to turn over. He spent a sleepless night tossing and turning to try and avoid the loose springs. By morning he was shattered.

Next morning Chris rose early and had a solitary breakfast. Vickie was nowhere to be seen and presumably fast asleep. He cursed his temporary bed and his ex wife for causing him so much pain and trouble. After breakfast, Chris went down to the workshop and moved the chaise back again so he could make a start on it. He knew it was useless as it was. No one would buy it in the state that he had found it during the night. He put on a face mask to keep out the dust and ripped off the cover. Underneath the old material he found a mass of dusty horsehair and rusty springs. The chords holding the springs in place had rotted and ceased to hold them. He ripped out the lot and got back to the bare mahogany frame. All the while he was working, Chris kept an ear open for signs of his ex wife, but she did not put in an appearance and no sound came from the bedroom. Unlike him, she must have slept well!

Once he'd knocked the chaise frame apart with a rubber hammer, Chris removed the old animal glue from the joints and filed them down smooth. He cleaned the polished surface of the frame and legs and applied French polish to them to give them back a pristine finish. With the frame ready, he clamped and glued the whole thing together then stopped for a

157

break. When he checked the clock he found it was almost nine o'clock and time to open up the shop, but there was still no sign of his unwanted guest. 'What is she playing at?' he muttered under his breath.

Chris made himself a strong coffee and  sat down. His poor night's sleep was catching up with him and he really needed that dose of caffeine. When he'd finished the drink, he decided to run a duster over the shop stock making it look pristine and desirable. He was just polishing the sewing box that Sara had reserved, when she drove up in her car, parked it at the front and came into the shop.

'Morning Chris. I have the cash for the box.' She ran her fingers appreciatively over the polished lid and handed him a wad of notes.

'Thanks. That's good. Do you want me to deliver it?'

'I think I can load it into my boot. I'll take it now.'

Chris was pleased to see her again and invited her to sit down for a few minutes. 'Would you like a coffee?'

'No thanks. I've just had a full English breakfast.'

The words had hardly  left Sara's lips when a female voice called from the workshop. 'That's just what I could do with.'

Chris frowned. Sara looked surprised!

Vickie came into the sales area. She was  wearing  a pair of Chris's slippers, far too big for her feet, and his towelling dressing gown over the thin nightie she had donned the night before. She smiled at Chris and asked. 'Any more milk, Chris. I had a good night's sleep in your bed and now I fancy some breakfast.'

Sara rose from her chair, a thunderous look on her face. She turned to Chris and grabbed back her money. 'That woman again! She's obviously stayed with you all last night. You can stuff your sewing box. I am finished with you.' She marched out of the shop before Chris could offer a word of explanation. He stood in the shop looking completely lost.

'She's a pretty girl but it's a pity she's so highly strung.' Vickie smiled cattily at her ex.

Chris blew his top. 'You come here and take advantage of my soft heart. You  wanted the divorce and now you  seem to want to start all over again. Well you can want. I want you out of here and out of my life today. No ifs and no buts. Out! '

Vickie was taken aback at his anger.   She had secretly hoped they could make up their differences and start again as she had made such a mess of being in business on her own account. She turned and went back up the stairs.

Chris despised his ex wife and knew there was no way he could tolerate her interfering any more in his life. He followed Vickie as she climbed the stairs to get dressed and shouted after her. 'Half an hour, then I need to go into Oakham. I want you out and the doors locked behind you before I leave here.'

Vickie knew she had overstepped the mark. She dressed and loaded her things into her car, not even bothering with breakfast. Without a backward glance or a word of thanks or goodbye, she drove out of the village and out of his life.

# Chapter Twenty Six

When Chris returned from Oakham, he slowed down and as he drove by the pub, hoping to catch sight of Sara, but she wasn't there. However, he did see Sara's mother, Mrs Goodacre, and the vicar talking earnestly together at the church gate. He put his hand up to acknowledge John Smyth as he drove by them.

Later at his flat, Chris stripped his bed and made it afresh with clean linen. He could still smell Vickie's perfume on the sheets and wanted to be rid of any signs of her. He filled the washing machine and put it on the hottest wash. Down stairs once more in the workshop, he made himself a coffee then took the clamps off the chaise frame to check the joints. The glue had done it's work well and the frame was sound, with no loose parts. He put new springs into the frame, securing them with string to hold them firmly in place, then he covered the springs with a modern filler to replace the dusty horsehair that the Edwardian furniture maker had used. Finally, he covered the surface with a layer of upholsterer's Dacron to make a smooth and lump free surface. He was just stretching a layer of linen over the finished surface and tacking it down, when the shop bell announced the arrival of another visitor. He took off his apron and went into the shop to find both John Smyth and Mrs Goodacre standing in the sales area.

'Hello, what have we here?' From their serious expressions he knew something was amiss. He smiled at John and looked questioningly at Brenda Goodacre. She had never been into his shop before and had always seemed uninterested in him or in antiques. Getting no reply from her, he turned to the vicar and asked 'What can I do for you?'

'I don't know, but Brenda and I, want to ask a favour of you.'

Chris smiled at them both. 'Go ahead, ask away. If I can do anything for you I will.'

Mrs Goodacre frowned and looked at the vicar for reassurance.

John continued. 'We know you are friendly with Brenda's daughter and we want to ask you to have a word with her.'

Chris was about to correct them and tell them he may well have been friendly with Sara but that was before the confrontation with Vickie that morning. Before he could tell them, Mrs Goodacre spoke.

'I'm worried to death about my daughter. John tells me the O'Conlans and the Psychic College are dangerous. I want... '

160

The vicar interrupted her. 'I've told Brenda a little of what you saw the other night, and what we both saw in the vestry. She is worried about her daughter studying at the college...for that matter, so am I.'

Chris shrugged his shoulders helplessly. 'What am I supposed to do about it?'

Brenda spoke up again. 'You and Sara are very friendly. I know you've taken her out to dinner and I've seen you laughing together over the bar. I have spoken to her to warn her off the college courses and John has done the same, but she won't take any notice of us.' She shook her head desparingly as if she had done all she could. 'Sara's like her dad used to be. She's as stubborn as a mule when she has her mind set on something. Nothing we can say makes any difference. Please, will you speak to her. You're more her age and she might listen to you.'

Chris shrugged his shoulders again. He was equally concerned at the girl's involvement with the O'Conlans and with Dave Porter but he doubted he had any influence on her after that morning's affair. He was about to explain when he caught sight of Mrs Goodacre's pleading expression. He shook his head but decided to try and help. 'I will speak to Sara, but don't expect miracles. I don't know that she will welcome my interference in her plans, either.'

Mrs Goodacre smiled her thanks and left the shop. John Smyth, however, had detected Chris's hesitation and reluctance to help. He remained behind and questioned the dealer. 'Chris, do I sense a problem in our request?'

Chris nodded glumly. 'It's not that I don't want to help or that I don't share your concerns. I was thinking along the same lines myself.' He hesitated trying to think of the best way to explain the situation.

John asked ' Well? What's the problem?'

Chris sighed. 'Sara and I fell out this morning. She saw my ex wife here dressed only in a nightie and assumed there was something going on.'

The vicar raised his eyebrows.

'Vickie, my ex wife has been thrown out of her flat for non payment of rent. She came here and pleaded for a bed for the night as she had nowhere else to sleep last night. I let her stay and she slept in my bed while I spent an uncomfortable night down here on a clapped out chaise. Nothing happened between us, but Sara walked in just as Vickie came downstairs still dressed in her night clothes. Sara got the wrong idea and stormed out of the shop. I haven't seen her since and I don't think she will want to see me.'

John looked glumly down at his feet. 'Oh! That's very inconvenient. You were our last hope of talking some sense into Sara. She's a grown woman and free to do what she pleases. Her mother and I can't dissuade her from her involvement with the Psychic College. She's dug in her heels and refuses to listen to us.'

Chris sighed again. 'I will try and speak to her, John, but don't hold your breath.'

The vicar put his arm around Chris's shoulders and patted him on the back. 'Do your best, Chris. No one can ask any more.' He went out of the shop leaving the dealer in a quandary.

Later that evening, just after opening time at the pub, Chris went to see Sara. She was on her own and the bar was empty. At first she looked as if she would walk out on him but finally she offered to serve him.

'A pint of bitter and a word with you.' Chris said.

Sara pulled his pint and stood it in front of him at the bar. Before he could speak she said. 'This is the third time to my knowledge that you and your ex have got together. The pair of you looked very cosy together this morning. Why did you ever get divorced?'

Chris shook his head. 'Vickie was sleeping upstairs last night at my place because she has been thrown out of her flat in Stamford. She had nowhere else to go and begged me to give her a bed for the night. I slept down in the shop on a chaise and...'

Sara let him get no further with his excuses. 'You must think I'm daft! I don't believe a word of it. I gave you the benefit of the doubt last time, Chris, but this time is once too often. I don't believe you.' She threw her glass cloth down on the bar and stalked off to the kitchen.

Chris called after her. 'Sara, your mother and the vicar want you to forget your ideas of more involvement with the Psychic College. They are worried about you... and for that matter, so am I.'

Sara stopped and turned to face him. 'You, worried? You are a two timing rat! Why should I listen to you? As for my mother and the vicar, they see problems everywhere. They told me some cock and bull story about you seeing demons in the church yard. Were you drunk, Chris?'

He tried to reason with her but she ignored him and went into the kitchen leaving him alone in the bar. He had had no chance to discuss the Psychic College with her and she refused to speak to him any more.

Chris drained his glass and walked home feeling miserable and inadequate. He could understand her feelings; he himself was as upset with the situation, but he was worried about her involvement with the O'Conlans and just prayed that dowsing would be the full extent of her studies.

Back at the pub, Mrs. Goodacre had heard the exchange between her daughter and the antique dealer. She went into the kitchen to remonstrate with Sara. 'Why do you want to study this Wicca business? Surely that's just witchcraft under another name?'

'Oh mother! Wicca is the old religion that studies plants and things. It only tries to do good for people. Tanith told me she practices it and it's harmless. Why can't you be pleased I'm trying to better myself with my studies?'

'John tells me studying these things could be dangerous. It's pagan and it's not Christian.'

'He would, mother! You and your precious vicar! I'll study what I like, whatever you say.' With that threat, she stormed out of the kitchen and left her mother to manage the bar. Sara was adamant she would do as she pleased in her free time, neither her mother nor her mother's friend, the vicar, would put her off the courses she had set her heart on. As for Christopher Doughty, he could go to hell! In a defiant mood, she contacted Tanith and enrolled on the Wicca course that very morning.

## Chapter Twenty Seven

Chris Doughty eventually stopped going to his local pub. He tried once or twice soon after his break up with Sara, but she just refused to serve him and walked away when he tried to talk to her. Vickie, the cause of all the grief, lost her business in Stamford and moved away from the area so he had no further problems with her. The clock he had taken from Vickie in lieu of payment for his work, was put into an antique auction and sold for enough money to cover his outlay on the restoration of it. His business in Barrowick gradually picked up as his regular customers found him and returned to do deals with him. Chris was pleased with the way the antique shop progressed that summer but he still missed his daily contact with Sara.

At one of the farm auctions in rural Lincolnshire, Chris bought a portfolio of old prints. They were in a bad state but he knew they dated from the early 1800's and were on hand laid paper. Some of them had frayed edges. Many were intact but they were very discoloured. He knew enough about prints to realise this set were all produced from copper engravings. The prints all bore the imprint of the copper plates where the paper had been pressed against the metal in a printing press and they all had the same watermark from the tray where the paper pulp was laid in the paper production. The poor state of the prints ensured he got them very cheaply; in fact he bought them with his low maiden bid.

Chris was not familiar with the restoration of paper antiques, like maps and prints, as his real expertise was in working with wood, but he was a quick learner and willing to try anything A few visits to the library and further research online, soon convinced him he could undertake that sort of work. The prints he had bought, were badly foxed and not very valuable in their present state, so he had little to lose and much to gain by learning to treat and conserve them himself.

The foxing of paper is a condition caused by damp. It is the result of a fungal infection that attacks the old paper and glue. The results of this problem are there for all to see; brown rust marks discolour the paper and lower its value. Old books, maps, prints and other paper antiques are very prone to the problem. Chris chose the worst one of the foxed prints to experiment on and learn how to bleach out the brown marks. He managed to buy some chloride of lime and some hydrochloric acid solution online, then he found two plastic trays large enough to hold a sheet of glass, which was slightly larger than the biggest print.

In his workshop he dissolved the chloride of lime in soft water and filled the tray with the bleaching solution. He dampened the print by spraying it with soft water as it lay on the glass sheet.

Paper loses all its strength when wet, so the glass support was essential to stop it tearing and turning to pulp under its own weight. He immersed the glass sheet bearing the print, in the chloride solution and waited for the brown fungal marks to fade. Slowly the fox marks vanished before his eyes. When he was satisfied all the offending marks had gone, he transferred the glass and its paper covering to a bath of dilute hydrochloric acid to halt the bleaching process. After a few minutes in the stop bath, he plunged the glass and its paper into a bath of clean soft water to remove all traces of the chemicals.

He was pleased with the appearance of the bird print after all that treatment. The initial experiment had been on a badly damaged picture of a Peregrine Falcon on its nest. He knew that birds of prey were always a favoured subject with serious collectors of wildlife pictures. There was something majestic about a falcon that seemed to have a universal appeal to bird watchers and print collectors alike. The Peregrine picture was allowed to dry on the glass sheet until it pealed off of its own accord. The paper was a bit uneven when it had dried, but a careful ironing between two sheets of blotting paper produced a flat, pristine print, which would grace any collection.

Chris made himself a coffee and laid the finished print on a table in his front shop, where the daylight from the large display window helped him asses it properly. As that had been the worst of his portfolio of prints, he was thrilled with the result, which promised a good return on his time and his investment. Nicely framed bird prints from the early part of the 19th century, could sell for as much as £200 each, depending on the subject and the frame. He was just admiring his work and finishing his coffee before he put another damaged print through the bleaching process, when the shop bell rang announcing a customer. He turned to see who had entered the shop.

'Hello. Nice to see you again.' It was the Reverend Smyth, vicar of the local church, on one of his regular calls.

John Smyth joined the dealer at the table and saw the Peregrine print. 'That's nice, Christopher. I'd give that room on my wall when it's mounted and framed. I have always fancied a print of a Peregrine falcon'

Chris smiled with satisfaction. The vicar was a knowledgeable collector of antiques and had a good eye for quality. 'I didn't know you collected bird prints, John'

'I don't, but I do a bit of bird watching at Rutland Water and that print has taken my fancy. Tell me, do you come by many like that?'

The dealer smiled. The vicar's reaction was very welcome. 'I have a few more but they all need to be restored. When I have cleaned and framed them you are welcome to see them all.'

John stroked his chin thoughtfully. 'You know, that sort of print, in the right frame, would sell well at the Rutland Water Bird Fair. Why don't you stand this August and try to sell them. I'm sure you might sell a few bits of antique furniture as well. It is a prestigious event. You would be seen by thousands of people and it could do your business a lot of good.'

Chris smiled. 'You sound very knowledgeable about retail business. How come you know so much about it?'

It was the vicar's turn to smile. 'You know, I wasn't born a vicar. I used to be a buyer for a top London store before I took to the cloth. You don't forget all you've learned just because you become a priest.'

Chris laughed at this but he knew the old man was talking sense. If he could stand the Bird Fair and sell his stock, it would do him a lot of good and get him an entirely new clientele. 'It's a pity you didn't mention that idea before. I bet you need to book a stall at the fair well in advance.'

John stroked his chin again. 'I believe you do, and it's probably far too late for this year. However, I have a few contacts in this area and one of them is a book seller who's standing this year's fair. He deals only in books but he may have room for one or two good quality prints on his stand. Let me use your phone. I'll check if he is amenable to the idea. That's if you would like to come to some arrangement with him.'

Chris made an instant decision. Of course he'd like to exhibit there. He was local, he would have enough bird prints to show once he had cleaned and restored them. What could be better? It would give him the incentive to clean and frame the whole collection.

The vicar made his call and arrangements were made for Chris to take a couple of the framed prints to show the book dealer. Now he had to work hard on the remaining prints to make them ready for the August fair. He thanked the vicar for his help and set to work with renewed urgency, restoring and framing the rest of the soiled bird prints.

Many months before he'd bought the prints, Chris had bought a load of old frames from the Oakham auction room and had spent many

166

hours restoring them. Whenever he had time on his hands and no business, he had set to work on one of those picture frames. Some of them were gilt, swept frames, the kind used for oil paintings but many of them were plain wood or veneered examples. He had several Oak frames and a few Burr Walnut ones. Those would be ideal for displaying his prints. A few of them had sold but the majority were still stored up in his flat waiting for him to find a use for them. Now he knew what to do with them.

As each bird print was restored, he cut a mount for it and set it in one of the restored frames. One or two of them, which were more frayed, he mounted in oval mounts to hide the damaged edges. At the end of all his work he had twenty good looking bird prints. Many of them were of foreign birds like Parakeets and Parrots but among the birds of prey were three prints of Ospreys. As the Osprey had nested at Rutland Water in recent years and they had become synonymous with the lake, he knew they would cause a stir at the Bird Fair and attract punters to the book stall. He decided to save those especially for the occasion.

Weeks slipped by. Chris kept himself busy and rarely caught sight of Sara. When he felt like a meal out, he drove into Oakham and ate at one of the pubs in the town. Occasionally he would catch a glimpse of the girl as she walked up Main Street, but he avoided contact with her and she never returned to his shop. His ex wife had done a thorough job alienating him from his friend. August came all too quickly and the preparations for the Bird Fair took up more and more of his time.

The Rutland Water Bird Fair is a prestigious event, which attracts thousands of visitors from all over the world. If Chris could build a good reputation there, he knew it would help his business in the future.

The Reverend Smyth called every few weeks, when he came to check on the Barrowick church. He kept an eye on the progress of the bird prints and admired each one as it was framed and stored. On one of his visits he asked Chris about Sara.

'Do you see much of Sara Goodacre these days?'

'No,' The dealer shook his head.

'I understand from Brenda Goodacre, you and Sara were quite good friends at one time.'

Chris nodded agreement but kept his gaze down and carried on working on a picture frame.

John continued. 'It's a pity you aren't still friendly with her. Her mother and I are still very worried about her. She seems to have become very involved with the Psychic College. We don't understand why she would want to study Wicca as she was brought up in a good Christian household. Still, if she wont listen to Brenda, I doubt anyone else could influence her.'

Chris frowned. He was also worried about the girl but she had told him, in no uncertain manner, that what she did in her free time was non of his business. He turned to the vicar. 'She wont listen to anything I have to say, but I do share her mother's fears for her. From what I have seen of the Psychic College, no good will come of studying there.'

John shrugged his shoulders; there was no use pursuing the subject if Chris and the girl weren't friendly any more. That was the end of the matter.

When the vicar had left his shop, Chris paused from his work and made another coffee. He deeply regretted his split from Sara and was worried about her, but he felt there was little he could do about it. She had made her feelings eminently clear to him.

During August, the Rutland Water Bird Fair was held. It was a large event, one of the largest of its type in Europe. The twitching fraternity and the businesses dependent on them, turned out in force. Chris closed his shop for a few hours and went to view the marquees at the fair.

The antique bird prints caused a stir when they were put on display at the back of the book dealer's pitch. People stopped at the stall and admired the Osprey prints then took the time to look at the books. Soon the pictures were selling and the dealer was selling more book. He asked Chris if he had any more of his prints to sell.

Sara's mother visited the fair along with John Smyth. They made a beeline for Chris when she saw him talking to the book dealer.

'So, you took my advice and you seem to be doing well.' The vicar beamed at Chris.

'You were right, John. This is certainly the place to sell bird prints.'

John looked over the stock that was left and saw the Peregrine Falcon he had admired at the shop. 'I see you still have my favourite. How much are you asking for it?'

Chris hesitated. If it hadn' t been for John's insistence he would never have contemplated standing the fair. He made a snap decision. 'It's £200 but you can have it for the price of the frame.'

John grinned but shook his head. 'I know you must be paying commission to sell here, Chris. I wont ask for any favours from you. I will take the Peregrine and pay you the £200 for it.' He reached up and unhooked the print from the wall then immediately wrote out a cheque for it.

Chris wrapped the picture up in bubble wrap and handed it to his friend.

Brenda Goodacre had stood by watching the transaction now she spoke to the dealer. 'You know, you and my daughter used to hit it off rather well. Is there nothing we can do to get you two together again?'

Chris shrugged his shoulders. 'Sara decided to end our friendship. I wouldn't dream of causing her any problems so I've stayed away from your place. Unless she relents I don't see what I can do.'

Mrs Goodacre shook her head in despair and walked away from the stall. John thanked Chris for the print and hurried after her.

Chris considered the landlady's comments. She knew he was divorced and that must have gone against her Christian principles but she was still hoping he would make it up with her daughter. Things must be very fraught in their relationship for Mrs Goodacre to contemplate him as a boyfriend for Sara. It was a measure of how worried she must be.

After lunch, on the first day of the event, Chris toured the whole fair. He had a look around the other marquees to see what else was on offer there. It was very busy. The morning wildlife lectures had finished and the afternoon sessions, with a couple of well known TV presenters, had not yet got underway. The book stall sold several more of his prints and took quite a bit of money for him. When he returned he was thrilled with his takings.

'If you fancy a look around the fair or you want to get some food , I will mind the stall for you,' he told the book dealer.

The book stall owner was ready to stretch his legs, he jumped at Chris's offer. While he was manning the stall, Chris was surprised to see Tanith O'Conlan was mingling with the punters and handing out leaflets advertising the Psychic College. She stopped at the book stall in front of the dealer who was busy totting up his takings from the bird prints. At first she didn't recognise him with his head down and approached him to hand him a leaflet and to chat about the college. When he looked up and smiled at her, her expression changed to a frown.

Chris spoke first. 'Hello. I am surprised to see you here. Tanith isn't it?'

She nodded.

The dealer continued. 'I would hardly think a bird fair was the place to advertise your sort of courses. But then, I'm selling antiques prints here so maybe you'll do well. Have you had much interest?'

She was about to answer when Francis O'Conlan arrived on the scene. She stepped away to join her husband. A whispered conversation took place between them, with a few furtive glances towards Chris. Finally she walked a little further on and the professor came and spoke to Chris.

'Hello again. It seems most of the local businesses are here this year.' He hesitated then changed the subject abruptly. 'Tanith tells me you read the Tarot cards. Where did you study them?'

Chris laughed out loud. 'No, not me. I just make it up as I go along.'

O'Conlan smiled, but it was clear from his expression he didn't believe Chris's denial.

The book dealer returned to his stall as the two men were speaking. Chris decided he'd seen enough of the O'Conlans. He made an excuse and moved to the next display, which was advertising Mediterranean bird watching holidays, but he couldn't help noticing Francis and Tanith were still watching him closely as he walked away from them.

## Chapter Twenty Eight

Weeks drifted into months and the summer passed by in Barrowick. Chris saw Sara occasionally as he walked the village but they never spoke to each other. At the end of October, just after the clocks were put back, the dealer was working in the evening in his shop when the Reverend Smyth called to see him.

'John. Nice to see you again.'

The vicar looked around the shop and admired one or two old oak carved pieces that Chris had in stock.

'You interested?' Chris asked hopefully.

'Not really. I dropped in to see how you were. I also made a point of coming to Barrowick this evening because it's the 31st of October, All Hallows Eve.'

Chris shrugged his shoulders and smiled. All Hallows Eve sounded like some church festival, but he wasn't familiar with it.

'It's All Hallows Eve, Chris. You are probably more familiar with it as Halloween.'

'Ah! The night the kids light candles in pumpkins and frighten themselves with ghost stories.'

'Actually it is a church festival. Tomorrow is All saints Day and the evening before used to be a night for prayer and vigil.'

'Didn't the festival start in pre Christian times?' Chris was trying to recall all he'd read about it.

'Yes, some say it did. It was called Samhain by our Celtic forebears. It was really just an end of summer festival, an excuse to have a feast, but some folk think the veil between the living and the dead is at its thinnest and the spirits of their ancestors walk abroad. It's only superstition of course.'

'So why are you really here?'

'Halloween has been taken over by witches since the middle ages. If you believe the old stories, tonight you will see crones on broomsticks crossing the night sky.'

Chris laughed and ushered the vicar through to his workshop where he switched on the kettle to make some coffee.

John continued. 'To be serious, Chris, after what happened here on St John's Eve I thought it wise to check on the village tonight. Halloween is the main witchcraft festival for modern witches and warlocks. It will be interesting to see what occurs here after dark.'

Chris nodded; he remembered the previous problems they had with the Psychic College and the terrifying atmosphere in the church. The two friends drank their coffee and stood in amiable silence.

Finally, John put his empty coffee cup down. 'I'm going to have a beer at the local pub. Come with me.'

Chris shook his head.

'I know you haven't set foot in the place lately, but come on Chris. You needn't speak to Sara and we can sit at a table by the door.'

The dealer had to admit he missed his drink at his local after work. He occasionally drove into Oakham to a pub there but it wasn't always convenient, and he was wary of drinking and driving home. He relented, washed his hands and put on his jacket. 'Ok John. Just this once and just for you.'

The two men walked the length of the village to the Barrowick Arms and passed by more and more cars being parked along the village street.

'This looks familiar, Chris. What does it remind you of?'

Chris nodded, tight lipped and serious, as a couple drew up in a large expensive car, got out and took two small cases from the boot, then they walked across the road and went into the Psychic College grounds.

John continued. 'It looks as if we may have a repeat performance tonight. I'm glad I came.'

The two friends went into the pub where the vicar ordered two beers and took them to a table near the door. Chris looked around the room and was surprised to see Sara wasn't serving. Her cousin, the lad who had helped when the psychic night was held, was busy behind the bar helping Mrs Goodacre serve the punters. When the vicar had sat down next to Chris she came over to speak to them.

John smiled at the landlady. and asked her. 'Sara not on duty tonight?'

Brenda shook her head and sat down heavily between the two men. 'Sara has been gone all afternoon. She went across the road earlier for her class and was due back here at tea time, but she's not come home.'

Chris could tell the woman was worried from her serious expression. John patted her hand and tried to reassure her. 'I'm sure Sara is fine. Maybe she stayed on at the college to help prepare for the evenings entertainment.'

Mrs Goodacre queried this. 'What entertainment? She never mentioned it to me.'

172

'There appears to be something on at the college. There are cars parked all along Main Street and people going in there. Maybe she's just giving them a hand.'

Brenda returned to the bar but she didn't look convinced by the vicar's suggestion.

When they had finished their drinks and left the pub, the vicar went across to the church, while Chris walked home to his shop and went up to his flat. As the evening wore on, the village quietened down. No more cars arrived and nothing seemed to be happening at the college. Chris sat in his flat, reading. He kept breaking off from studying his clock books to think about Sara. Although she had made it very obvious she would have nothing more to do with him, he felt a bit uneasy when he considered the trouble she may be in. He reminded himself, she was no longer his concern, and in some ways he was pleased about that; his experience with Vickie had made him very wary of getting too close to another woman. He was still hurting from the divorce and didn't need another experience like that. He placed his book on the table and sat considering his real feelings towards Sara Goodacre.

Chris got up from his chair and walked to the French windows. He opened them wide and stepped out onto the balcony to look over the village street. In the dark he could just make out that Main Street was lined with car, many of them large expensive models. There was no sign of activity at the vicarage but lights were burning in most of the rooms. On impulse he decided to walk down to the pub to see if Sara had returned home. If she was still missing he would take the path alongside the reservoir and pass by the rear of the vicarage grounds to see at closer quarters what was happening there.

At the Barrowick Arms, Mrs Goodacre was still waiting for her daughter to return. 'I'm worried Mr. Doughty. It's not like Sara to stay away for so long and not let me know what she's doing.'

Chris nodded sympathetically. 'I'm sure there's a simple explanation. She'll be home soon enough. I wouldn't worry if I were you.' He reassured Sara's mother but he did not feel that confident himself. There was a lingering doubt in his mind and a very uneasy feeling about Sara and the people she had joined. He left the pub and walked down the track to the water's edge and the path that passed behind the vicarage.

At the gate into the vicarage grounds, Chris hesitated and stopped to look and listen. There seems to be nothing happening in the barn or at the vicarage. All those people who had arrived in those cars must be

173

somewhere, but where? He jumped over the locked gate and walked quietly up the yard to the barn. At the new barn door he stopped and listened intently. There was no sound and the building was in darkness. He tried the door and found it unlocked.

Curious about the barn, now it had been renovated, Chris peered around the door into the building. He was surprised at what he saw there. In the gloom at the far end of the building, just in front of the raised area that reminded him of an old minstrel gallery, was what appeared to be a raised dais with a cloth covered table set on it. The rest of the room was bare; there were no chairs or other furniture. It certainly wasn't like any lecture room he had ever seen. He revised his ideas about the use the barn would serve for the new college. As his eyes became accustomed to the poor light he spotted a familiar looking object on the balcony overlooking the raised table. He stepped into the empty barn and walked quietly to the far end of the room to get a closer look. He was amazed to find it was the stone goddess from the nearby churchyard. It was stood on the very edge of the balcony, directly overlooking the dais and table. The large sandstone figure, which must have weighed a lot, appeared to be secured by a rope around its neck and tied to the rails of the balcony. How they had managed to move it and get it lifted into that position was a mystery as it was so very heavy. But they had succeeded in moving it, even though they had no right to take the stone statue from the churchyard.

Chris stopped immediately in front of the dais and looked up at the sandstone Shelagh. Then he looked down at the floor at his feet and noticed the dais was surrounded by a painted circle. There were several unusual symbols painted on the circumference of the circle. He knelt down to look more closely and realised some of the symbols resembled ones he had seen on the blade of the Athame when he'd inspected it at his shop. It appeared the table was some kind of altar and the stone figure was set above it to be used in some sort of ceremony. John had been right to suspect there could be trouble in the village that night.

Chris stood for some minutes taking in the scene and trying to understand it. He was about to walk back to the main door and leave the barn, when he heard voices. From the approaching sounds, he realised there were several people coming to the building, and he didn't want to be found there. He looked around for a way to escape but could see only one way out of his dilemma. Hiding on the balcony was his only chance of avoiding detection. He ran up the wooden steps to the balcony above the altar and hid behind the stone goddess

174

Just in time, Chris managed to get in the shadow of the ancient Shelagh. The lights came on and a procession of people, walking in pairs, proceeded into the barn from the new doorway. Chris peered down from his hiding place and took in the strange scene. Each of the participants wore a cloak and a mask. As their legs were bare it was impossible to know if they had anything else on underneath. The masks were like Venetian carnival masks, similar to the one he had seen in the pub at the time of the previous gathering on St John's Eve. The cloaks were of velvet or some similar soft and expensive material, and were made in various colours. From the way they walked and their general demeanor, he guessed each pair was a man accompanying a woman. At the head of the group was the tall figure of a man in a crimson mask and cloak, walking with his arms around a girl, helping her along as if she was having some difficulty walking. Chris's heart missed a beat. It was unmistakably Francis O'Conlan and the girl he was supporting was Sara!

Chris dodged behind the stone figure and sat with his back to it. Once the procession had come into the barn, the main lights were turned off and small lanterns, held by the participants, lit up the area below him. It all looked very theatrical and mysterious.

Around the circle on the floor, several large bowls of incense were lit, their pungent smoke spiralled up into the roof of the building. Chris sniffed cautiously at the aromatic smoke, wondering if it was from some hallucinatory drug. The masked figures looked very spooky in the dark with only the faint glow of the lanterns to illuminate the scene. From below, in the barn, he heard Dr O'Conlan addressing the gathering and realised the ceremony had started. The doctor's voice rang out loud and clear as he addressed his flock. They answered him with well rehearsed responses. It reminded Chris of a church congregation when the worshippers and the priest were reciting the creed together. The voices grew louder and sounded more enthusiastic. Some of the people started dancing, others went into close clinches and hugged each other.

Chris detected a subtle change in the atmosphere as the participants grew more rowdy. He peered down to see what was happening and saw Francis O'Conlan standing just below him, facing the gathering. Standing beside the professor was his wife, dressed in a golden robe with a red pentagram embroidered on the front of it. She was wearing a gold face mask, which completely covered her face, but Chris recognised Tanith by her red hair, which tumbled down her back.

175

When Chris looked down, he became aware of the naked body of a girl, laying prone on the altar. Chris peered through the gloom at the nude figure and was shocked to see it was Sara! He looked closer and realised she seemed to be in a daze; her eyes were glazed and staring up towards the ceiling; she seemed totally unaware of her surroundings and the tumult going on around her. The congregation crowded forward to surround the altar; all eyes were on the naked girl. Chris sat back and tried to make sense of what he was witnessing. Smoke from the incense bowls swirled around him as the warm fumes rose into the roof space, concentrating there. From below him the chorus of voices grew louder, the calls and responses sounded more and more frantic. Things were getting out of hand and the ceremony seemed to be heading for some kind of climax.

## Chapter Twenty Nine

When he had time to absorb what was happening in the barn, Chris was sure that Sara was not a willing participant in the scene below him. She seemed oblivious to her predicament and lay naked on her back on the altar as if she was in some kind of trance. She was not moving at all nor was she calling out the responses as all the other people were. He was sure she must have been drugged to take part in the ceremony and be so detached from it. What could he do about it? He was completely outnumbered by the group below him. He searched in his pocket for his mobile phone and sent an urgent text message to John Smyth. The vicar was his only hope, the only person he could contact who would immediately understand the urgency of the situation. He carefully spelled out his message in the shadow of the stone goddess.

'HELP. SARA BLACK MASS. BARN. POLICE'

Chris sent that cry for help and prayed the vicar got his call before it was too late. Below him in the barn, the scene was growing ever more frantic. Voices were raised, people were throwing off their cloaks and dancing naked around the altar, their inhibitions completely lost. Bare breasts and torsos, glistening with sweat, reflected the light from the lanterns they held. He guessed, from their frenzied actions, they must have taken some kind of drug before the ceremony.

Throughout the whole of this, Sara lay unmoving. It was as if she was sound asleep but with her eyes wide open, staring up into the darkness of the barn roof and oblivious to her surroundings. Chris searched the group and thought he recognised a few of the participants. Apart from O'Conlan and his wife, he was sure he saw Dave Porter and the two women he had seen previously in the Barrowick Arms on St John's Eve. Suddenly, his attention was drawn to a tall thick set man near the back of the crowd. He recognised the man as DC Phillips. His previous suspicions about the detective had been right all along.

As the people below him became more abandoned, Chris knew he would have to act to stop the proceedings. He couldn't let anything serious happen to Sara, who seemed completely unaware of the danger she was in. Whatever ceremony was being celebrated that evening, be it a Black Mass or some other witchraft gathering, he was sure she was not a willing participant. He considered how he might create a diversion and halt the proceedings. He knew if he shouted out and showed himself at the edge of the balcony, it would temporarily halt the proceedings but the diversion would be only temporary and he would be seen by the crowd below. He would be liable to attack, but such an action would buy him and Sara some valuable time. He crept slowly towards the stone goddess, stopping every few steps to try and clear his head as the fumes from the smoking bowls were beginning to have an effect on him. Below him, in the hall, the chorus of voices grew ever louder and more urgent.

As Chris watched the scene and considered his options he saw Francis O'Conlan take up a vessel in his hands. He recognised at once it was the bronze chalice he had bought from Steve Mattock. It was empty, there was no wine in it. The doctor held the chalice aloft for all to see and shouted words in a language Chris couldn't understand. The congregation answered with a roar; their voices growing hoarse from shouting. All the time this was going on, Sara lay perfectly still, seemingly unconscious of her surroundings. O'Conlan placed the chalice on the altar between the girl's feet. Suddenly the room went silent. Tanith, produced the bronze Athame from under her robe and handed it to her husband. He held the bronze dagger up high for all to see. There was a roar of approval from the crowd.

Chris was shocked. Surely they weren't going to sacrifice Sara? He watched in horror as Francis O'Conlan raised the dagger even higher and stepped back to show everyone what he was doing. Chris hesitated no longer. He stepped forward hoping to stop the ceremony but the fumes from the bowls finally affected him. His head swam, he lost consciousness and stumbled helplessly against the stone figure of the Goddess.

The ancient figure rocked and slowly began to tilt forward, putting an intolerable strain on the rope tethering it. With a resounding crack, the rope snapped and the heavy stone block fell forward. Chris fell back unconscious onto the wooden platform, oblivious to the accident.

In the barn, time stood still. The stone column slowly overbalanced and plummeted to the ground gaining speed and momentum as it fell. The massive figure seemed to fall in slow motion and turned in its descent. It landed on top of the man who was standing directly in its path. With a sickening crunch the heavy statue cracked Francis O'Conlan's skull and pushed him to the ground. The congregation stopped their frantic shouting and stared in disbelief at the spectacle. It took them several seconds to realise what had happened.

Stunned by the incident, the Black Mass celebrants milled around in the dark, their lanterns bobbing up and down. Suddenly, someone threw a switched and the barn was flooded with bright light. Naked men and women hurriedly picked up their cloaks to cover their bodies. Tanith, screamed her husband's name and fell onto her knees beside him trying to roll the sandstone block off of his motionless body. Two of the men nearest to the dais, rushed to her aid and rolled the heavy stone off her husband. Inevitably, someone looked up to where the statue had stood and spotted Chris, lying unconscious on the balcony above them. The crowd was alerted to the intruder. A shout went up from a dozen throats and several of the congregation pointed at Chris. While this was happening, Tanith was still trying to revive the lifeless body of her husband. She cried out his name and cradled his body close to her.

Some of the men in the group started to run towards the wooden steps leading up to the balcony, shouting and shaking their fists. Chris was in real danger, but he was oblivious to their threats; he had lost consciousness, poisoned by the fumes that had concentrated in the roof space.

Dave Porter recognised the inert figure and shouted at him. 'You're outnumbered Doughty. We will get you. You're dead meat this time.'

Several men rushed up the wooden steps to where Chris lay drugged and helpless. They lifted him up, intending to throw him off the balcony onto the stone floor below them.

Just as the dealer was being lifted into the air, there was a loud splintering sound. The barn door was forced open. Suddenly, dozens of uniformed police rushed into the area. The naked men who had attacked Chris, stopped in their murderous act, dropped him onto the balcony and stood sheepishly, in full view of the police officers below them. The men and women below them in the barn screamed and tried to escape but their escape was cut off. They were rounded up and allowed to cover their nakedness with the discarded cloaks.

The Reverend John Smyth, dressed in his full church regalia, had immediately followed the police into the barn, bearing a large silver cross before him and reciting Christian prayers in a loud voice. It was like a scene from some apocalyptic film.

When the door was broken down, fresh air entered the building and Chris slowly regained consciousness. He dragged himself to the edge of the balcony and saw Sara, still laying on the altar below him, oblivious to the chaos around her. He made his way falteringly down the steps and covered her naked body with one of the discarded cloaks. The vicar came over to his side and looked down at the body of Dr O'Conlan. He turned to

179

Chris. 'Are you alright, Chris. You look awful.'

'I must have fainted from the fumes, but I'm OK now. What about him?' He pointed to O'Conlan.

John shook his head. 'If you live by such evil you may perish by it. Francis O'Conlan was a wicked man, but I will pray for his soul.'

Tanith broke into loud sobs and stared up at Chris with wild eyes. She pointed at him and shouted. 'You predicted this! You are the cause of all this!'

Chris ignored her rantings and turned to the vicar. 'We must get Sara to a doctor. I'm sure she's been drugged. She hasn't moved during this whole ceremony. I suppose we ought to get a doctor to him as well.' He pointed to O'Conlan who lay with his head in a pool of blood beside the stone goddess.

The vicar shook his head. 'I think he's beyond our help. I'm sure he's already dead, but I think you ought to see a doctor as well. You must have breathed in too much of that drugged incense. You were unconscious when we broke into here.'

# Chapter Thirty

After Chris was seen at the hospital, he spent the remainder of the night with the police in Leicester, explaining all he had witnessed. His story was corroborated by their forensic examination, which confirmed the rope holding the sandstone goddess had snapped under the weight of the stone block and Francis O'Conlan's death had been accidental. The members of the witchcraft coven were all rounded up and charged with kidnapping and drugging Sara. The news of the ceremony and the death of Dr Francis O'Conlan was broadcast on all the national TV news bulletins.

Early next morning as Chris was leaving the police station he came face to face with DC Phillips who was handcuffed and being moved to another cell. The dealer couldn't resist a wry smile as they passed each other in the corridor. He turned to the sergeant on duty. 'That detective knows a lot more about other crimes that the group may have committed. Ask him about the recent suspicious death of Steve Mattock in Barrowick.'

The sergeant raised his eyebrows. 'I think we'd better come and get a statement from you Mr Doughty in the next day or so. There's no rush. We have enough work on our hands for now, questioning this lot. We'll be in touch.'

In the small hours of the morning, Steve took a taxi home and went straight to bed, exhausted by the night's events. He knew Sara had been taken to hospital for observation, where she would be well looked after. He also knew that John Smyth would have spoken to Sara's mother, reassuring her that her daughter was going to be fine and explaining what had happened. He fell asleep as soon as his head hit the pillow and did not wake up until later that afternoon. The only lasting effect he had from the fumes in the barn, was a splitting headache, which he treated with a strong coffee and a couple of pain killers.

When he was properly awake and recovered, Chris decided to take the day off and leave the shop closed. He looked in the mirror in the bathroom and saw his sad reflection; he had a badly bruised face and a split lip, the results of his fall and the manhandling he had suffered the previous night. His cheek was so sore, he decided not to shave that day, to save himself further discomfort. He dressed leisurely and cooked a full fried breakfast while he listened to Radio Rutland reporting the events of the previous night in their local news bulletin. The bald facts that the police had raided a gathering in a barn in the village of Barrowick and one man had died  during the event, seemed all too brief to account for what he had experienced on  that All Hallow's Eve. He had almost finished eating when someone knocked loudly and insistently on the shop door.

Chris was in two minds whether to answer the caller; it was probably only a punter wanting to look around the shop, but then again it could be the police wanting an interview. He decided to go downstairs and see who wanted him.

The Reverend Smyth stood on the pavement outside the shop, a broad smile on his face. 'Can I come in, Chris? I left it late before I called as I guessed you'd be shattered after last night.'

Chris let the vicar into the shop and locked the door behind him. 'Come up to the flat, John. I have just had my breakfast and was going to make myself another coffee.'

Up in the flat the two men sat opposite to each other and sipped their coffees. Finally, John put down his cup and grinned at Chris. 'You did a very brave thing last night. I shudder to think what would have happened to Sara if the Black Mass had gone on uninterrupted. '

Chris shook his head. 'I shudder to think what would have happened to both Sara and myself if you hadn't arrived with the police when you did.'

The vicar held up his hand in protest. 'That was only because of your phone message. I was praying in the church when my mobile rang. I had been hoping for some sort of sign telling me what to do.' He leaned forward and looked concerned. 'When I came into the barn last night you were being manhandled and about to be thrown off that balcony.  I see you have facial injuries. Are you alright?'

Chris grinned 'I'm fine, but what's the news about Sara?'

'She's also fine. She was heavily sedated but the effects are gradually wearing off. The hospital are keeping her in for observation for a few days but her mother tells me they've identified the drug and don't expect her to suffer any permanent damage.'

Chris nodded. 'Good.'

'Mrs Goodacre will probably come up to thank you after I call and tell her you are OK. Is that alright with you?'

Chris shook his head. 'She's no need to bother. Tell her I'll probably go down for a pint later this evening and I'll see her then.' He drank the last of his coffee and changed the subject .  'Tell me, what about the stone goddess?   Is it badly damaged from the fall? It's a shame such an antiquity can survive thousands of years just to be trashed in this modern age.'

John nodded agreement. 'There was some damage to one of the corners at the base of the stone but really it stood up to the impact very well. I am getting a local builder to move it back into the churchyard once the police have finished with it. We'll get it cleaned up; there are blood stains on it now as well as the lichens and moss. Let's hope it stays in the curchyard undisturbed for another five thousand years.'

'Francis O'Connel? What about him?'

'He died instantly. They have moved the body to the morgue and there will be a post mortem, but I would think the result is a foregone conclusion. I will pray for his soul. It was a bad day for this village when that man moved here. Let's hope any new owners of the vicarage are normal, ordinary people.'

'And Tanith? She seems to be blaming me for her husband's death.'

'Yes, that's a mystery. What did happen between you two?'

Chris put down his mug and explained. 'She read the Tarot for me at the psychic night they held at the local pub. I wasn't interested, but Sara insisted I had a go as she had a spare free session. Tanith read my cards and I gave her an alternative reading. I hadn't a clue what it was all about and was only messing about, but she took umbrage at it.'

'Curiouser and curiouser. Can you recall the reading?'

Chris furrowed his brow as he tried to remember the cards. 'There was the Fool. I do recall that because she said that was me! Then she turned up the Tower, then the Magician, then the card with the skeleton on it; Death, I believe it was called. I can't remember exactly what she said next except that I was the Fool and the Tower showed I was the bringer of change.'

The vicar frowned and asked Chris to continue.

'I asked her if the Death card meant she could see my death coming but she shook her head and said it only meant change or new beginnings. Anyway, I said the Magician was nearer the Death card than the Fool, so it must apply to him.' Chris shrugged his shoulders, that was all he could recall and he didn't understand what the fuss was about.

'What happened next?'

'Tanith seemed upset by my interpretation. She stopped the reading rather abruptly and went to the ladies.'

'Right. Now I understand. To someone like Tanith, who obviously believes in the Tarot's ability to predict the future, you had just predicted the death of the magician. To her mind that magician was her husband. She regarded him as a Magus; that's a high ranking magician in the old meaning of the word.'

Chris was shocked. 'Oh! I didn't understand that.' He stroked his chin thoughfully then continued. 'When you think about it, that's exactly what has happened. I was involved, things did change drastically and her husband is dead. How strange.'

John put his cup down and got up to leave. 'I must be off. Church duties call. Do look after yourself Chris. If you need any counselling over this affair don't hesitate to ring me.' He tipped his coffee dregs into the kitchen sink and was about to leave when he remembered something else he needed to say. 'You may not believe the idea that someone could be a Sensitive, but from what I've seen and heard of you, I believe you are one. I hesitate to use the word psychic, but I suppose some would call it that. Think about it Chris, those strange feelings with the chalice and your Tarot prediction. There seems to be something unusual going on with you. There are more things in heaven and earth than we are permitted to understand.'

Chris just shook his head and laughed.

## Chapter Thirty One

Tanith O'Conlan left the vicarage two days after her husband's death. The place was emptied almost immediately and was put back on the market. The estate agent removed the Psychic College sign and erected a new 'For Sale' notice. The village was stunned at the things that had occurred in their midst without them realising it was happening. The affair would be the talk of the pub bar for a long time to come. Sara eventually was allowed home from hospital but she was weak from her ordeal and the lingering effects of the strong drugs she had been given. Her mother insisted she go straight to bed and rest until she was fully recovered. Chris was not sure how the girl felt about their relationship as they had parted on such bad terms so he did not visit her, but waited patiently for her to make the first move. He was busy French polishing a small tripod table when the telephone rang in his shop.

'Barrowick antiques. Can I help you'

'Mr Doughty? This is the estate agents who are handling the sale of the old Barrowick vicarage. I believe you handled the clearance of the property for the previous owners?'

'Yes. Why?'

'We need to completely clear the place. The late owner's wife left in a hurry and there are some oddments still in there. We've been told to get rid of them. Being in the village and close at hand, we thought of you. Can you help us?'

Chris considered the request. He wasn't looking forward to going into the barn again but it was business he could ill afford to turn down. 'OK. When do you want it done?'

'As soon as possible. You'll understand when I tell you I have a client already interested in the vicarage, but he has heard about the recent goings on there and is reluctant to inspect the place. I need to be sure there is nothing left that would remind anyone of the last owners. The police tell us they are done now so we can get it cleared.'

Chris understood the urgency. He checked his watch. 'OK. I'll get onto it straight away. Can you meet me there in an hour with the keys?' He had nothing pressing to do that day at the shop and wanted the job over as soon as possible. Later that morning he picked up the keys from a young lady who'd been sent by the estate agent.

'Hi.' She greeted him at the vicarage front door, unlocked the house and went in. Chris followed her, not sure what he expected to find inside.

'Aren't you the man who saved that girl's life from the Witches? You must be very brave.' The girl looked admiringly at Chris.

He shook his head and denied the suggestion. 'It's all been exaggerated by the press and the TV news. It was nothing.'

She seemed disappointed at his reticence and handed him the keys. 'Here. When you've done, lock up and push them back through the letterbox. We have a spare set at the office.' She turned and left Chris inspecting the mess that Tanith had left behind when she and her staff vacated the vicarage in a great hurry.

There were hundreds of papers and folders thrown onto the floor in several of the downstairs rooms. The kitchen was the worst room with dirty pots and pans abandoned in the sink and a fridge full of rotting food and sour milk. The cupboards, which he opened one by one, still had tins of food in them and several half empty boxes of cereals and other foodstuffs. Upstairs, Chris found the bedrooms were mainly empty but the master bedroom had split pillows and feathers strewn all over the carpet. It was painfully obvious they had left in a great hurry and had not bothered to take any care about it. He could understand Tanith's state of mind but couldn't forgive her for what she and her late husband had planned for Sara. No doubt the police would be investigating her involvement in the affair. She deserved all she would get.

When he'd finished in the house he went to the barn to see what state it was in. He didn't need a key to get into there as the shattered door was still loosely swinging on its hinges where the police had forced an entry. He stood just inside the doorway and looked the place over. Most of the remains of the witchcraft ceremony had been removed by the police. There were no masks or cloaks left behind but the table that served as an altar was still standing there on the dais. He walked over to it and stood looking at it. With the cloth cover removed he could see it was just an ordinary modern oak dining table. In the cold light of day it was almost impossible to believe what had happened there on Halloween. He swept up what few bits and pieces remained and loaded the table into his van.

The last thing he did was to fetch a mop, bucket and some bleach from his shop and remove the dark traces of Francis O'Conlan's blood from the barn floor. He hesitated at the door as he left the barn, taking a last lingering look around him. That was one place he would never forget.

By late afternoon, Chris had cleared all the rooms in the house, filling his van with the rubbish. He had not stopped to eat and decided to have a late lunch at his flat before he drove to the local refuse tip. Back in his flat he fried himself egg and bacon and ate the meal sitting by the open window. The curtains were blowing into the room on the breeze coming off the reservoir. He sat and watched them flapping gently in the wind and occasionally wrapping their hem around the ebonised grandfather clock case he had placed against the wall. It was a pity he had never found the movement for that clock. It deserved to be whole and ticking in his sitting room. As this would be his last opportunity, he decided to make one last effort and search the entire vicarage for the missing clock parts before he gave up the keys.

After lunch Chris searched every room in the old vicarage. There were several bedrooms that had not been used by the O'Conlans, and there was a large utility room, which was now empty of any washer or dryer, but there was no sign of the missing clock works.

Finally he stood in the hall and looked around him. It had been worth checking everywhere but it had been in vain. He knew he had a very slim chance of finding what he wanted but it was worth one last try. It was then he happened to glance up at the high ceiling and spotted the hatch to the loft space above the landing. He was reluctant to go up there. In his experience lofts were notoriously dirty and always full of worthless rubbish, but something prompted him to try. He knew sometimes people did banish unwanted things to the loft, and that clock case had been discarded in the barn so it had not been valued at the time. He had a funny feeling the loft might be worth searching. John Smyth's suggestion that he might indeed be psychic, crossed his mind. Why not go with his gut feeling, he had nothing to lose.

Chris remembered seeing a wooden ladder hanging on the garage wall in the vicarage grounds. He decided to fetch it and a torch from his van and to search the loft, the last possible hiding place for the clock movement. When he'd climbed into the loft, Chris instantly regretted it. It was a large area, being the roof space of a very large house. It was terribly dusty and full of cobwebs, which hung from the beams like black drapes. It was obvious no one had disturbed the area for years. He walked carefully across the ceiling taking care to step only on the beams and not onto the plastered areas. He found discarded cardboard boxes all over the place and decided to throw them down into the hall to take them to the tip with the rest of the rubbish. It was when he went to lift one of those crumbling boxes he felt something very heavy inside it.

He pulled open the box and shone his torch inside. There, lying on its face, was a small blackened clock dial with a movement attached. His heart missed a beat! He used his fingers to wipe off the accumulated dirt and cobwebs of decades of neglect.

The square dial was less than ten inches across; a similar size to the hood of the ebonised clock case he'd restored. There were four brass angel heads set at the corners. He knew these were Cherub Head spandrels, the earliest style of spandrel and used mainly in the 1600's. The chapter ring was narrow and engraved with Roman numerals showing the hours and the five minute intervals. He looked below the chapter ring on the square brass dial, searching for signs of a maker's signature. By the light of his torch, he was excited to see there were words engraved there. He spat on his finger and scrubbed the lettering, then held the torch closer to it. He couldn't believe his luck! Clearly visible was the legend 'A Fromanteel Londini.'

This was a rare find indeed. Ahasuerus Fromanteel was the man who advertised the first pendulum clock to be made in England in the mid 1600's. He was the man who helped develop the pendulum clock, which led to the birth of the English grandfather clock. This was amazing! He held in his hands a piece of priceless horological history. Chris was thrilled. There was no doubt in his mind, this movement and dial must fit the case he had back at his flat. It was a very valuable find but one he knew he could never part with; his pleasure at owning such an early example would far outweigh any monetary value the longcase clock might have. He could hardly wait to reunite the movement with its clock case. It was a dream come true.

## Chapter Thirty Two

The day after his marvelous find at the vicarage, when Chris had time to try the Fromanteel clock in the ebonised case, he found it fitted perfectly. He didn't rush to restore the dial and movement but decided he must do some serious research before he ventured to work on such an historic example. He wrapped the clock movement and dial in an old sheet and left it undisturbed in his bedroom while he undertook some in depth reading about the subject. Meanwhile, his business still needed his attention. He was busily polishing an oak bedding chest in his back shop, getting it ready to sell, when the doorbell rang announcing another caller.

Chris put his polishing cloth down, intending to join the customer but before he had time to go into the shop, the newcomer had let herself into the shop and walked through to his work room to join him. He was pleasantly surprised to see it was Sara.

'Hi. Feeling better?' Chris threw his arms around her and gave her a hug, he was so thrilled to see her again.

Sara burst into tears and clung onto him for some minutes. Finally she regained her composure and broke away. 'I've come to apologise and to thank you.'

Chris locked the shop door, ushered her up to his flat and made them both a coffee. He stood and watched her as she relaxed in his armchair by the window. She looked very subdued, still somewhat pale and shaken from her ordeal. He put a mug of coffee on the table beside her. 'Here drink this. You had a lucky escape the other night. What's the hospital got to say? Are you OK?' He had so many questions they all came out at once.

'Yes, thanks to you, I'm fine.' She smiled at Chris and continued. 'I have been very silly over this psychic business. I trusted the O'Conlans and they took advantage of me. Mum, the vicar and you warned me, but I took no notice. I'm so sorry.'

She looked closely at Chris's face and could see the bruise on his cheek, which was beginning to fade to yellow but still clearly visible. She also noticed his split lip. 'John explained to me what happened and how you saved me. What can I say? I'm very grateful to you.'

'As long as you're OK now. That's all that matters.' He thought back to the rows they had had before she joined the Psychic College and started to explain. 'You needn't worry about Vickie, my ex. She's gone. She was desperate when you saw her here. She'd lost the shop, had all her

189

stock taken by the bailiffs and had nowhere to stay. She finished up on my doorstep because...'

Sara put down her mug, stood up and pressed her finger to his lips to stop him speaking. 'I know. I had plenty of time to consider things while I lay in hospital.' She threw her arms around his neck and gave him a passionate kiss, which hurt his damaged lip, but he enjoyed it so much he didn't complain. She broke away from their embrace and grinned at him. 'We must go out for dinner again as soon as we're both fit and able.'

**Other Fiction by this Author**

**The Runford Chronicles.**
(Adult fantasy novels)

The Faerie Stone  9781902474012

The Tomatoes of Time  9781902474007

The Pied Punch & Judy Man  9781902474069

The Archdruid of Macclesfield  9781902474090

Oswald Gotobed & the Cambeach Ghost  9781902474199

**Historical Novels**

St. Anthony's Piglet  9781902474175

Deeping Fen  9781902474243

**Non-Fiction Books by this Author**

The Spalding Bird Museum  9781902474236

Animal Taxidermy 9781902474137

Bird Taxidermy  9781902474144

Fish Taxidermy  9781902474151

Taxidermy Trophies  9781902474168

Traditional Taxidermy (The above four books in one volume)
9781902474212

Care of the Longcase Clock 9781902474182

Self-Publishing Books  9781902474250